SEEDS OF HOPE

Tree of Life Book 1

BY: KEVIN MORTLEY

CHAPTER 1	- 1 -
CHAPTER 2	- 15 -
CHAPTER 3:	- 36 -
CHAPTER 4:	- 43 -
CHAPTER 5	- 50 -
CHAPTER 6	- 57 -
CHAPTER 7	- 67 -
CHAPTER 8	- 79 -
CHAPTER 9	- 93 -
CHAPTER 10	- 112 -
CHAPTER 11	- 125 -
CHAPTER 12	- 131 -
CHAPTER 13	- 137 -
CHAPTER 14	- 145 -
CHAPTER 15	- 153 -

CHAPTER 16	- 161 -
CHAPTER 17	- 173 -
CHAPTER 18	- 188 -
CHAPTER 19	- 197 -
CHAPTER 20	- 206 -
CHAPTER 21	- 216 -
CHAPTER 22	- 230 -
CHAPTER 23	- 238 -
CHAPTER 24	- 248 -
CHAPTER 25	- 258 -
CHAPTER 26	- 267 -
CHAPTER 28	- 282 -
CHAPTER 29	- 291 -

Chapter 1

Roman woke abruptly and looked around to try to get his bearings. "Where am I?"

There was nothing in sight but tall waist-height grass, a large cluster of trees to his left, and a large walled city to his right.

As soon as he saw the city a bulb went off in his mind and he got excited.

"I was actually Isekai'd...no truck-kun this time though." He said and looked around as the excitement started building. He got to his feet, almost expecting his intro music to start but hearing nothing but nature around him as the wind danced through the grass.

He stood there for several long moments waiting to hear something.

"I mean, the world isn't supposed to be this quiet, is it?"

He looked at the large walls, expecting maybe some sort of warning horn or something to herald his arrival but there was nothing. Just eerie silence that seemed to be choking out the world.

"Hello!" He yelled out when he walked through the gate and still saw nobody. The inside of the city was a mess, it looked like he was walking through the aftermath of a war. Bodies strewn all over the place, pools of blood...just pure destruction and...death.

"W-what happened here?!" He whispered to himself, taking in everything around. He had never seen anything like this. He came from a peaceful time...yeah there was still violence but nothing on this scale. He was used to people getting gunned down by the police, by family, by neighborhood thugs but had never seen chunks of people strewn across the ground. He could take seeing a dead body with a few holes but not...in six pieces.

He threw up...all over his shirt.

Soon he couldn't hear the eerie silence as his heart started assaulting his eardrums, making its presence known and the harder it beat the harder it was for him to control his emotions until finally, he was a mess on his knees in a pool of vomit heaving as he struggled to catch his breath.

"Get it together, get it together, get it together, getitogether, getittogether." He kept muttering to himself, his whole body violently shaking as the panic attack rampaged through him. This went on for about 30 seconds until he remembered something his mom used to tell him.

"Whenever you are stuck and feel like you're losing control just remember to pray. Seek out your Jesus and He will calm your heart and mind." She said smiling down at him and kissing him through space and time.

He dragged his mind back around and focused forward, picturing it like a massive steering wheel and turning it until he found the bright light in the corner of his mind that he honestly had been neglecting recently. once it got there it clicked and he gained a small bit of peace, enough for him to say the words.

"Dear heavenly Father..." he prayed and the more he said the more his mind calmed until he slumped to the ground and took deep breaths.

"Thank you," he finished the prayer and stood up. He glanced around, searching for anything useful— someone who could help or perhaps even some water to clean himself. After about ten minutes of walking through the devastated city, stepping over the bodies of humans, horses, and even a few strange-looking creatures that might have been pets, he noticed something. Some of these creatures resembled oversized, furry felines, with whiskers and ears that reminded him of the stray cats he used to feed back in his neighborhood.

Eventually, he stumbled upon a well, though it was draped with a dead body. "I'm so sorry," he murmured as he pushed the body aside to access the water. He pulled up the bucket and, to his relief, the water was clean—none of the blood had tainted it. He sniffed it cautiously and took a tentative sip.

"Whoa!" he exclaimed. It was the best water he'd ever tasted, refreshing him to his core. He took his time washing off before searching the nearby bodies for something to hold the water in. Given the medieval feel of the place, he doubted he'd find anything like a Yeti bottle; more likely, they would have leather water skins. The stone and wood buildings, the people dressed in tunics and iron armor, armed with swords, shields, pitchforks, and spears—all confirmed that he was in a medieval world.

After some searching, he found a leather bag slung across one of the corpses. It seemed suitable for now—until he reached inside and his hand kept going, up to his elbow.

"Magic bag! Awesome!" he exclaimed before reality hit him again, and he sobered. He tried to search the bag, but his hand continued to sink deeper.

"Maybe I need to give it a command or something? Inventory. Bag. Status." He tried various commands, and finally, when he said "Status," a blue window appeared in front of him.

Status
Name: Roman
Race: Human
Age: 19
Title: [World Walker]
— *World Walker* is a title earned by traversing the cosmos to arrive on another world capable of sustaining life and with access to the System. This title is currently incomplete; the user has only the lite version. Levels and stats are unavailable.
Title: [Exponential Growth]

— The user's growth in all areas increases exponentially. All activities completed by the user are influenced by this title until the body can no longer sustain it. Once this limit is reached, the user must improve their body's cultivation level for continued growth.

Title: [Cultivator's Body]
— The user has the ability to enhance bodily functions through cultivation.

"Uh... that's it? A bit more detail would be nice!" Roman muttered in frustration. The titles on his status screen seemed sparse. The *World Walker* title appeared to be incomplete, leaving him without access to stats or levels. But as he looked closer, his initial disappointment turned into excitement. The synergy between the other two titles—*Exponential Growth* and *Cultivator's Body*—was incredible. With the right training and hard work, he could push his limits far beyond the ordinary.

Having read countless cultivation novels and gamelit books, the concept of cultivating to grow stronger was familiar territory for him. Traditional cultivation involved meditation and specific breathing techniques, but he had none of those at his disposal. He'd have to figure it out on his own.

"Okay, focus," he muttered, glancing around the desolate city. "First, I need to find somewhere safe." Just because it seemed deserted now didn't mean it would stay that way. While he hoped to encounter someone friendly, he wasn't keen on running into hostile beings without a way to defend himself. *Exponential Growth* was great, but it wouldn't help if he couldn't protect himself right now.

He spotted a sword lying next to one of the bodies and picked it up. The weight felt awkward in his grip, but he resolved to make it work. Leaving the city, he approached a nearby tree and took a few tentative swings, imagining an enemy before him.

<Sword Proficiency Gained>

"Whoa!" he exclaimed as the message popped up. The more he swung the sword, the more natural it felt. Within a few minutes, he moved as if he'd been training with this blade for years.

<Sword Proficiency Level 1 Attained. Damage caused by wielding swords increased by 5%, stamina cost decreased by 5%, and critical chance increased by 15%.>

Roman grinned. He wasn't defenseless anymore. The increase in critical chance intrigued him, though he wasn't sure how it would play out in actual combat. "I should probably test this on something," he murmured, scanning his surroundings.

The forest around him was alive with vibrant colors and the melodic chirping of birds. It was stunning, and he realized with a start that he hadn't noticed its beauty before. The trees swayed gently in the breeze, and the air was filled with the crisp scent of pine. It felt as though the world itself had just awakened, vibrant and full of life.

"How did I miss this?" he wondered aloud, his eyes widening as he took in the scenery.

After a few minutes of wandering, he stumbled upon a small clearing. A low, guttural noise caught his attention. Peering around a tree, he saw a strange sight: a small creature locked in combat with a large brown bear. He squinted, trying to make out what the creature was.

<Observation Proficiency Attained>
<Far Sight Proficiency Attained>

Now he could see the creature more clearly. It stood just over four feet tall, covered in thick fur from head to toe. Large canines jutted out from its upper jaw, and a bushy tail flicked behind it. *I've never seen a bunny like this,* he thought, watching the bizarre scene unfold. Despite its resemblance to a harmless rabbit, the creature's sharp claws and teeth, combined with its quick, agile movements, indicated it was anything but defenseless.

Roman hesitated. He wanted to intervene but remembered that both animals were enemies. The bear might be dangerous, but this rabbit-thing was clearly no ordinary prey. He decided to wait, observing as the two continued their strange battle.

The bear lunged, swiping at the bunny, but the agile creature leaped out of reach each time. This dance of attack and evasion went on for about thirty seconds. The bear roared in frustration, unable to keep up with the smaller creature's speed. Then, in a sudden shift, the bear's body glowed red. It tilted its head back, releasing a roar that seemed to shake the very air around them.

The bunny froze, its body quivering. Roman's heart clenched as he watched the bear charge, its jaws snapping down on the creature. It pinned the bunny with its massive paws, shaking its head violently, tearing flesh and fur. Blood sprayed across the ground as the rabbit's life ebbed away.

"OH!" Roman gasped, a mix of excitement and fear coursing through him. The bear's head snapped in his direction, and it let out a deafening roar that sent a shiver down his spine.

"Oh, crap!" He gripped the sword tighter, his knuckles turning white. "I guess now's as good a time as any to try this out." Steeling his nerves, he sprinted toward the bear, not entirely sure what he was doing but knowing he couldn't just stand there.

He slashed at the bear's shoulder, and to his shock, a glowing red bar appeared above the bear's head. *Is that its health bar?!* He watched it decrease by a mere 1%. His attack barely scratched the beast, but it certainly got its attention. The bear dropped the bunny's limp body, turning its bloodied maw towards him with a roar.

"Uh, oh!"

The bear charged, swiping a massive paw at Roman. He raised his sword in defense, the impact sending him stumbling back several feet. His arms ached from the blow, but the sword held firm, absorbing most of the force.

"What was I thinking?!" he shouted as the bear struck again. He barely managed to duck under the next swipe, the air whistling above his head as the claws passed by.

<Blocking proficiency gained.>

Shut up! he mentally screamed at the notification. He had no time for distractions. The bear lunged again, and he rolled away, narrowly avoiding its jaws.

"Come on, Roman... You've got this," he muttered to himself, his confidence building as he found a rhythm in dodging the bear's attacks. After each missed strike, he saw brief openings—a chance to counter. He waited for the bear to swing its left paw, then ducked and darted forward, thrusting his sword beneath the bear's arm. The beast roared, swiping faster and with greater ferocity.

Roman backed off, his breathing heavy. He couldn't afford to get cocky. Every time he dodged and struck, the bear's movements grew more sluggish, blood pouring from its wounds. Minutes passed like hours as they fought, Roman dancing around the massive creature, avoiding its powerful blows.

Finally, the bear slowed, its massive chest heaving as it struggled to catch its breath. Blood matted its fur, and its once ferocious roars had turned to labored growls. Roman could see the weariness in its eyes, and he knew the fight was nearing its end.

Roman saw an opening and surged forward, swinging his sword upward. The blade connected with the bear's chin, sending it reeling back. Seizing the opportunity, he rushed in, driving the sword into the exposed neck and out through the back. The bear collapsed with a heavy thud that reverberated through the ground, making Roman stumble slightly.

"That was way too close," he gasped, dropping to his knees as he struggled to catch his breath. His entire body trembled from the adrenaline and exertion. Images on his mistakes throughout the fight flashed through his head...while the chin hit helped expose the throat...that wasn't where he was aiming if he was being honest.

Just as he tried to regain his composure, a strange mist began to rise from the bear's body, swirling toward him. It happened so quickly that he barely had time to react before the mist surged into him, filling him with an overwhelming sensation. It was like having a huge meal and then, despite being full, eating a rich dessert on top of it. His stomach twisted as if it might burst.

I'm gonna puke! he thought frantically, his mind scrambling for a way to cope. Then he remembered his titles. I need to cultivate! But how? He tried to recall what he'd read in the books. Cultivation usually involved drawing in energy, but he had already done that. What came next? Move the energy around the body, strengthen the meridians and core, right? But he hadn't even created a core yet. How was he supposed to start?

Dropping to the ground, he squeezed his eyes shut, forcing himself to focus inward. His heart pounded like a war drum, his breath coming in ragged gasps. He could feel his body trembling as he desperately tried to visualize his inner workings. Slowly, faint tendrils of energy began to appear in his mind's eye, swirling in his chest like a chaotic, writhing nest of serpents. Sweat dripped down his brow as he reached out mentally, trying to grasp the energy, but his imaginary hand passed right through them.

"No, no, no!" he growled, his frustration mounting. His whole body felt like it was on fire, every nerve alive with the pulsing, uncontrollable energy. He looked down and saw that his hand was made of light, flickering and unstable. Panic surged through him. *I can't even hold on to it! How am I supposed to control it?*

He forced himself to breathe, to concentrate. Slowly, he tried to solidify his hand, compacting his energy until it felt more substantial. His pulse raced as he extended his hand again, trembling as he reached for one of the writhing tendrils. This time, his fingers closed around it, and he almost screamed as it squirmed in his grasp like a live wire, shocking him with each pulse. It felt wrong, alien, like trying to hold onto pure lightning.

"This feels so weird," he whispered, his voice shaking. Every instinct screamed at him to let go, but he gritted his teeth and began coiling the tendril around itself, forming a tighter and tighter spiral. His head throbbed, and his vision blurred, but he kept going, grabbing another tendril and twisting it around the first, each one joining the others until he held a tightly wound ball of energy. It vibrated violently in his hand, sending jolts of pain up his arm. His whole body felt like it was being torn apart from the inside.

"Come on... come on!" he muttered desperately, his heart racing out of control. He took a deep, shuddering breath and pushed inward with all his strength, trying to compress the chaotic ball of energy. It fought him every step of the way, pushing back with a force that made his bones ache. His hands began to glow brighter, the ball of energy humming louder and louder until it felt like the sound was tearing through his skull, resonating with his very soul.

His mind felt like it was splitting in two, the pressure building to an unbearable level. The humming grew into a deafening roar, his vision turning white as if he were being consumed by the energy itself. Panic clawed at him, and he bit down on his lip, forcing himself to keep going. *I have to control it. I have to…*

The energy surged, wild and uncontrolled, threatening to tear him apart. He screamed, the sound lost in the cacophony inside his mind. Every muscle in his body tensed as he pushed harder, forcing the energy to compact further, his teeth grinding together as he struggled to contain it. Just when he thought he couldn't take it anymore, that he would explode from the pressure, something inside him shifted.

With a sudden, almost audible *click*, the chaos transformed. The ball of energy, once a raging storm, now purred softly, a gentle, soothing vibration spreading through his body. The agony melted away, replaced by a warm, calming sensation. His breathing slowed, and he let out a long, shuddering sigh of relief.

He'd done it. Somehow, he'd managed to control the energy. For now.

Grinning like a fool, Roman released the compressed energy. He watched in awe as the shining orb floated in the air before him. It spun slowly at first, then drifted down from his chest level until it settled into his solar plexus. Once in place, it began to spin faster, the purr turning into a powerful, steady hum that radiated through his entire being.

The sensation was incredible, unlike anything he'd ever felt. It was as if pure power was flooding his body, rejuvenating him from the inside out. He couldn't help but picture that iconic scene from a superhero movie when a certain man of iron created a new element to power his suit.

Roman opened his eyes, feeling completely transformed. The energy pulsing from his chest was like a beacon of strength and vitality. He had no idea how he ended up in this world or what awaited him, but for some reason, the fear and confusion had faded. He felt calm, almost accepting. Whatever happens, happens, he thought.

Then he heard a soft voice, clear and commanding. Move.

It was so familiar that he jumped, glancing around to see who had spoken. Then he remembered. It was a voice he would never forget, one that had been a constant presence in his life. Smiling warmly, he realized he was being guided, just as he had been so many times before. It had been a long time since he'd gone to church or opened his Bible, but that voice was unmistakable.

He stood, unsure of where he was going or what he would find, but with faith in his heart, he took a deep breath and, without hesitation, moved forward.

Chapter 2

A few miles north of Roman's location…

"I have a report, Sire!" a young voice echoed through the grand hall, filled with noblemen dressed in their finest attire. The only one seated was the ruler of the county, Count Kenan.

"Speak!" Count Kenan barked, his anger still simmering from the previous report. "Have you found those monsters?"

"We have, my lord. They've been traced to the Merkwood Forest." The young squire's announcement was met with shocked gasps from the assembly. Everyone knew the terrifying tales of that forest and the surrounding lands; no one dared to venture that far north within the county.

"Mobilize the army! I want every last one of those beasts dead by the end of the month! Do you hear me? Not a single one of those filthy creatures is to live after ransacking one of my cities! They slaughtered thousands in a week—KILL THEM ALL!" He leaped from his seat, his voice booming as his fury was met with the roaring approval of the gathered nobles.

One of the knights standing beside the Count stepped forward, bowing slightly and saluting with his right hand over his chest. The other knights followed suit, their synchronized gesture drawing the Count's attention and silencing the room.

"We shall hunt those orcs to the ends of the earth, Sire. You have my word," Knight Commander Dalf vowed solemnly.

"I leave it in your hands," Count Kenan said, his tone quieter but no less intense. He sank back into his chair, his mind already shifting to the next issue at hand.

Roman

Roman had been walking for hours, losing track of time without a watch. The sun blazed overhead, but a gentle breeze kept the heat from becoming unbearable. He admired the stunning scenery—the vibrant green of the trees, their dark bark almost black, creating a stark contrast that felt both eerie and captivating. Bright bushes and colorful plants dotted the landscape but vanished as soon as he got too close. They seemed to shy away, as if hiding.

"I should probably keep moving. I need to find somewhere safe to rest," he thought, taking a step forward—only to be knocked down flat.

He rolled to his feet, sword at the ready, expecting an attack. But nothing happened. Confused, he took another step, only to be knocked down again. Frustration flared within him.

"What the hell is going on? Am I being attacked?" he muttered, spinning around, his eyes darting in every direction.

Still nothing. He was about to move again when he noticed something peculiar. Surrounding him were tiny, fluffy balls bouncing up and down, as if waiting for him to make his next move.

"What are you?" he wondered aloud.

A screen appeared before his eyes:

<Observation Proficiency leveled up> <Far Sight Proficiency leveled up>

The creatures were undeniably cute—until they weren't. The moment he thought this, they transformed into something out of a nightmare. One was covered in fur with six arms, each wielding a tiny dagger. Another had four snarling, foam-mouthed heads. But the one that truly unnerved him was the headless figure, cloaked in a hood that floated as if it had a life of its own.

"I'm not sure which is worse," he muttered, eyes darting between the horrifying forms.

"Roo!" one of the smaller furballs cried, leaping up to bounce off his leg before retreating back to the group. They repeated this action several times, almost playfully, before suddenly launching into an attack. Now that he could see them clearly, Roman easily dodged their advances, using his sword to push them back without harming them. He moved in a wide circle, gradually backing away from their cluster of trees. It was clear they were protecting their home, and he didn't want to hurt them for that.

As the creatures realized he wasn't fighting back and was instead retreating, they, too, began to fall back, letting out a collective "Humph," as if to say, "Yeah, you better leave." Roman chuckled at the thought, turning his back and continuing on his way.

After a few steps, a thought struck him. *Why didn't I get any proficiency?* Then he remembered: *Oh right! I turned it off.* With a quick mental command, he reactivated the system.

Status:

- **Name:** Roman
- **Race:** Human
- **Age:** 19
- **Titles:** [World Walker], [Exponential Growth], [Cultivator's Body]
- **Skills:**
    - **Sword Proficiency Level 2**
    - **Observation Level 3**
    - **Far Sight Level 2**
    - **Blocking Level 2**
    - **Evasion Level 3**
    - **Cultivation Level:** Broken Core

He skimmed through the familiar information until his gaze settled on his cultivation status.

Cultivation Level: Broken Core

A core has formed but possesses only limited functionality. Energy absorption is significantly reduced due to the core's incomplete creation and imperfect seal. Supports only one Seedling. A Seedling grants access to the core's power and can be placed in extremities, senses, and five locations between the brain and gut. Each Seedling type unlocks different abilities.

"Okay, so my core is incomplete, but I can place a Seedling for additional power. Once I improve my core, I can add more Seedlings…" Roman murmured, thinking it over. Cultivation novels usually laid everything out clearly from the start, but this felt much more... real. He tried questioning the system, but it didn't respond—it wasn't sentient, just a repository of information that became available as he met certain criteria.

As he puzzled over the system, he heard that familiar voice again: "Trust." More words followed, but they blurred together, leaving only a single word echoing in his mind. Yet, that one word filled him with a sense of certainty, guiding him toward what he needed to do.

Roman sat down, leaning against a tree. He focused inward, visualizing his core not as a sphere but as a small bonsai tree growing in a pot. Taking a deep breath, he pulled in more energy, watching the leaves glow as they absorbed the energy, channeling it through the branches and trunk. He imagined the roots, hidden but essential, and was thrilled to see the tree grow ever so slightly.

He continued this process, his core growing inch by inch until it stood almost three inches tall.

"There," he whispered.

A soft crunch interrupted his concentration. Roman scanned the area, his eyes locking onto a bush just as it shifted. Pain shot through his head. *I've reached my limit,* he thought, struggling to his feet. His body felt sluggish, exhaustion pressing down on him like a heavy weight.

As he stood, waiting for the dizziness to pass, he noticed something remarkable—his fatigue melted away almost instantly. Power surged through him, more potent than before, like the rush from three espressos followed by a shot of adrenaline.

"This feels incredible!" he laughed, exhilarated. He took a step and stumbled, covering twice the distance he expected. *Am I tripping?* he wondered, testing it again. Each step carried him farther, his speed and strength seemingly doubling.

"Thank you, Lord," he whispered, closing his eyes and smiling as he prayed. This place, this experience—it was already a thousand times better than he could have imagined. For so long, he had been a doormat, bullied and abused, but he had always held onto his faith, seeking those moments of peace that reminded him he wasn't alone. Now, he had a chance to change things, to be someone who mattered.

His joyous thoughts were interrupted by a series of growls. Normally, those sounds would have frozen his blood, but now he grinned, gripping his sword. A pack of nine large, brown wolves, led by a larger gray one, surrounded him. The alpha's eyes narrowed, questioning why he wasn't afraid. Most people would have run, but Roman charged straight at the gray wolf instead.

Don't kill them—just hurt them enough to scare them off, he felt more than heard. Adjusting his strike, he slashed at the wolf's face. It yelped, and the pack sprang into action. Roman moved like a whirlwind, dodging and striking with precision. In less than thirty seconds, the wolves realized they hadn't landed a single hit and retreated. The gray wolf glanced back one last time, its eyes filled with fury as blood dripped from a cut near its eye.

Roman looked at his sword, now glowing faintly. Messages flashed before his eyes:

<Sword Proficiency Level 4> <Evasion Level 5> <Far Sight Level 3> <Observation Level 4> <Title Bestowed: "One with the Blade">

He focused on the new title:

One with the Blade: *The user can wield their sword as an extension of their body, enhancing its durability and sharpness proportional to their proficiency level. Additionally, the blade's edge can extend up to one foot.*

"Oh, that's awesome!" he exclaimed, envisioning himself as his favorite game character, slicing through enemies from a distance. He practiced, imagining a large radius around him as the sword's reach. After several failed attempts, he finally felt the pull, his energy draining as the blade's edge glowed bright blue, extending and slicing through the air.

He continued until he could sustain the technique for a few swings, then looked up. The sky was darkening.

Might as well set up camp, he thought, gathering sticks for a fire.

Roman gathered a bundle of sticks and branches, arranging them into a makeshift fire pit. As he worked, he realized that aside from his sword and some water, he had no other supplies. Despite the lack of provisions and the discomfort of sleeping on the ground, his excitement overshadowed any sense of inconvenience. He lay down next to the fire, feeling its warmth seep into his bones. Though the day had been pleasantly warm, the temperature had plummeted sharply after sunset. Pulling his cloak tighter around himself, he listened to the crackling of the fire and the soothing symphony of the forest night. A deep sense of peace enveloped him, and he closed his eyes.

Wake up.

Roman's eyes snapped open, his heart pounding. He sat up, every muscle tense, and looked around. The fire was now just a heap of glowing embers, casting a faint red glow. The moon hung high in the night sky, bathing the clearing in a pale, silvery light that made the shadows stretch and sway like ghostly figures. His eyes darted around, scanning every shadow, straining to hear any sound out of place.

There.

He spotted it—a small, black blur flitting at the edge of his vision. It moved swiftly toward him, but the moment his eyes locked onto it, the shape froze and seemed to dissolve into the darkness. Roman leapt to his feet, drawing his sword, his senses heightened and alert.

What is that? An animal? Another monster? A person? His mind raced through the possibilities, none of them comforting. He forced himself to take slow, measured breaths, trying to calm his nerves.

Movement again. This time, it was larger and darker, creeping toward him at a deliberate, menacing pace. Roman focused all his willpower, trying to pierce the shadow's veil. For a brief moment, he saw something—patches of light and dark shifting behind the shadowy form. But just as he began to make sense of it, the image shattered, leaving him with a splitting headache. Gripping his sword tighter, he braced himself, frustration mingling with fear as he prepared for whatever was coming.

A cold chill ran down his spine, the hairs on the back of his neck standing up as if warning him of imminent danger. The shadows around him seemed to ripple and move, but the figure that had approached him vanished as silently as it had come.

Was it scouting me out? he wondered, his thoughts a jumbled mess. I can't stay here. Without another thought, he turned and ran, pushing himself harder than ever before. It felt as though the wind itself was propelling him forward, his feet barely touching the ground. Trees blurred past, the forest a whirlwind of dark shapes as he sprinted deeper into the woods. Even with his newfound speed, a persistent sensation nagged at him, as if he were being watched, stalked by that same shadowy presence.

"What the hell?!" he shouted, coming to an abrupt stop. He turned sharply, sword raised, his chest heaving. "Come on then! If you want to fight, let's do it!"

His voice echoed through the silent woods, his challenge ringing out. Sweat dripped down his forehead, and his grip on the sword was so tight that his knuckles turned white. He scanned the area, every sense on high alert, but saw nothing. Minutes passed, his initial adrenaline beginning to fade, leaving behind a tense, coiled readiness.

Then he saw it—a shadowy figure to his right, moving with a slow, deliberate gait. As it drew closer, the darkness peeled away, revealing a young man dressed in black, his features sharp and his eyes wary. A long dagger was strapped to his right hip, the blade gleaming faintly in the moonlight.

"I mean you no harm," the stranger said, raising his hands in a gesture of peace.

Roman kept his sword raised, his instincts screaming that this could be a trap. "Who are you? And why were you stalking me?"

The man's expression was calm, almost apologetic. "I sensed a strong presence and came to investigate. When you started running, you passed through one of my shadow puppets—it stuck to you until you slowed down. I followed it here. I was going to step behind a tree and de-stealth myself—I've learned it's less creepy that way."

"Shadow puppet? Stealth?" Roman echoed, his mind racing to piece together what the stranger was saying.

"Oh, yeah, I'm a Shadowwalker." He shrugged as if that explained everything. "I can move through shadows, become invisible, manipulate darkness. All that fun stuff."

"What's your name?" Roman asked, still wary.

"Oh, sorry! I'm Seth. And you are?"

"Roman," he replied curtly, not lowering his guard.

"Nice to meet you, Roman. But this isn't really the safest place to be having a chat. What are you doing out here, anyway?" Seth asked, glancing around nervously.

"I don't know," Roman admitted. "I woke up here."

Seth's eyes widened slightly. "Woke up here? Man, someone must really have it out for you. This is the Merkwood Forest, one of the most dangerous places in the kingdom!"

"So why are you here?" Roman countered, his curiosity piqued despite the situation.

"I'm here with my party. We came to train, fight some monsters, and level up. It's rough, but you get stronger that way." He paused, scrutinizing Roman. "Wait, are you saying you don't know about the System?"

"Levels? System?" Roman asked, feigning confusion to glean more information.

Seth nodded. "Yeah, most people are blessed with the System at birth. It quantifies their abilities, attributes, everything. You gain Experience Points from various actions, and once you've gathered enough, you level up."

Roman frowned, thinking about his own situation. "What does leveling up do for you?"

"It gives you a boost in stats, depending on your class. I'm a Shadowwalker, so my stats focus on dexterity. You also get a few free stat points to allocate as you see fit," Seth explained. "But you can still get stronger without it—there are many who aren't blessed with the System but can still hold their own, especially if they have unique Titles."

"Titles?" Roman's mind raced. He thought of his own Titles, powerful in their own right.

"Yeah, Titles are like special acknowledgments from the System. They're incredibly rare, given for unique accomplishments, and they grant bonuses. The King has the Title of Sovereign, which makes him a more effective ruler. Most people are lucky to get even one Title in their lifetime."

Roman nodded, absorbing this new information. His Titles were extraordinary, and it seemed others didn't have a way to see them. That gave him an advantage, but also a reason to be cautious.

"Why don't we head back to my camp?" Seth suggested. "It's not safe to be out in the open like this."

"Right," Roman agreed, his wariness still intact but his curiosity winning out. "Lead the way."

Seth turned, and Roman followed, the forest around them filled with unfamiliar sounds. They moved quickly but cautiously, Seth leading them through the dense underbrush. Roman's mind was a whirlwind of thoughts, trying to process everything he'd just learned.

When they arrived at the camp, Roman saw a small clearing with a blazing fire in the center. Three figures sat around it—two were seated, and a third stood near the edge of the trees, eyes alert.

"Everyone, we've got company!" Seth called out, his voice cheerful. He plopped down next to a girl with almost white-blonde hair. Roman quickly took stock of the group—the standing figure was a woman with a bow slung across her back, while a man in full plate armor lounged by the fire.

"Hey there, nice to meet you all," Roman greeted, raising a hand.

"Hey, I'm Jessika," the blonde girl in the long flowing robe type dress said, waving back.

"I'm Zorin, but people call me Z," the armored man added, nodding.

"Alexia, but you can call me Lexi," the woman with the bow said, giving him a friendly nod.

"And I'm Roman," he replied, feeling a strange sense of camaraderie despite the circumstances.

"So, where did you find him?" Zorin asked, a faint smile on his lips.

"He was in the middle of the woods, alone," Seth said. "He doesn't remember much."

"How did you survive out there?" Zorin asked, a hint of incredulity in his voice.

"I'm tougher than I look," Roman said with a grin.

"Well, you're welcome here. We don't turn our backs on people in need," Zorin said, and the others nodded in agreement.

"Thank you. I really appreciate it," Roman said sincerely. He felt a strange sense of relief, as if a weight he hadn't realized he was carrying had been lifted.

"So, do you remember anything at all?" Lexi asked, curiosity glinting in her eyes.

Roman hesitated, then decided to tell them part of the truth. "I woke up in the middle of a grassland near a city. The city was destroyed, everyone dead. I ran and ran until I ended up in the forest."

"The only city near here is Eidon," Zorin said, the mood around the fire growing somber. "We were headed there to set up a base. If it's destroyed, we need to alert the kingdom."

"Did you see anything that could tell us who did it?" Jessika asked, pulling out a leather-bound notebook.

"I saw a lot, but nothing I could make sense of at the time," Roman admitted. Jessika nodded, scribbling something down before tearing the page out and tossing it into the fire. It burst into flame and vanished.

"That's amazing," Roman muttered, impressed.

"Magic book," Jessika said with a smile. "I've linked it to my mom back home. I just sent her a message to alert the authorities."

"Thanks," Roman said, feeling gratitude and a strange sense of hope for the first time since he'd arrived.

The group chatted more as the night went on, sharing stories and laughter. Jessika and Seth served food—

something like meat and potatoes, though Roman had no idea what kind of meat it was. It tasted amazing, and he ate with a hunger he hadn't realized he'd been holding back.

For the first time in what felt like forever, Roman felt a sense of belonging. Whatever challenges lay ahead, he knew he wasn't facing them alone.

"Oh, okay, that's pretty cool. You mentioned you were headed to Eidon. Why is that?" Roman asked, his curiosity piqued.

"We came here to train for the next year," Lexi explained, leaning back and stretching her legs toward the warmth of the fire. "Since Eidon is the closest city, we thought it would be a good place to set up base. The plan was to go there first, get settled, then head out here. But SOMEONE—" she shot a playful glare at Z— "couldn't wait and dragged us into the forest."

Z grinned, unabashed. "It ain't my fault! You saw that orc! It looked too cool to pass up. We *had* to fight it."

Lexi raised an eyebrow, her expression skeptical. "And how did that go, exactly?"

"Fine!" Z defended, crossing his arms. "We did just fine! I only broke a sword."

Jessika burst into laughter, wrapping her arms around Z in a playful hug. "You were amazing," she said, planting a kiss on his cheek. Z's confident demeanor faltered as he blushed, turning his head away to hide his embarrassment.

"You two are together?" Roman asked, a smile tugging at his lips.

"Oh no, he's like my big brother," Jessika said, her smile softening. There was a genuine warmth in her voice, and Z's expression turned from embarrassed to affectionate.

"Ah, got it. So, you've mentioned the kingdom a couple of times now. Can you give me more details about it?" Roman inquired, eager to learn more about this world.

"Yeah, sure," Z said, his voice taking on a more serious tone. "This is the Kingdom of Meridia. It's ruled by King Juelius and Queen Willemina. We're the easternmost kingdom on the Northern continent."

"There are three other kingdoms on this continent," Seth added, gesturing with his hand as if mapping out the region. "Fairen, Akilus, and Darnison. To the south, there's the Southern continent, which has five different kingdoms, all ruled by a High Emperor."

Roman nodded thoughtfully, absorbing the information. "And where exactly are we now in Meridia?"

"We're near the southwestern border," Lexi said, poking the fire with a stick. "Just past Eidon lies the boundary we share with Fairen."

"So, do you think it was Fairen that attacked Eidon?" Roman asked, his mind flashing back to the destroyed city he had seen.

"Maybe," Lexi said cautiously. "There's been a lot of tension recently, but an attack like that without warning? It could start a continent-wide war. Meridia is allied with Darnison to the west, and Fairen is allied with Akilus to the south. If they were behind it, things could get messy."

"Who has the strongest military? Is Meridia powerful?" Roman asked, trying to gauge the kingdom's strength.

"Meridia is one of the strongest," Z said confidently. "But all four northern kingdoms are pretty evenly matched. Darnison is usually considered the weakest, but that's mostly because it's smaller and has fewer people."

"That makes sense," Roman replied, his mind racing as he tried to piece together this new information. The mention of alliances and potential conflict made him uneasy, but it was clear that understanding the political landscape would be crucial for his survival.

Their conversation shifted to lighter topics as they shared stories around the fire. They talked about how they had met, the adventures they'd had, and the close calls that had bonded them together. Jessika and Seth moved around the campfire, serving up portions of the meal they had prepared. Roman accepted a wooden bowl filled with what looked like meat and potatoes. He didn't recognize the meat, but it was tender and flavorful, filling him with a warmth that spread through his body.

He hadn't realized how hungry he was until he began eating. Each bite felt like a small victory, the simple act of eating grounding him amidst all the chaos and confusion of the past few days. For a few moments, the fear and uncertainty faded away, replaced by the camaraderie and comfort of the shared meal.

"So, how did you all meet?" Roman asked between mouthfuls, genuinely curious about this group that had so readily accepted him.

"It's a bit of a long story," Jessika said with a laugh, her eyes sparkling in the firelight. "Z and I are actually from the same village. We've known each other since we were kids. When we both got our System Blessings, we decided to travel together. Seth joined us a few months later."

"Yeah, I was wandering around, getting into trouble," Seth added with a grin. "I heard about these two crazy adventurers who took down a wyvern all by themselves and figured I had to meet them."

"We didn't know what we were doing back then," Z said, shaking his head. "We just saw it terrorizing a village and jumped in."

"And nearly got ourselves killed," Jessika interjected, laughing. "But Seth showed up and helped us finish it off."

"And Lexi?" Roman asked, glancing over at the archer, who had been quietly listening to the conversation.

"I joined a little later," she said, her voice soft but firm. "I was tracking a band of slavers that had kidnapped some villagers. Ran into these guys while they were fighting off a group of bandits. We decided to join forces, took down the slavers together, and I've been with them ever since."

Roman nodded, feeling a sense of admiration for these people. They were brave, resilient, and seemed to genuinely care about each other. He glanced around at the group, a strange warmth spreading through him. It had been so long since he'd felt like he belonged anywhere.

"Sounds like you've been through a lot together," he said quietly.

"We have," Z said, his voice filled with a quiet pride. "But it's made us stronger."

A comfortable silence settled over the camp as they finished their meal, the fire crackling softly. Roman leaned back, gazing up at the stars that twinkled in the clear night sky. For the first time since he had woken up in this strange world, he felt a glimmer of hope. Whatever challenges lay ahead, he wasn't alone anymore.

"We should get some rest," Jessika said, breaking the silence. "Tomorrow, we'll need to decide what to do about Eidon."

Everyone murmured their agreement, and the camp slowly quieted as they settled in for the night. Roman lay down, wrapping his cloak around him. The ground was hard and the night air cool, but he felt a deep sense of peace.

He closed his eyes, his thoughts drifting. He still didn't know why he was here or what his purpose was, but for now, it was enough to know that he was no longer wandering aimlessly. He had found allies, maybe even friends, and for the first time in a long while, he felt like he was exactly where he was meant to be.

Chapter 3:
Bonds Forged in Battle

The morning sun filtered through the canopy of leaves, casting dappled shadows on the forest floor. Birds chirped overhead, and the air was crisp with the scent of pine and damp earth. Roman stretched, feeling the stiffness in his muscles from sleeping on the ground. Around him, the others were already up and about, preparing for the day.

"Morning," Seth greeted, tossing Roman a piece of bread. "Sleep well?"

"Yeah, as well as you can on the ground," Roman replied with a grin, taking a bite. It was dry and crumbly, but it filled his stomach.

"We've got a full day ahead," Z said, sharpening his sword. "We'll head deeper into the forest, find some decent monsters to train on. There's no telling what's going on in Eidon, so we need to be ready for anything but we'll stay in the area until we get word on what they want us to do."

Roman nodded, feeling a thrill of excitement. He had spent most of his life reading about adventures, and now he was living one. But there was also an undercurrent of anxiety. He still didn't fully understand his abilities or the System. And he had to keep the fact that he was from another world a secret.

After they finished eating and packed up their camp, they set off. The forest seemed almost alive, the trees whispering secrets as the wind rustled their leaves.

Roman felt a strange sense of familiarity, as if the forest itself were welcoming him.

"So, Roman," Lexi began as they walked, "you said you don't remember much, but you've got some serious skills. How did you learn to fight like that?"

Roman hesitated. He needed to be careful. "I used to train a lot... before I lost my memory," he said, choosing his words carefully. "I don't remember specifics, but I think I was good at it."

Seth nodded, accepting his answer. "Makes sense. You definitely handled yourself well last night."

"Thanks," Roman replied, relieved that the conversation hadn't gone deeper. He still wasn't sure how much to reveal.

They moved steadily through the forest, the terrain becoming more rugged as they went. The underbrush thickened, and the trees grew taller and closer together. After about an hour of trekking, they came to a clearing where the ground was littered with the remains of what looked like a fierce battle.

"This looks promising," Z said, surveying the area. "Let's split up a bit. We'll cover more ground that way. Lexi, keep an eye from up high. Jess, you're with me. Seth, take Roman and scout around."

Roman glanced at Seth, who nodded. "Ready?" Seth asked, his eyes scanning the surrounding trees.

"Yeah, let's go," Roman replied, gripping his sword.

They moved cautiously, keeping to the edges of the clearing. Seth was light on his feet, moving almost silently. Roman found himself following the

Shadowwalker's lead, trying to match his steps and keep his senses alert.

<Skill learned- Stealth>

"So," Roman said quietly, "you've been with them for a while?"

"Yeah, about a year now," Seth replied, his voice low. "They're good people. Best I've met."

"You didn't have a group before?" Roman asked, curious.

Seth hesitated, glancing at Roman. "Not really. Grew up in the capital. It's... complicated."

Roman raised an eyebrow. "The capital? What's that like?"

"It's—" Seth started, then caught himself. "It's not what you'd expect. Lots of politics, you know? Everyone trying to outdo everyone else. It's exhausting." He shook his head as if to clear away the memory. "I prefer the simplicity of this. You fight, you survive, you get stronger."

Roman could sense there was more to the story, but he didn't push. Instead, he nodded and kept his eyes on the forest, trying to pick up on any signs of movement. They continued in silence, the only sound the rustle of leaves underfoot.

They were about to turn back when Roman caught a glimpse of something between the trees—a flash of scales and a low, rumbling growl.

"Did you hear that?" Roman whispered, stopping in his tracks.

Seth nodded, his eyes narrowing as he focused on the spot where Roman had been looking. "Yeah. Let's check it out, carefully."

They moved forward, each step deliberate and cautious. As they rounded a large tree, they saw it—a massive creature, its body covered in dark, glistening scales. It was about the size of a horse, its long tail whipping back and forth as it sniffed the air.

"A drake," Seth whispered, his voice tense. "Not fully grown, but dangerous."

Roman felt his pulse quicken. He had read about creatures like this, but seeing one in real life was something else entirely. He tightened his grip on his sword, feeling the weight of it in his hand.

"We need to be smart about this," Seth said, his eyes locked on the drake. "It's got tough scales, and it's fast. We'll have to hit it hard and keep moving."

"Got it," Roman said, steeling himself. He focused inward, feeling the energy of his core pulsing in time with his heartbeat.

They spread out, flanking the creature. Seth moved like a shadow, circling to the drake's left, while Roman took the right. As they approached, the drake's head snapped up, its yellow eyes narrowing as it spotted them.

Seth struck first, darting in with a quick slash at the drake's flank. The creature roared, its tail lashing out, but Seth was already gone, slipping back into the shadows.

Roman saw his opening and charged, his sword slicing through the air. He aimed for the drake's leg, hoping to cripple it. His blade struck, but the scales were tougher than he'd anticipated, and the sword glanced off with a harsh screech.

The drake reared back, its mouth opening to reveal rows of sharp teeth. It lunged at Roman, but he rolled to the side, narrowly avoiding the snapping jaws.

"Nice move!" Seth called, his voice filled with adrenaline. He appeared behind the drake, slashing at its tail. The creature bellowed in pain and fury, its massive body thrashing as it tried to turn and face both opponents at once.

Roman got to his feet, his heart racing. He could feel his body responding, his reflexes sharper than ever. He darted forward, feinting to the left before slashing at the drake's exposed belly. This time, his sword found purchase, cutting through the softer scales.

The drake roared, whipping around to strike at him, but Roman was already moving, dodging to the side. Out of the corner of his eye, he saw Seth dart in and land another blow, this one deeper than the last.

The drake staggered, its movements slowing. It turned its head, yellow eyes glaring at Roman with a fury that sent a shiver down his spine. It lunged, and Roman barely had time to brace himself before the creature's weight slammed into him, knocking him to the ground.

He felt the air rush out of his lungs as he hit the dirt. The drake's claws raked at him, and he barely managed to twist away, the sharp talons tearing through his shirt but missing his skin. Pain flared through his shoulder, and he struggled to get back on his feet, his vision swimming.

"Roman, get out of there!" Seth shouted, his voice tinged with panic.

Roman rolled to the side, narrowly avoiding another swipe. He could feel the energy in his core surging, the power flooding through his limbs. He focused, pushing the pain aside, and got to his feet just as the drake lunged again.

This time, he was ready. He sidestepped, slashing his sword across the drake's neck as it passed. The blade bit deep, and the creature let out a choked roar, its body collapsing in a heap.

For a moment, everything was still. Roman stood there, panting, his sword dripping with dark blood. Then Seth was beside him, his hand on Roman's shoulder.

"Are you okay?" Seth asked, his eyes scanning Roman for injuries.

"Yeah... I think so," Roman replied, his voice shaky. He looked down at the drake, its body lying still at his feet. The realization of what they had just done hit him like a wave. "We did it."

Seth grinned, the tension easing from his face. "Yeah, we did. You were amazing."

Roman laughed, the sound a little wild with relief. "You weren't too bad yourself."

They both turned as they heard footsteps approaching. Z, Lexi, and Jessika emerged from the trees, their expressions a mix of worry and admiration.

"Holy crap, you guys!" Lexi exclaimed, her eyes wide as she took in the drake's body. "That's a drake! A real, freaking drake!"

Z clapped Roman on the back, nearly knocking him over. "You guys did great. That's no small feat."

Jessika rushed over, her hands hovering as if she wanted to check Roman for injuries but wasn't sure where to start. "Are you okay? You're not hurt, are you?"

"I'm fine, I promise," Roman said, his heart still pounding. "Just a few scratches."

"So since you're ok…I gotta ask…at any point during that fight did either of you think to call the rest of us? The whole point of this is to fight these monsters to train." Lexi said sarcasm pouring from her.

"Oh right…I forgot." Roman said and scratched the back of his head.

"Whatever." Lexi shook her head and walked closer to the drake like she was annoyed but Roman saw the smile on her face so he relaxed.

They spent the next few minutes inspecting the drake, discussing the battle and what they had learned. As they talked, Roman noticed something in Seth's demeanor—a pride that seemed almost out of place, like he was used to being praised for his skills but was trying to downplay it.

Chapter 4:
Strength in Unity

The afternoon sun cast long shadows across the forest floor as the group moved deeper into the woods. The air was filled with the scent of pine and earth, the occasional rustling of leaves hinting at creatures hidden just out of sight. Roman's heart raced with anticipation as they ventured into an area that seemed to teem with life—and danger.

"Stay close," Z said, his voice low but commanding. "There are usually packs of monsters around here. We don't want to get separated."

They formed a loose circle, weapons ready. Lexi took point, her bow nocked and eyes scanning the tree line. Z moved into the front line next to Lexi to fulfill his role as tank, Seth and Roman took the flanks, moving with quiet precision, Jessika held the rear, their eyes alert for any signs of movement.

They didn't have to wait long. As soon as the fighting started Lexi did an acrobatic flip and ended up next to Jessika at the rear. She didn't need to risk herself being up front if there was no scouting to be done.

A rustling from the underbrush caught their attention, and a moment later, a pack of creatures burst from the trees. They were wolf-like, but larger, with twisted limbs and dark fur matted with mud and blood. Their eyes glowed with a predatory hunger as they snarled and snapped, circling the group.

"Dire wolves," Z muttered, raising his sword. "About six of them. Lexi, take out the leader first."

Lexi nodded, drawing her bowstring back and letting an arrow fly. It struck one of the largest wolves in the eye, and it dropped instantly, the other wolves hesitating for a split second.

Roman didn't wait. He felt the energy surging through his core, his muscles thrumming with a power that begged to be released. He launched himself forward, his sword slicing through the air. One moment he was standing beside Seth, and the next he was in the midst of the pack, his blade cutting through the nearest wolf like it was nothing.

The creatures barely had time to react. Roman moved with an almost unnatural speed, his body a blur as he weaved between the wolves, striking with precision and power. Each step seemed to carry him ten times as far as it should, his sword flashing in the dappled sunlight as he struck again and again. To the others, it looked as though he was teleporting, his form flickering in and out of sight as he darted around the battlefield.

"Holy—!" Jessika's exclamation was cut off as she swung her staff, knocking a wolf aside that had tried to flank her.

Roman's sword struck another wolf, cleaving through its shoulder. He spun away from a snapping maw, his movements fluid and effortless. The wolves were fast, but he was faster. He could feel the power coursing through him, each strike landing with deadly precision. It was as if time itself slowed down for him, every motion calculated, every step perfect.

Seth moved in tandem with him, his own style complementing Roman's speed. He darted in and out of the shadows, his daggers flashing as he struck at exposed flanks and vulnerable joints. Together, they carved through the pack, the wolves howling in pain and fury as they tried and failed to counter the relentless assault.

Z charged forward, his shield raised as he bashed a wolf aside, his sword coming down in a heavy arc that cleaved through bone and sinew. "Keep it up!" he shouted, his voice filled with the thrill of battle.

Lexi loosed arrow after arrow, each one finding its mark with deadly accuracy. The wolves fell one by one, their bodies littering the ground. Jessika moved behind them, her staff glowing with a soft light as she cast spells that bolstered their strength and healed their minor injuries.

Roman felt invincible. He moved faster and struck harder than he ever had before, his sword an extension of his will. He slipped between the wolves like a shadow, his blade cutting through them with ease. The last wolf lunged at him, its jaws snapping shut just inches from his face. He pivoted, his sword slicing through its neck in a single, clean motion.

The clearing fell silent, save for the labored breathing of the group. The ground was strewn with the bodies of the wolves, their dark blood soaking into the earth. Roman stood amidst the carnage, his chest heaving, his sword dripping with blood. He glanced at the others, their eyes wide with a mixture of shock and awe.

"That was... insane," Lexi breathed, lowering her bow.

"You moved like—like you were teleporting," Jessika said, her eyes wide. "How did you do that?"

Roman hesitated, wiping the blood from his sword. "I don't really know," he said truthfully. "It just... happens."

Z clapped him on the shoulder, nearly knocking him off balance. "Whatever it is, it's incredible. I've never seen anyone move like that."

"Yeah, no kidding," Seth added, his eyes narrowing slightly as he studied Roman. "That must be an awesome skill like Swift or something."

"Actually I don't know. How can I search my skills?" Roman asked playing dumb while also trying to see how their systems worked. He saw the notification when he learned <Flash Step>, but didn't want to say anything in case it was a rare skill or if obtaining skills the way he did was weird.

"Oh you need to visit a temple for that and use the Searching Stone. It pretty much does as it says, it searches your body and soul for your levels, titles, and skills. Or if you could afford a searching stone you could do it outside of the temple but those are insanely expensive." Seth answered and Roman nodded.

They spent the rest of the day training together, honing their skills and learning to fight as a unit. Roman found himself slipping into a rhythm with the others, their movements becoming more coordinated as they took on more packs of creatures. He used his speed to draw attention, darting in and out of reach, while Seth struck from the shadows. Lexi provided cover from a distance, her arrows never missing their mark, and Z and Jessika held the line, their combined strength a solid bulwark against any threat.

With each battle, Roman's confidence grew. He learned to control his speed better, focusing the energy in his core to move even faster, strike even harder. He felt the thrill of combat, the exhilaration of testing his limits and pushing beyond them. But he was careful not to let himself go too far. He didn't want to reveal too much, to show them just how different he really was.

As the sun began to dip below the horizon, casting the forest in hues of gold and crimson, they finally made their way back to camp. They were all tired, their bodies sore and bruised, but the camaraderie between them was palpable.

"Not bad for a day's work," Z said, dropping heavily onto a log by the fire. "We made some real progress today."

"Agreed," Seth said, stretching his arms over his head. "Roman, you were incredible out there. I've never seen anything like it."

Roman shrugged, trying to downplay his abilities. "I just do what I can."

"Well, whatever it is, it's working," Lexi said, handing him a water skin. "You're a natural."

Roman took the water skin, his thoughts swirling. He couldn't deny the sense of satisfaction he felt, the pride in what they had accomplished together. But there was also a nagging worry. He was getting closer to them, feeling a bond forming, but he still had to keep his secrets.

As the night deepened and the stars began to twinkle overhead, they sat around the fire, sharing stories and laughter. Seth regaled them with tales of growing up in the capital, his words slipping here and there, hints of a life much more privileged than he wanted to admit.

"You know, back when I was a kid, we had this huge banquet hall," Seth said, then caught himself, glancing around quickly. "I mean, not *we*—one of the noblemen my dad worked for in the capital did.

Z raised an eyebrow, smirking. "Oh really? A banquet hall in the capital? What kind of kid gets to see that?"

Seth coughed, looking away. "Just, you know... those official tour things. For kids. To see the, uh, history and stuff."

Roman hid a smile, listening to Seth's awkward attempts to cover his slip. It was becoming clearer that Seth wasn't just an ordinary adventurer. But he wasn't about to press the issue. They all had their secrets.

The conversation turned lighter as the night wore on, the fire crackling softly as they shared more about themselves. Roman felt a strange warmth spread through him, a sense of belonging he hadn't felt in a long time. He still had a lot to learn, a lot to figure out, but for now, he was content.

As they settled down to sleep, Roman lay on his back, staring up at the stars. He didn't know what the future held, but he knew he was no longer alone. He had allies, friends even, and together they were stronger than any of them could be alone.

Tomorrow would bring new challenges, new battles to fight.

Chapter 5
In the Capital of Meridia

"Your Majesty, Baron Clyburn is requesting an audience with you," announced a deep, silky voice. The speaker, a tall, thin man dressed in immaculate black attire with pristine white cuffs, bowed deeply as he stepped to the side of the golden throne. The King, seated regally, gazed down at the long line of petitioners. He loathed these endless sessions of hearing noble complaints and petty grievances more than anything else.

"Who?" the King snapped, his eyes narrowing. "How dare some minor noble demand my time!"

The outburst echoed through the opulent hall, the nobles shifting uncomfortably at the display of royal temper. After a moment, the King took a deep breath, reigning in his irritation.

"Fine, bring him in," he said, his voice calmer but no less commanding.

"Yes, Your Majesty," the head butler replied, bowing again before turning to fetch the Baron.

A few moments later, the double doors at the far end of the room swung open, and a man of average height and build entered, his velvet tunic clinging slightly to his sweat-slicked skin. His face was flushed, his forehead gleaming, and his hands trembled as he bowed deeply before the throne.

"Your Majesty," he said, his voice shaky with nerves. He waited, bent low, until the King gave a slight nod of acknowledgment.

"Rise, Baron. What is it you wish to discuss?" the King asked, impatience clear in his tone.

"Your Majesty, I received an urgent message from my daughter," the Baron began, his voice thick with anxiety. "She and her party went into the Merkwood Forest to train, and she has informed me that the city of Eidon has been sacked!"

"What? Sacked?!" the King exclaimed, his eyes blazing. "How do you know it's not a mistake?"

"My daughter is a powerful mage, Your Majesty. She used a special parchment spell to send the message directly from the forest. I trust her judgment implicitly."

"Damn it!" the King cursed, his knuckles whitening as he gripped the arms of his throne. "Do we have anyone stationed on that side of the kingdom to verify this?"

One of the generals stepped forward, his face grave. "No, Your Majesty. We've redirected all our forces to the northwest to deal with the orc incursion."

The King's face contorted in fury. "DAMN IT!" he roared, his voice booming through the hall. "Where are the Hydra Knights?"

Merkwood Forest

"You all should get some rest. I'll take the first watch," Seth said, standing from the fire and moving towards the tree line. He positioned himself just outside the circle of light, where the shadows cloaked him, allowing his eyes to adjust and his senses to sharpen.

"I can take a shift too, if you need," Roman offered, feeling a twinge of guilt that the others were looking out for him while he had yet to fully contribute.

"Don't worry about it, man," Z said, stretching out beside Jessika and Lexi. "You're new here, and you seem a bit out of place. Best you conserve your strength and get some sleep."

"Thanks. I guess I will," Roman replied, lying down near the fire. The warmth of the flames was a welcome contrast to the chill that settled over the forest as night deepened. He closed his eyes, listening to the wind rustling through the leaves and the rhythmic chorus of chirping insects. But sleep eluded him, his mind racing with questions and doubts.

Is it really possible to level up and become stronger? he wondered. *The system doesn't seem to work for me. I've grown stronger since I woke up here, that much is clear, but is that considered strong in this world?*

He had nothing to compare his abilities to. Sure, he had survived fights against creatures that would have killed any ordinary person back home, but how would he fare against a trained human opponent? And what about this group he had fallen in with? They seemed trustworthy, but what if they were just lulling him into a false sense of security?

What if they're planning to rob or kill me? His thoughts spiraled further. *What if they're cannibals and want to eat me?*

His heart pounded in his chest, anxiety tightening its grip. He took a deep breath, forcing himself to calm down. He needed to think rationally, to plan.

Okay, he thought, trying to organize his jumbled thoughts. *I'm in a world similar to Earth, but people can get stronger, fight monsters, and use magic. There's political tension, and war could be on the horizon. But what's my role in all of this?*

His thoughts drifted to cultivation—something that seemed unique to him in this world. *Should I ask them about it?* he wondered. But if cultivation wasn't common knowledge, revealing it could make him a target. Better to keep that secret for now.

He opened his eyes and glanced around the camp. The fire burned low, its embers glowing softly. Seth was a dark silhouette against the backdrop of the trees, standing vigilant. Roman got up quietly and approached him.

"Hey, Seth. I have a lot of questions. Do you mind if we talk for a bit?" Roman asked, sitting down as Seth turned to face him.

"Sure," Seth said, his expression curious. "What's on your mind?"

"First off, I know you guys have levels and classes, but are there levels for skills too? Like, does practice make you better?"

Seth nodded slowly. "Yeah, there's something called Proficiency. It's not something most people can see until they're highly skilled in a particular area, though. You've got to be close to mastery before it becomes visible."

"Mastery?" Roman repeated, intrigued.

"Right," Seth continued. "My dad once told me about a blacksmith who reached mastery rank in his craft. Everything he makes is automatically considered Epic grade now. It's rare, though. Most people never reach that level."

"That's incredible," Roman murmured, the concept of Proficiency making sense now. He must have been building Proficiency all this time, even if he couldn't see it.

"What about titles?" Roman asked, trying to sound casual. "How do you get those?"

"Titles are given by the System for unique achievements," Seth explained. "They're even rarer than Proficiencies. A title can grant you powerful abilities or bonuses. Like the King—he has the Sovereign title, which makes him a better ruler. Most people are lucky to get even one title in their lifetime."

Roman's mind raced. *So, titles are supposed to be rare... but I have three.* He wondered what it meant that he had been given so much power, yet he couldn't even access basic parts of the System. He decided not to press Seth for more information; he didn't want to reveal too much.

"What about you?" Roman asked, changing the subject. "You mentioned you grew up in the capital. What's that like?"

Seth hesitated, his gaze shifting away. "It's... different. I was... well, my family was pretty influential. Lots of expectations, lots of rules. But it wasn't the life I wanted."

Roman sensed there was more to the story, but he didn't push. "I get that. Sometimes you just have to find your own way."

"Exactly," Seth said, looking relieved. "That's why I left. Being out here, fighting, training—it's what I want to do."

They sat in companionable silence for a while, the crackling of the fire and the quiet sounds of the night their only company. Roman's mind was still buzzing with questions, but he knew he'd have to find most of the answers on his own.

"Thanks for answering my questions," Roman said finally, standing up. "I think I'll try to get some sleep."

"No problem," Seth replied, giving him a nod. "Get some rest. We'll need our strength tomorrow."

Roman lay back down by the fire, pulling his cloak tighter around him. His mind still raced with thoughts and uncertainties, but there was a strange sense of peace too. He was starting to understand this world, bit by bit, and though there were still countless mysteries to unravel, he felt more prepared than he had before.

As he drifted off, he wondered what the next day would bring. More battles, more training, more secrets to uncover. But whatever it was, he would face it head-on, just as he always had.

The last thing he heard before sleep claimed him was the soft rustling of leaves and the gentle crackle of the fire, a soothing lullaby that carried him into a dreamless slumber.

Chapter 6

Roman's mind spun wildly. He felt an intense pull to be honest with Seth, as though some invisible force was urging him to reveal everything. He struggled against it, the rational part of his mind screaming to keep his secrets hidden. He barely knew these people, after all!

Trust. The word echoed in his mind again, and the tug became almost unbearable. With a sigh, Roman looked into Seth's eyes, searching for any sign of deceit.

"I need to tell you something, Seth. Can I trust you with a secret?" Roman asked, his voice steady but his heart pounding.

"Of course," Seth replied, sincerity etched on his face. "I know we haven't known each other long, but I feel like I can trust you completely. It's almost like fate brought us together, like you were meant to be here."

Roman swallowed hard. The thought had crossed his mind too—some unseen hand guiding his every move, but for what purpose? Before he could respond, a voice interrupted them.

"Do you mind if we join?" Roman's head snapped up. A man stood just a few feet away, a twisted grin on his face. Roman hadn't heard a thing—not a single footstep. He jumped to his feet, mirroring Seth, but before they could react, a sword was at each of their throats.

"Don't even think about it," the man sneered, his foul breath washing over them. He stepped closer, and

Roman gagged at the rancid stench emanating from him—a putrid mix of sweat, urine, and decay.

"Damn, dude, ever heard of soap?" Roman muttered, recoiling.

"Shut up!" the man growled, swinging a fist into Roman's face.

"Roman!" Seth shouted, stepping forward, but his movement was halted as the sword at his neck bit into his skin, drawing a thin line of blood.

"Stay put and shut up!" the man barked. He turned to his companions, a cruel grin spreading across his face. "We'll take your gold, have some fun with your women, and be on our way."

Roman's stomach churned with rage as he watched four more men drag Jessika and Lexi toward the campfire. Z was on the ground, two more thugs pinning him down as he struggled violently.

"Don't you dare touch them!" Z roared, his voice thick with desperation. One of the attackers laughed and tore at Jessika's dress. Z surged up with a roar, knocking one of his captors aside and tackling another. He landed a few solid punches before being struck from behind. He fell to the ground, limp, and the men quickly bound him.

"Get these two tied up as well, and bring that one over here!" the leader commanded, glancing around nervously. "We need to finish before the rest of the army catches up."

Army? Roman's mind raced. "Who are you? What do you want?" he spat, his voice strained as he struggled against the thug holding him down.

"Shut up!" the man barked, stomping on Roman's back and shoving his face into the dirt. Roman could no longer see what was happening, but the sounds of Jessika and Lexi screaming as their clothes were ripped away filled his ears. Rage and fear twisted inside him, his heart pounding like a war drum.

No. Not like this. Roman's breathing grew rapid, his vision narrowing. A surge of anger and despair twisted in his chest, and suddenly, he wasn't in the forest anymore. He was back on Earth, reliving the darkest night of his life.

The scene shifted around him, the smells of pine and fire replaced by the acrid stench of asphalt and gunpowder. He was back in that grimy alleyway, his body pinned to the cold, wet ground. His limbs felt leaden, useless, the throbbing pain in his chest making it hard to breathe.

"Please, just let her go!" he had screamed, his voice hoarse with desperation. His eyes were locked on her, on his girlfriend, Jamie, her body trembling as she was held down by two men. Her face was streaked with tears, her eyes wide with terror. He had fought so hard to reach her, his muscles straining against the unseen force that kept him pinned. But it was no use.

"Shut up!" one of the men had barked, his voice rough and filled with a cruel pleasure. He struck Roman across the face with his pistol, and Roman's head snapped to the side, the metallic taste of blood filling his mouth.

"Jamie, I'm so sorry," he had whispered, his voice breaking. He had felt so powerless, so utterly helpless. All he could do was watch as they assaulted her, their laughter echoing through the narrow alley, drowning out her sobs.

He had begged, pleaded, screamed until his throat was raw, but they hadn't listened. They had stripped away every shred of dignity, every ounce of hope. And he had been forced to watch, every second of it burning itself into his memory like a brand.

Then came the gunshots. He still remembered the sickening sound of the bullets ripping through her body, the way she had crumpled to the ground, her eyes losing their light as her blood pooled around her. He had screamed her name, his voice a raw, broken thing, but she was already gone.

His heart had shattered in that moment. He didn't remember the next few seconds clearly—only flashes of pain, the sound of his own scream echoing in his ears as a bullet tore through his spine. The world had gone black, and when he woke up, he was paralyzed from the waist down, lying in a sterile hospital room.

Jamie was dead, and he had been left behind, broken and alone, trapped in a body that no longer obeyed his will. He had wanted to die then, to follow her into whatever lay beyond. But he hadn't been given that mercy.

The memory of that night had haunted him ever since, the pain and rage festering in the darkest corners of his soul. He had buried it deep, hidden it behind a facade of strength and determination. But now, here in this alien world, faced with a group of men trying to hurt the only people who had shown him kindness, it all came rushing back.

No. Not like this. The words echoed in his mind, and something snapped. He couldn't let it happen again. He wouldn't be helpless this time.

He was back in the forest, the sights and sounds of the camp flooding his senses. The air was thick with the smell of pine and sweat, the crackling of the fire mingling with the cruel laughter of the men. Jessika's scream cut through the haze like a knife, sharp and piercing.

Roman felt the rage rise within him, a tidal wave of fury and despair that threatened to drown him. But this time, it wasn't paralyzing. It was empowering. He felt his muscles tense, his senses sharpen, every fiber of his being humming with energy.

The ropes binding his hands snapped like dry twigs as he surged to his feet. The thug standing over him barely had time to react before Roman's fist connected with his jaw in a devastating uppercut. He felt the bones shatter beneath his knuckles, the man's head snapping back with a sickening crunch. The spray of blood felt almost surreal, and the camp fell silent as everyone turned to look.

But Roman didn't care. He was beyond caring. He moved like a force of nature, his body a blur as he crossed the camp in a single step. His hand closed around the throat of the man assaulting Jessika, and he hurled him away like a rag doll. The thug hit the ground hard, his windpipe crushed, his body twitching as he gasped for air.

The world was reduced to a series of disjointed images: the flash of his sword as it materialized in his hand, the terrified look on the face of the man standing over Lexi, the way the blade slid through flesh and bone like it was nothing. He barely registered the warm blood splattering across his face, his body moving on instinct.

He was everywhere and nowhere, his movements so fast that it seemed as though he was teleporting, appearing in one spot, then another. The attackers had no chance. He cut them down, one after another, the rage in his chest like a fire that wouldn't be quenched until they were all dead.

Not like this. The memory of Jamie's broken body, the sound of her final breath echoed in his mind. He couldn't save her then, but he could save them now. Each blow, each swing of his sword, was fueled by that memory, by the promise he had made to himself to never be powerless again.

He didn't stop until the last man lay dead at his feet. The camp was a scene of carnage, bodies strewn about like discarded toys, the ground slick with blood. Roman stood amidst the chaos, his chest heaving, his vision blurred with tears and rage.

But then he saw Lexi, huddled on the ground, her body trembling. And the look on her face—it was fear. Not of the men who had attacked them, but of him. She was afraid of him.

The realization hit him like a punch to the gut. The fire in his veins died, leaving only a cold, empty void. His sword slipped from his fingers, clattering to the ground. He took a step back, then another, his heart hammering in his chest.

"I'm sorry," he whispered, his voice breaking. "I'm so sorry."

He couldn't do this. He couldn't be this person. The rage, the violence—it had consumed him. He looked down at his hands, stained red with blood, and felt sick. This wasn't what Jamie would have wanted. This wasn't what he wanted.

He stumbled backward, his vision swimming. The forest seemed to close in around him, the trees towering like silent sentinels, their branches reaching out like skeletal fingers. He needed to get away, to escape this nightmare.

He turned and—Step.

50 Miles from Eidon

The commander stood on a rise, looking back toward the smoldering ruins of the city they had just left. His heart ached with rage at the senseless destruction. Innocent lives had been snuffed out, and they had heard nothing—no warnings, no rumors. How had they been so blind?

He clenched his fists, the leather of his gloves creaking under the strain as his nails bit into his palms. Blood dripped from his fingers, but he didn't notice. He had sworn an oath to protect his people, and he had failed.

"Sir, we've returned," a voice called out, drawing his attention. The scouting party he had sent into the Merkwood Forest approached, their faces grim. Behind them, he saw four figures, their armor dirty and bloodied, their expressions hollow. The commander's eyes narrowed as he took in their condition. The tall, broad-shouldered man with the shield must have been their frontline, bearing the brunt of the fight to protect the others.

"Who are you, and what happened?" the commander demanded, his voice harsh. His gaze lingered on one of them, recognition flashing in his eyes. He looked away quickly when the man gave a slight shake of his head. *What are you involved in?* he wondered. This could complicate things far more than he had anticipated.

"Good day, Commander. My name is Jessika," the blonde girl said, stepping forward. "This is Seth, Z, and Lexi. We were training in the forest when we were attacked by a group of men. There was another with us, a man named Roman. He saved us but... he left after."

The commander studied them intently. They looked battered but resilient. There was strength in their stances, experience in their eyes. They weren't mere novices. Jessika's posture, the way she held herself, suggested she was more than capable despite her lack of visible weapons. The archer, Lexi, moved with the grace of a predator, her dark leather armor blending into the surroundings.

"Good day, Commander, we were out here to train. My name is Jessika, this is Seth, Z, and Lexi. There was one more that we met a couple of days ago but he ran off after protecting us from a group of men trying to attack us in the night." The blonde girl says, Commander Athel looked at her intently. She called him Seth so she obviously had no clue who he actually was either. He looked at the rest of the group, they had good armor, seemed to hold themselves like fighters so they weren't newbies. The blonde was on the shorter side but there was something about her that made you want to avoid fighting her and she had no visible weapons either...must be a caster. He looked to the other girl, archer, she was tall and lithe, dark green and black leather armor and even her hair was a dark brown. She would blend into the woods with ease. The big guy was the front line for sure. Full plate armor, giant shield and sword, black hair and bright observant blue eyes....then there was Seth...like a shadow itself, the ultimate rogue, which from his family wasn't entirely a good thing.

"You were attacked? By who? Where are they now?" He asked.

"Dead, the guy we met yesterday, Roman, killed them all after they tried to..." Jessika cut off, unable to finish her sentence but he was able to connect the dots: group of bandits come across a small group, overpowered them and they happened to have two pretty ladies there...unfortunately wasn't a rare occurrence. When might makes right, justice and honor usually are hard found.

"How many men were there?" He asked on.

"Ten." Seth said and then quickly added. "He took them all out with only a few strikes while the rest of us were tied up. He brought his bindings and attacked them. He was terrifying and fast, we couldn't even follow his movements."

"I see." The commander said. To be able to take on ten men on his own was impressive. But why run away after? "Have you seen any signs of the bandits or this Roman anywhere else?" He asked.

"I don't think they were bandits. I heard them mention an army. I think they are what happened to Eidon. They must have been a scouting party." Z stepped forward and answered.

"So it begins." The commander mumbled to himself. "We will head back to the capital and I will let them know what happened. If there is an army that destroyed a city that is a force to be reckoned with. Lindt, form a portal for and these folks! Rest of you! Head to Kenan and wait for me there. Smithson, you're in charge until my return. Move." He ordered and everyone burst into activity. A bright blue portal appeared and without even turning to tell them to follow, the commander stepped through.

Chapter 7

*****

Roman

The world slowed, as if time itself recoiled from him. Roman dropped to his knees, the weight of his body pulling him down like lead chains. His breaths came in ragged, uneven gasps, each one a reminder of the battle that had just taken place. His heart pounded furiously in his chest, the adrenaline that had kept him alive now abandoning him, leaving him hollow and trembling. His limbs felt impossibly heavy, as if he were sinking into the earth, drowning in his own despair.

What's happening to me? The thought whispered through the haze of his mind, but it was weak, drowned by the rising tide of panic and guilt. *Is this because of the skill I used?* He tried to rationalize the weakness, but the truth gnawed at him, sharp and relentless. *Or did I go too far?*

A tremor ran through his body, violent and consuming. His strength, the power he had reveled in moments before, now seemed like a curse, draining him, punishing him for his sins. His mind lurched to another, darker thought—a truth he couldn't ignore any longer. *Is this because I killed those men?*

His gaze fell to his hands, still stained with their blood, and a sickening wave of revulsion surged through him. The red was vivid against his skin, an accusation, a brand marking him for what he had done. He recoiled, disgusted, his stomach twisting into knots as if the blood had seeped through his flesh and into his soul, corrupting him at his core.

His hands—once vessels of strength and hope—now trembled as if they could barely hold the weight of his guilt. *How could I?* The memory of those men—human lives—flashed in his mind, each face twisted in fear, in pain, in the final moments before he took their lives. They weren't monsters. They weren't mindless creatures like the wolves. They had families, they had histories, and now, because of him, they had nothing.

Roman bent over, retching, the bitter bile burning his throat as his stomach turned. The taste lingered, acrid and sharp, like the consequence of his actions—impossible to swallow, impossible to spit out. His body shook violently, the weight of his sin pressing down on him, suffocating him.

What have I done? His heart cried out in anguish, but there was no answer, no comfort, only silence. He felt like he was alone in the universe—abandoned. *Is this what it means to be forsaken?*

Roman's mind swirled in chaos, his guilt spiraling into something darker, something deeper. The faces of his new companions flashed before him—Seth, Lexi, Jessika, Z. They had trusted him, accepted him even though they barely knew him. And what had he done? He had run. He had abandoned them after the violence he had unleashed, after losing control in front of them. They had seen him for what he truly was—a monster.

You're nothing but a coward. His own voice echoed in his mind, dripping with disgust. "Coward," he spat, his voice a broken whisper. *You should've stayed.* His heart pounded in his ears as shame coiled around his throat, choking him. *You should've stayed and made sure they were safe. But instead, you ran. You always run.*

His breath came quicker, shallow and uneven, as the magnitude of his failure overwhelmed him. *What if there were more bandits? What if the army they mentioned is already closing in on them?*

He squeezed his eyes shut, his mind grasping for the teachings of his old life—teachings that now felt distant, almost forgotten. *Lord, is this my punishment? For everything I've done? For all my sins?* He had always believed there was redemption, always believed in a second chance. But now, in the wake of the blood he had spilled, those beliefs seemed hollow, unreachable. *Am I beyond saving?*

His chest ached with the weight of his guilt, each breath harder to take than the last. He had killed. Not just in battle, not just to defend himself—he had *enjoyed* it. For a brief, horrifying moment, he had reveled in the power, in the destruction. *How could I have let myself sink so low?* He bent his head, feeling the sting of tears at the corners of his eyes, shame scorching through him.

He thought of his old life, his beliefs, the lessons he had once clung to. *Thou shalt not kill.* The words rang in his mind like a bell, a commandment he had shattered. The burden of it weighed on his soul. He had lost his way. *How could I face them now?* The thought of his companions, the looks of horror they must have worn, twisted his stomach further. What must they think of him now?

A part of him wanted to lay down and never rise again. *You don't deserve to go back. You don't deserve forgiveness.* The voice in his head was relentless, cruel. *You should have been the one to die.*

But even in the midst of the storm inside him, a spark flickered. His friends—Seth, Lexi, Jessika, Z—they were still out there. He had left them vulnerable, alone. If there was any chance that they were in danger, he couldn't just sit here, drowning in his own self-hatred. *They trusted you once. You owe them that much.*

Roman's hands dug into the dirt beneath him, his fingers curling into fists. He gritted his teeth and forced himself to rise, though every fiber of his being screamed at him to stay down. The weight of his guilt didn't lift, but the thought of his friends, the thought of their safety, gave him enough strength to stand.

"I have to go back," he whispered, his voice barely audible. He stumbled forward, his legs shaking, but he moved. His heart still ached, his soul still felt tainted, but he couldn't abandon them. Not again. *Not this time.*

Roman glanced around, his vision still hazy, but he caught sight of a thin path through the underbrush. The branches were broken, evidence of his reckless escape. It had to be the way back.

I can't change what I've done, he thought, his jaw clenching. *But I can still do something right.*

"Alright, Roman. Pull it together." His voice was a harsh whisper, barely audible over the pounding of his heart. He forced himself to breathe deeply, trying to calm the storm raging inside him. *You've got to go back. Make sure they're safe.* The words echoed in his mind like a mantra. He swallowed hard, pushing the fear aside. *Then get everyone out and report those bastards. If that army really is the one that attacked Eidon...*

His throat tightened as the image of Eidon's destruction flashed before him—the streets littered with bodies, the city a smoking ruin. He couldn't let that happen again. *I can't let them get ambushed.*

Roman looked around, his gaze landing on a tall tree nearby, its sturdy branches far above the ground. *I need to get my bearings. Find them.* Without hesitation, he sprinted toward the tree, his legs surging with power. He leaped, muscles coiling as he shot upward, grabbing a thick branch seven feet above the ground. The strength flowed through him, almost startling in its intensity, but it was quickly tempered by the purpose driving him.

A brief, fleeting grin tugged at the corners of his lips. *Out-jumping LeBron, huh?* For a split second, the thought was almost amusing, a spark of normalcy in the chaos. But it faded just as quickly, and he pushed it aside, focusing on the task at hand.

He climbed higher, his movements swift and agile, driven by desperation. His muscles burned with the effort, but the urgency of his mission dulled the pain. He scaled the tree quickly, the branches thinning as he neared the top, until finally, he broke through the canopy. Below him, the forest stretched endlessly in every direction, a sea of green swaying gently in the wind.

"Wow..." he breathed, the word slipping out unbidden. For a moment, he allowed himself to marvel at the beauty before him—the towering peaks of mountains to the north, the plains rolling into the horizon to the south, and far to the east, the gleaming outline of a city nestled against the curve of a wide, winding river. That must be where they'd head next, but his attention was locked on something far more immediate.

His heart leaped as he spotted movement—a small black dot moving along a narrow path through the trees. His friends. Relief surged through him, a brief flicker of hope.

But that hope was short-lived.

Something else caught his eye—something much larger, moving with terrifying speed from the north. An army. Roman's blood ran cold as he squinted, trying to make out the details. Even from this distance, he could see the dark mass of soldiers, an unstoppable wave bearing down on the small dot that marked his friends.

"No..." The word barely escaped his lips, a hoarse whisper of disbelief. His mind flashed back to Eidon—the broken city, the devastation, the bodies. *If this is the same force...* He couldn't let them reach his friends. He *wouldn't*.

"I have to get to them before the army does!" Roman's voice shook with urgency, his fear morphing into something sharper, more determined. Without wasting another second, he launched himself from the tree, letting gravity take him. His body dropped like a stone, free-falling for several heart-stopping seconds before his hand shot out, grabbing a branch to slow his descent. He hit the ground hard but rolled with the impact, already on his feet and sprinting before the dust settled.

The forest blurred around him, branches snapping at his face, tearing at his clothes, but he didn't slow. Tears stung his eyes, a mixture of wind, pain, and the weight of his guilt, each drop a plea for forgiveness, for strength. His lungs burned, his legs ached, but none of it mattered. The only thing that mattered was reaching them—before it was too late.

Faster. The thought pulsed in his mind like a heartbeat. *Faster.*

He pushed harder, his feet pounding the earth in a frantic rhythm, the wind rushing past him in deafening roars. It felt like the very forest was trying to hold him back—branches clawing at him, roots tripping him up—but every time he stumbled, he caught himself, refusing to stop. He couldn't stop.

Lord, I know I've failed. I know I've sinned. The prayer formed in his mind, unbidden, desperate. *But please, just give me enough time. Just let me make it in time.*

His breath came in ragged bursts, his muscles screaming for him to slow down, but he wouldn't. He couldn't. His friends' faces swam before his eyes—Seth, Lexi, Jessika, Z. He had left them behind, vulnerable. He had abandoned them when they needed him most. *Coward.*

The word cut through him like a knife, but this time, it drove him forward. He had to be more than what his doubts told him. He had to be the person they needed.

Branches whipped at his face, cutting into his skin, but Roman barely felt it. The pain in his legs was secondary, the burn in his lungs a distant concern. All that mattered was the looming shadow of the army, and the small, fragile hope that he could make it to his friends before the nightmare descended.

As he tore through the forest, his heart thudding in his chest, the memories of his guilt, his failure, tried to drown him again. *You can't save them.* The voice was there, a cruel whisper at the edge of his mind. *You failed before. You'll fail again.*

"No," he whispered, shaking his head violently. *Not this time.* His body hurtled forward, a blur of desperation and determination.

Please, God. Don't let me fail again.

His legs carried him faster, his feet barely touching the ground as he sprinted through the undergrowth. He knew he was running on borrowed time, but for once, he prayed it would be enough.

The trees began to thin, and he knew he was close. "Seth! Lexi! Z! Jessika!" he shouted, his voice hoarse with desperation. But there was no answer, only the rustle of the wind through the leaves.

"Jessika! Lexi!" He broke through the tree line and skidded to a halt, his heart plummeting at the sight before him. A group of armed men stood in a clearing, their weapons drawn. Roman's eyes darted frantically around, searching for his friends.

"Halt!" A commanding voice rang out, cutting through the silence. "Identify yourself!"

"My name is Roman!" he called, his voice shaking with fear and adrenaline. "I was with a group of friends in the forest, but we got separated."

"What are their names?" the man demanded, his hand resting on the hilt of his sword.

"Lexi, Seth, Z, and Jessika," Roman answered, his heart hammering in his chest as he prayed they were safe.

"Stand down, men," the leader ordered, and the tension in the air eased as the soldiers lowered their weapons. "You match the description and you know their names. You must be the one."

"Where are they?" Roman asked urgently. "Are they okay?"

"They're not here," the leader said. "They went with the commander to report the attack to the King. We're heading to Kenan to meet up with them. We'll escort you there."

Relief washed over Roman, the fear that had been gripping his heart easing slightly. "Thank you," he said, his voice thick with emotion. But then he remembered the army he had seen. "Wait! There's a massive army heading this way, over the hill! I was running to warn you."

He looked around at the soldiers—there were maybe fifty of them, well-armed and disciplined. But against the size of the force he had seen...

"I'll climb that tree," he said, pointing to a tall oak nearby, "and get a better look at what we're facing."

The leader nodded. "I have a scouting party out as well. If there's something out there, we'll know soon enough."

Roman ran to the tree and jumped, the strength in his legs propelling him high into the air. He grabbed a branch and began to climb, his heart pounding with urgency. Within minutes, he was at the top, his eyes sweeping the landscape.

What he saw made his stomach drop. A vast sea of men was moving toward them, their armor glinting in the sunlight. Thousands of soldiers, marching in tight formation, their banners fluttering in the breeze. But that wasn't the worst of it.

Farther back, beyond the initial force, was an even larger army, stretching as far as the eye could see, their ranks darkening the plains like a shadow. They were headed straight for the city he had seen in the distance.

God, there are so many... Roman dropped from the tree, his heart racing as he sprinted back to the leader.

"It's worse than I thought," he panted, struggling to catch his breath. "There's an army heading toward us—thousands of men. But there's a much larger force heading toward the city."

The leader's eyes widened. "How many?"

"Thousands," Roman said, shaking his head. "I don't know exactly. But it's huge."

The sergeant cursed under his breath. "We have no choice. We have to get to the city before they do. We might not be able to stop them, but we can warn them and help fortify the defenses."

He turned to his men. "Double time! We move fast and try to reach the city before the enemy does."

The soldiers snapped to attention, their faces grim. Roman followed them, his mind racing. He had to get back to his friends, to warn them about the danger heading their way. But more than that, he had to face the consequences of his actions.

The fear of losing control again, of hurting the people he cared about, gnawed at him. But he couldn't let that stop him. He had to be better, stronger. He had to protect them, no matter the cost.

He took a deep breath, steeling himself as they set off. The path ahead was uncertain, but he would face it head-on. He had to.

For them.

For Jamie.

For himself.

Chapter 8
Roman

Roman and the soldiers ran as one, their collective movement like a well-oiled machine surging through the forest. The sound of their footfalls and the rhythmic clink of armor filled the air as they pushed forward. Roman felt the wind rushing past him, his feet barely touching the ground. Despite the pace, his breathing was steady, his muscles humming with energy.

After a while, the Sergeant, his brow furrowed in confusion, glanced over at Roman. Finally, he couldn't hold back his curiosity any longer.

"How are you able to keep up with us? Who are you really?" the Sergeant asked, his voice tinged with suspicion.

"I already told you. I'm Roman," he replied, keeping his tone casual. "I was training with some friends when we got separated. And why wouldn't I be able to keep up? We're not exactly sprinting, and I'm not weighed down with armor like you guys are."

The Sergeant gave him a skeptical look. "That may be true, but the average person would be struggling to keep this pace. Yet here you are, running like it's a leisurely afternoon stroll. You're not even winded. What are your stats?"

Roman feigned a look of mock offense, his voice dripping with exaggerated indignation. "Whoa there, Sergeant! I might not be from around here, but I thought it was common knowledge in this kingdom that asking about someone's stats is incredibly rude."

"Usually, yes," the Sergeant agreed, his eyes narrowing. "But when an entire city is destroyed, and a blood-covered stranger runs out of the woods claiming to have been separated from his friends, I think it's a good time to make an exception."

Roman shrugged, nonchalant. "Nah, I don't see how those things are related. Either way, I'm not giving you that information." He pointed to the left, where enemy soldiers were beginning to charge toward them, weapons raised and shouting battle cries. "And look, now you've got bigger things to worry about than prying into my business."

The alarm spread quickly. Drums and horns blared from the other side of the hill, their ominous tones rolling across the battlefield like a thunderstorm. The enemy was close now, almost cresting the hill. Roman watched as the soldiers around him sprang into action without hesitation, their movements precise and coordinated. This was no ordinary unit—they were elite, honed by years of training and experience.

"Sea Squad, flank left! Earth Squad, right! Everyone else, Richter maneuver!" Sergeant Smithson bellowed, his voice carrying above the din of approaching battle.

The soldiers moved in perfect unison. Two squads broke off to the flanks, creating a pincer formation that forced the enemy to choose their targets carefully. The remaining men spread out, forming a solid line that bristled with shields and spears. They were outnumbered and had the disadvantage of being on lower ground, but they moved with confidence, their focus unwavering.

"Impressive," Roman admitted, casting a sideways glance at the Sergeant, who nodded smugly.

"This is nothing," Smithson replied with a proud grin. "When the Commander returns with the main force, it'll look like a work of art. He's spent years crafting this unit into the finest on the continent." His words were cut short by the earth-shaking collision as the two forces met.

The clash was brutal. Metal clanged against metal, and the ground shook with the impact of bodies colliding. Roman's heart pounded as he watched the carnage unfold, a strange exhilaration mingling with the unfamiliar sense of guilt and horror. It was surreal—on one hand, he felt out of place, as though he were watching some grotesque play unfold before him. On the other, he felt a thrill, a surge of adrenaline that made him want to leap into the fray and test his strength against these foes.

He could almost see the world as a game, each enemy a target to be eliminated, each move a chance to rack up a higher score. His mind raced with thoughts of combos and tactics, of maximizing efficiency. But deep down, a voice whispered that these weren't just enemies—they were people, with lives and families and stories of their own. It was a truth he didn't want to face, not now.

I have to hold back, he thought, clenching his fists. *If I lose control again...* He glanced at the Sergeant, who was barking orders and directing the men with calm authority. *I can't let them see what I'm capable of. Not yet.*

But then another thought crept in, dark and insidious. *What does it matter? I'm not beholden to these people. I serve no one here. Why should I care what they think?* He didn't even know if he was on the right side. Who were the good guys in this war? Who were the bad guys? The lines blurred and twisted in his mind, leaving him feeling lost and unmoored.

He took a deep breath, searching for the calm, still voice that usually guided him. But there was only silence. Ever since that night at the campsite, since he'd let the rage take over and killed those men, he had felt utterly alone. It was as if the rage had severed his connection to something greater, something that had once given him clarity and purpose.

"Sea Squad, push!" the Sergeant shouted, snapping Roman out of his thoughts.

"Uh, how do you expect them to hear you over all of this?" Roman asked, gesturing to the chaos around them.

"They hear me," the Sergeant replied confidently, his eyes never leaving the battlefield. "I know every one of these men, and they follow me because they trust me. It's a bond that's unbreakable."

Roman smiled faintly. It sounded like something his father used to say, back when faith had been a comfort instead of a burden. "It's impressive," he admitted, watching as the soldiers followed the Sergeant's orders, driving the enemy back despite being outnumbered.

"They've got this under control," Roman said, nodding as the soldiers continued their relentless advance.

"This is nothing for them," the Sergeant agreed, his voice filled with pride.

Commander Athel, Capital of Meridia

"This way, Commander." The young servant's voice trembled as he led Commander Athel and his entourage through the gilded halls of the royal palace. The Commander moved with purposeful strides, his portal master, Seth, Jessika, and Z trailing behind him. There was no time for formalities. The situation was dire, and every second counted.

"My King!" Athel called out as he pushed open the massive doors to the throne room, not bothering to wait for the usual introductions. "We are under attack and need to respond immediately."

King Juelius stood from his throne, his expression shifting from irritation to concern. "Commander Athel. You and your unit were not due back for another week. What has happened?"

"Your Majesty, we made it to the Merkwood Forest after finding Eidon reduced to nothing more than a ghost town," Athel reported. "We found these young people there, training."

The King's gaze shifted to the group standing beside the Commander. His eyes narrowed as he recognized one of them.

"Seth! What in the world are you doing here?" The King's voice wavered between anger and relief. He took a deep breath, trying to compose himself. "Are you alright?"

"Yes, Father, I'm fine," Seth replied, his voice steady. A murmur rippled through the hall as the nobles realized who the young man was. Jessika and the others gasped in shock, they knew he was from a rich family but not a royal let alone the Crown Prince! The Commander shook his head slightly. This kid was always causing trouble, but at least this time it had led to something useful. They might not have been able to prepare in time without his warning.

"What did you see?" the King asked, his eyes narrowing.

Seth recounted the events in detail, his voice calm and clear despite the gravity of the situation. He described the army they had seen, the destruction of Eidon, and the fight in the forest. The King listened intently, his face growing darker with each word.

"I assume you have already begun mustering the troops?" Commander Athel asked as soon as Seth finished speaking.

The King nodded. "You are in charge. We did not leave many here in reserve, just about 2000, the rest went north. Get out there and do what you must."

"Sire," the Commander replied with a sharp salute. He turned and strode from the room, his mind already racing through strategies and tactics.

"We should help," Seth said, turning back to his father.

"Absolutely not!" the King snapped. "You should be on your way home. You should never have left the palace grounds in the first place. What were you doing in Merkwood?"

"Training," Seth answered, his voice firm.

"Training? In Merkwood? I have brought the best trainers in the kingdom here to teach you, and you sneak off to the most dangerous forest in the realm?"

"There's nothing else to learn from them!" Seth's voice rose, his frustration boiling over. "I need real challenges, not pampered instructors who are too scared of you to push me!"

The King's face flushed with anger, but before he could respond, a soft voice cut through the tension.

"Seth," the Queen's voice was gentle, soothing. She moved gracefully onto the dais, her presence calming the storm that had been brewing. "Your father is trying to protect you, and this kingdom. Think about it—what would happen if the heir to the throne were killed in battle? How would our people react?"

Seth looked down, his anger fading. "I just want to get stronger," he muttered. "I can't do that locked up in the palace."

The King's expression softened slightly. "We will find a way to help you train, but you must understand, your safety is paramount."

"What about that new dungeon in the Southern Ridge?" the Steward suggested, stepping forward. "It would be a perfect place to test his skills, and it's a controlled environment."

The King's eyes brightened. "Yes, that could work. Once the current crisis is dealt with, you can go with the Commander and clear it. You'll have the challenge you seek, without the risk of real death."

Seth's eyes lit up. "And I can bring my friends?"

The King hesitated, then nodded. "Yes, as a thank you for protecting my son I will also grant you all titles and the land out there will be split amongst you. Build, and protect it as we try to expand our borders into the untamed mountains and whatever may be beyond."

Seth turned to his friends, who grinned and exchanged excited and nervous looks. "There's one more, though. We met him in Merkwood, and he saved our lives."

"What do you mean?" the King asked, frowning.

"We were captured by what we thought were bandits, but they were scouts. They tied us up and were about to…" Seth's voice faltered, and he glanced at Jessika and Lexi, who both looked down, their faces pale. "They were going to hurt the girls. Roman, the guy we met, broke free and killed them all in a matter of seconds. Then he vanished. I think he moved so fast he got lost. We need to find him."

The King's eyes widened slightly. "He killed a group of trained scouts in seconds?"

Seth nodded. "Yes, Father. He was… incredible. I've never seen anything like it. He moved like the wind, faster than I could track."

There were gasps from the gathered nobles. The last person who had displayed such speed was the legendary hero Flash Step Morrow, who had died decades ago in the final battle of the Great War.

"Hmm," the King murmured, deep in thought. "I will have the Commander look for him. If he truly saved your lives, he deserves a reward. And if he is as strong as you say, he could be an invaluable ally."

Seth beamed. "Thank you, Father."

The King nodded, his mind already turning to the looming threat. "Prepare yourselves. Once the battle is over, we'll make arrangements for the dungeon."

Seth and his friends cheered quietly, the tension lifting from their shoulders. But in the back of his mind, Seth couldn't shake the image of Roman standing amidst the carnage, his eyes wild and desperate. He hoped they would find him before it was too late.

Roman

"Damn, so that's what a slaughter looks like up close, huh?" Roman murmured, his voice thick with a grim sort of wonder. Beside him, Sergeant Smithson chuckled along with a few of his men, their laughter tense but genuine.

"You'd better get used to it," the Sergeant replied. "Now, let's get to the top of this hill and see what we're really dealing with." He gestured forward, and the soldiers moved out, their faces set with grim determination. Roman fell in beside him, his heart hammering in anticipation.

They crested the hill together, and the sight that awaited them was beyond anything Roman had imagined. The breath caught in his throat, his mind struggling to process the sheer scale of the force arrayed before them.

"Oh... how?" the Sergeant stammered, his voice barely a whisper. His face had gone pale, and he stood frozen, staring out over the valley below. Some of his men stumbled to a halt beside him, their expressions mirroring his shock and fear.

Roman had expected a large force, but the reality was staggering. The entire valley seemed to be filled with soldiers, stretching as far as the eye could see—a sea of armor and steel, thousands upon thousands of men. And they weren't alone. Huge creatures lumbered through the ranks, chained and muzzled; their eyes gleaming with a terrifying intelligence.

Roman's eyes widened as he spotted a massive, scaled beast among them. It looked like a dragon, but its wings were stunted, and its movements were more lumbering, less graceful. *A drake,* he realized, recalling the wingless cousins of the dragons he'd read about in this world's lore.

The soldiers around him were paralyzed with fear, their faces drained of color. Roman locked eyes with the Sergeant, seeing his own shock reflected there. He nodded, and the Sergeant returned the gesture, a glimmer of relief breaking through his fear.

Let's get the hell out of—

"Alright, men!" The Sergeant's voice cut through the stunned silence, his tone sharp and commanding. "Now that our warm-up is done, who's ready for some real fighting?" His words were like a spark in dry kindling, snapping the men out of their stupor. Some even managed to chuckle, though their eyes were still wide with shock.

"Looks like they didn't bring enough men for all of us to have a fair fight, so some of y'all will have to share, okay?" The Sergeant's grin was fierce, and he slammed his fist against his chest, the sound like a drumbeat. The men around him echoed the gesture, the metallic thud reverberating through the air.

"These bastards dared to sneak into our country, attack our cities, and now gather in secret to assault another. Are you going to let that stand?"

The response was immediate. Fists struck against armored chests in unison, the sound building into a rhythmic, thunderous beat. It wasn't loud, but the energy in the air was palpable, a fierce determination that seemed to lift the spirits of everyone present—even Roman found himself caught up in it.

"I thought so," the Sergeant growled, his voice low and intense. "Let's show them who the Hydra Knights are. Let's make them earn every step they've taken into our land with blood. Are you with me?!"

The rhythmic thudding grew louder, each beat resonating through the ranks. Roman felt his own heart pounding in time with it, his blood singing with the thrill of the moment.

"I need a weapon. Armor, if you have any spare," Roman said, his voice steady.

The Sergeant looked at him, then nodded. "Glad to have you with us." He called over to the quartermaster, who eyed Roman critically.

"Sword's no good for you right now," the quartermaster muttered after a moment, his gaze sharp. "Glaive. This one's special. Brought it from home." He handed Roman a long, ornate polearm with a wicked curved blade mounted proudly atop it. The craftsmanship was beautiful, the blade gleaming in the light. It felt strangely familiar in his hands, as if it had been made for him.

"I've never used one before," Roman admitted, though the weight felt right, the balance perfect.

"Learn," the man replied simply, thrusting the weapon into his grip. As soon as Roman's hands closed around the shaft, a sense of calm and confidence washed over him, banishing the lingering traces of fear.

"Wow," Roman breathed, the words slipping out before he could stop them.

"I told you," The quartermaster said with a satisfied nod. He tossed Roman a set of light armor. "This should fit. Get ready."

Roman's confusion must have been obvious because one of the soldiers leaned over and whispered, "Don't question it. It's his skill. His magic lets him match the right gear to the right person for the right situation. It's amazing."

Roman nodded, his heart racing as he pulled on the armor. It fit perfectly, as if tailored just for him. He flexed his arms, testing the range of motion. It felt good. Better than good—it felt right.

"Alright, looking good," the Sergeant called out as Roman stood, the glaive held firmly in his hands. Roman felt a surge of energy, a sense of purpose and belonging that had been missing since he'd arrived in this world. It was back—that feeling of being on the right path, of being exactly where he was supposed to be.

This is it, he thought, his mind clearing. He focused, sifting through the different options available to him, letting that inner compass guide him. The path that resonated strongest was clear: *Fight as hard as I can to limit casualties among these men.*

"Sergeant, I know you don't know or trust me, but I can take out a lot of them on my own. Where would be the best spot for me to engage, alone, to help you?"

The Sergeant raised an eyebrow, clearly skeptical. "By yourself? Are you looking to die?"

"Not at all. I'm trying to keep your men alive. If I can draw enough of their attention, or at least disrupt them, you won't have to spread your forces so thin."

The Sergeant's gaze was sharp, assessing. "I'm not sure if you're crazy or just plain insane, but I can see you mean what you say." He pointed toward a ridge on the enemy's flank. "If you hit them there, right when we engage, it'll cause chaos. They'll focus on us first because we're the bigger threat. Once you start doing damage, you'll pull their attention, and we can exploit the confusion. If you're not strong enough, you die, and we fight like planned."

Roman grinned, his grip tightening on the glaive. "Sounds good to me. See you in the thick of it." And with that, he was off, covering the distance in a blur.

"Damn, he's fast," the Sergeant muttered, watching Roman disappear into the distance. "Maybe he wasn't bluffing after all."

He turned back to his men, his voice rising into a guttural roar. "Men! MAKE THEM PLEAD TO THEIR GODS FOR FORGIVENESS, MAKE THEM REGRET THE DAY THEY WERE BORN! MAKE. THEM. FEAR. YOU!"

Chapter 9
Roman

Roman felt the Sergeant's rallying cry reverberate through him, even though he was too far away to hear the actual words. The power behind it, the raw, primal energy, was enough to send a shiver down his spine. He bounced on the balls of his feet, expelling the last of his nervous energy, and muttered a quick prayer.

"Lord, I've made more mistakes than I can count, but I don't think this is one of them. I feel like this is where you want me to be. I know I'm new to this world, but I'm willing to fight for these people like they're my own. Give us the strength we need. Guide every step, every breath. In Jesus' name, I pray. Amen."

A warmth spread through him, a familiar, comforting presence that he had thought lost. He smiled, a fierce determination settling over him.

He pushed off with his left foot—and stumbled, his face planting into the dirt. He lay there for a second, stunned.

"Ah! Okay, let's try that again," he muttered, brushing himself off. *Glad no one saw that.* He took off again, more cautiously this time, making sure to watch his step. The enemy army loomed ahead, a dark mass bristling with weapons and armor. Roman could see some of them turning, pointing at the small group charging down the hill. Laughter rose from their ranks, but it died quickly as they saw the Hydra Knights' banner and the crest on Roman's armor.

"Hydra Knights!" one of the enemy soldiers shouted, his voice tinged with fear. "Commander!"

The opposing commander turned; his face twisted in confusion. "How many?"

"About fifty on one side, and one man alone on the left flank."

"Fifty and one…" The commander's eyes narrowed. "Why bother?"

"They came from the direction of the scouts, sir."

The commander's expression hardened. "So they killed an entire scouting party with just fifty men? And now they're charging? Men, I know this seems like a joke, but do NOT underestimate these soldiers!" He rose, his voice booming. "ARM UP!"

Roman grinned as he saw the enemy mobilizing, his pulse quickening. He pushed harder, feeling the wind whip past him as he ran full speed across the open field. He was moving so fast that the soldiers couldn't track him, their cries of confusion echoing through the air.

With a deafening boom, he hit their lines, tearing through their ranks like a force of nature. His glaive swung in a wide arc, cleaving through bodies with brutal efficiency. Ten men were hurled through the air with his first strike, another dozen cut down with his second. He moved like a whirlwind, a blur of steel and death, his momentum carrying him through the enemy ranks with terrifying ease.

He didn't bother blocking or dodging, simply plowing through them, his weapon slicing and crushing anything in its path. His speed was his greatest advantage; the enemy couldn't touch him, couldn't even see him clearly as he darted among them. He felt almost detached, as if he were watching from outside his own body, each kill a point on a scoreboard.

After a while, he stopped, panting, his chest heaving. The air was thick with dust and the stench of blood. He looked around, his eyes narrowing as he saw more soldiers rushing toward him.

"Now for the real fun," he muttered, ducking as an arrow whistled past him, striking one of the men charging at him. "Not a good idea to shoot at me here."

The archers seemed to get the message, stopping their volleys as Roman continued his assault. He moved through the ranks, his glaive a blur of deadly precision. He was in his element, his mind clear, his body moving on instinct.

But then a strange sensation began to build in his chest, a faint vibration that grew stronger with each breath. He frowned, focusing on it, and a series of screens flickered into view before his eyes. He had minimized them earlier, and now they sprang back to life, displaying information.

--Glaive Proficiency lvl 10 gained. Mastered. <You have reached maximum proficiency with this weapon and unlocked a Choice: Elemental Damage, Attack Speed, or Raw Damage Increase. Please select your Choice.>

Roman's eyes widened as he focused on just that section for now, ignoring the rest of the data. *I've mastered it already. That's insane!* He glanced around, still moving, and pushed the notifications aside. He'd deal with that later. For now, he needed to focus on the fight.

Gasp! Pain exploded through his side as an arrow struck, piercing his ribs. Roman stumbled, his breath hitching, the shock of the wound momentarily paralyzing him. He could feel the blood bubbling in his lung, each breath a struggle.

You can handle this. Run while you assess. He gritted his teeth and pushed himself forward, sprinting back toward the hill he had descended, his mind splitting between the physical and the mental. He focused inward, tracing the path of the arrow. The damage was bad—a punctured lung and a cracked rib.

He visualized his energy, directing it toward the wound. It flowed around the arrowhead, coating it, and then gently pushed, sealing the punctures as it moved. The arrow fell free, clattering to the ground. He sighed in relief, but the pain still burned in his chest.

Energy can't fix everything. I'll need proper healing for this. He tried to focus on his lung, but the energy wouldn't respond. He glanced at his hands, noticing the faint glow around the seedlings embedded in his palms. The energy swirled around them, as if trying to dig them out.

What are you doing? He pushed more energy toward the seedlings, willing it to work. It felt as though something was shifting, the sensation both thrilling and painful.

And then the pain exploded.

It wasn't just pain—it was agony, tearing through Roman's body like molten fire coursing through his veins. His vision blurred, and he collapsed onto the ground, his body convulsing uncontrollably. His scream was caught in his throat, muffled by the dirt pressing against his face. His muscles spasmed violently, betraying him as waves of sheer torment ripped through every inch of his being. He could hear the distant roar of the enemy's cheers, their laughter ringing out in celebration, thinking they had finally brought him down.

But inside Roman, the real battle had just begun.

Focus, he tried to tell himself, but it was hard to grasp even that simple thought in the hurricane of pain. His body felt as if it were being torn apart from the inside, each breath a new agony. Every nerve screamed for mercy, and for a terrifying moment, he felt utterly vulnerable, the sharp edges of mortality clawing at his mind.

Is this how it ends? The thought slipped through the chaos, cold and terrifying. For a fleeting moment, it felt possible. He was too broken, too weak. *I can't... not now. Not like this.*

He gritted his teeth so hard he thought they might shatter. He had been through too much, survived too many horrors to give up now. He couldn't afford to let go, not when he was so close. The seedlings in his palms throbbed painfully, something within them shifting, as though something inside him was clawing its way to the surface.

Just… a little… more, he thought, his vision fading to black at the edges. Every nerve screamed, his muscles burned like they were being shredded from the inside, but he forced himself to hold on. The seedlings shifted again, and then, with a sickening *pop*, something inside him snapped. The pain vanished in an instant, replaced by a strange, pulsing warmth that flooded his body.

Relief washed over him like a wave, so overwhelming he thought he might weep. He lay there for a moment, gasping for breath, his body trembling from the aftershocks. His muscles twitched involuntarily, but the agony was gone, replaced by a tingling sensation that coursed through him like liquid electricity.

Roman slowly pushed himself to his knees, panting heavily. The distant cheers of the enemy faded into the background, insignificant now. His hands still shook, but it wasn't from weakness—it was from something else entirely. He looked down at them, his breath catching as he saw the faint glow beneath his skin. The seedlings were pulsating, vibrant with life, energy radiating from them in waves. He could *feel* it, a power thrumming just beneath the surface.

Focus.

The word came unbidden, but he latched onto it, pulling himself together. He grasped at the raw, wild energy swirling within him, reining it in, shaping it. The power responded, and as he pushed against the barrier inside himself, he felt it give way. The flood of energy that followed was like nothing he had ever experienced before.

With one final, agonized scream, the last of the barrier shattered, and the power surged through him—pure, unbridled, electric. His fatigue disappeared in an instant, his strength returning with a vengeance. He felt *alive*—stronger, faster, sharper than he had ever been before. His body hummed with the energy coursing through him, and with it came a deep, intoxicating sense of control.

I'm back.

Roman pushed himself to his feet, rolling his shoulders, testing the new power. He felt invincible, every muscle in his body vibrating with energy. His senses sharpened, the world coming into razor focus. The arrows raining down around him seemed to slow, their deadly trajectory easy to dodge. With a grin, he ducked and weaved through them with effortless grace, the thrill of it sending a jolt of excitement through him.

Let's see what this new power can do.

Roman's eyes locked onto the struggling ranks of the Sergeant's men in the distance. Without hesitation, he sprinted toward the battle, his feet barely touching the ground as he tore through the rolling hills. Arrows zipped past him, but he didn't bother dodging them now—he didn't have to. The energy pulsed within him, and every step felt like he was flying.

He burst into the fray, his glaive already humming with power. He didn't slow down. He simply held the glaive out, letting his speed and momentum do the work as he cut through the enemy ranks like a battering ram. The first soldier barely had time to scream before the blade tore through him. The second and third followed in quick succession, their bodies collapsing in a heap as Roman sliced his way through the mass of enemies with almost comical ease.

Alright, time to get flashy.

Roman grinned, his grip tightening on the glaive. He could *feel* the raw energy in the weapon, waiting to be unleashed. He made his choice: *Elemental Damage*. Electricity crackled along the length of the blade, at first just faint sparks, then growing into a vibrant web of energy that danced up and down the weapon. Roman laughed, the sound sharp and wild, as the power surged through him.

"Oh, shocking development on the field!" he quipped, his voice taking on a playful, exaggerated commentator's tone. "Roman did not come to play today, folks!"

With a flourish, he slashed the glaive diagonally, sending a shockwave of lightning arcing out from the blade. The wave ripped through the enemy ranks, cutting through soldiers like they were made of paper. At least twenty men dropped in a single strike, their bodies convulsing as the electricity tore through them.

"He is putting on one *electrifying* performance today!" Roman laughed, reveling in the absurdity of it all. He spun, his glaive crackling with energy as he cut his way through the remaining soldiers, each strike accompanied by another quip.

"Who's next?" he called out, ducking under a wild swing from one of the enemies. "Come on, don't be shy! I've got plenty of volts left for everyone!"

Roman darted forward, his movements were so fast the enemy couldn't track him. He swept his glaive in a wide arc, lightning trailing behind it in dazzling streaks of light. Soldiers fell before him like dominoes, and he barely broke a sweat.

Before he knew it, he was face-to-face with the Sergeant, who was mid-swing, barely registering Roman's presence.

"Whoa there, buddy. It's me," Roman said, grinning as he effortlessly ducked under the Sergeant's swing and pushed him back behind the front lines. "You're going to hurt someone with that if you're not careful."

The Sergeant blinked at him, bewildered. "Roman? What the hell—"

Roman leaned in, lowering his voice conspiratorially. "We've got another dust cloud coming our way. Can't tell if it's friend or foe, though. Thought I'd let you know before I start *really* showing off."

The Sergeant blinked again, still trying to process what he was seeing. Roman just grinned wider.

"Well, let's hope it's friends, 'cause if it's more enemies, this is going to get real interesting, real fast."

With a wink, Roman spun on his heel, the electricity in his glaive crackling with renewed vigor.

"Now, where was I? Ah, yes—*shocking* the audience!" He quipped before launching himself back into the fray, laughing all the while. He slashed at a few folks before he heard the Sergeant call him back.

"Wait Roman!" When Roman approached, he continued. "

The Sergeant's eyes narrowed as he turned to look back in the direction Roman had pointed out to him. "It might be the Commander, but I don't see how he would've mustered the army and marched out here so quickly. The next closest city is Kenan, and I know Count Kenan would send reinforcements as soon as he heard, but they shouldn't be here already."

Roman shifted, the energy inside him still thrumming, making him almost jittery with anticipation. "If you need me to get a closer look, I can do it. You mentioned a black flag with two griffons? I can try to see if it's that."

The Sergeant nodded. "Yes, that's Knight Commander Dalf's family crest. If you see it, it's a good sign. If not, get back here quick."

Roman took off without another word, sprinting across the battlefield with a speed that left even the seasoned soldiers staring in disbelief. He barely felt the ground beneath his feet as he moved, the landscape around him blurring into streaks of green and brown. Each stride was effortless, as though his legs were carrying him on a gust of wind. He reached the ridge in seconds, not even winded, and came to a stop, his enhanced vision already kicking in as he scanned the horizon.

The dust cloud was massive, churning the earth in its wake, obscuring details from normal sight. But Roman wasn't normal—not anymore. He squinted, focusing on the distant shapes as his vision homed in, piercing through the haze as if the dust was no obstacle at all.

Come on, show me what you've got.

His eyes darted between the moving figures, taking in the gleaming armor and shifting formations. It was a massive army, no doubt, but he needed to know if they were friend or foe. His heart pounded with a mixture of hope and dread. He scanned the horizon for a sign, something the Sergeant had described to him in haste.

There!

Among the sea of bodies, horses, and weapons, his eyes locked onto a banner fluttering in the wind. It was adorned with a pair of griffons, just as the Sergeant had said. Relief washed over him, but he didn't let himself relax yet. The army was still far off, but he knew better than to take any situation lightly.

Better make sure, Roman thought, crouching lower to the ground to get a better angle.

Now that he had identified the banner, he took a moment to scan the rest of the army, trying to get a sense of their numbers. His vision, still enhanced by the strange cultivation power coursing through him, allowed him to see much farther and clearer than any ordinary scout could. It was a force to be reckoned with, thousands strong, but nothing compared to the army they had just fought. This might be the reinforcements the Sergeant had hoped for.

Roman grinned. Alright, looks like help is on the way. But then he paused. Something tugged at him—a sense of unfinished business. He had been pushing his limits, unlocking new abilities, and yet he hadn't truly taken stock of where he stood now. He had been so caught up in the rush of battle and survival that he hadn't even checked the full extent of his status since everything had started to change.

Let's see where I'm at.

He focused inward, pulling up the interface of his stat screen. The familiar transparent display appeared before his eyes, lines of data scrolling as his status materialized in front of him:

Name:	Roman
Race:	Human
Age:	19
Title:	[World Walker]
Title:	[Exponential Growth]

Title: [Cultivator's Body]

Cultivation Status: Empowered Core (Leveled up twice from Broken Core)

Skills and proficiency:

Sword Mastery: Lvl 10 (Mastered)

Glaive Mastery: Lvl 10 (Mastered)

Elemental Weapon Mastery - Lightning: Lvl 5

Weapon Proficiency - All Weapons: Lvl 6

Enhanced Agility: Lvl 9

Enhanced Strength: Lvl 7

Athleticism: Lvl 9

Healing Acceleration: Lvl 5

Split Focus: Lvl 4

Battle Instincts: Lvl 6

Combat Awareness: Lvl 7

Energy Manipulation: Lvl 5

Spiritual Connection: Lvl 7

Flash Step: Lvl 6

Leadership Presence: Lvl 5

<...>

Roman's eyes flicked over the screen, noting his progress. His Empowered Core stood out, the result of his cultivation finally breaking free from its broken state. That pop he had felt earlier, the surge of strength—it all made sense now. He was stronger than ever, and the skills he had unlocked reflected that. The glaive mastery, the lightning infusion, even his speed—everything was coming together.

But something else caught his eye. A new system alert had appeared in the corner of his vision, flashing faintly.

New Skills Learned:

Lightning Burst (Active): Release an explosive surge of electricity, damaging and stunning nearby enemies.

Kinetic Absorption (Passive): Absorb and store kinetic energy from physical impacts, converting it into a temporary boost of strength or speed.

Roman grinned, his confidence swelling. *Well, well, looks like I've been holding out on myself.*

He dismissed the stat screen, the numbers fading from view, but the knowledge of his newfound abilities lingered. He rolled his shoulders, feeling the energy still crackling beneath his skin, eager to be unleashed.

Alright, he thought, standing up straight and casting one last glance at the approaching army. *Time to get* back to the Sergeant and let him know we've got reinforcements on the way.

And with that, he sprinted off again, his body surging forward with newfound strength, the wind rushing past as the ground blurred beneath him. There was no hesitation now—just the thrill of speed, and the feeling that, for the first time in a long while, he had control over the chaos inside him. He raced back to the Sergeant, the wind whipping past him. He skidded to a halt in front of the man, a triumphant grin on his face. "I saw the flag you talked about."

"Really?" The Sergeant's face lit up. "Then we're saved! All we have to do now is hold out."

"Should we fall back a bit until they get here?" Roman suggested. "I think I've been pushing myself a little too hard..." He trailed off, noticing the Sergeant staring out over the battlefield, his face tense.

Roman followed his gaze and saw the enemy forces shifting. The massive army that had seemed so unstoppable was now retreating, the soldiers pulling back toward the forest in a hurried, chaotic mass.

"They're retreating!" A cheer rose from the soldiers around them as the Sergeant turned, his voice ringing out over the battlefield.

"Chase them down! Push, men!" The Sergeant charged forward, his sword swinging as he cut through the retreating soldiers. Roman followed, his glaive carving a path through the enemy ranks. This time, he moved at a normal speed, the earlier surge of energy starting to wane. He was exhausted, but there was a strange exhilaration in the fight—a sense of purpose that he hadn't felt in a long time.

He fought alongside the Sergeant, cutting down soldiers with every swing. The retreating enemy was in disarray, and Roman could see the fear in their eyes as they fled. It was almost too easy. He laughed, a breathless sound, as he imagined what his friends back on Earth would think if they could see him now.

I could really go for some Chick-fil-A right about now, he thought with a grin, the absurdity of the situation striking him. *The Lord's Chicken sounds perfect after this.*

"Alright, men, halt!" the Sergeant called out as they reached the edge of the forest. He stopped his men, letting them catch their breath as they watched the enemy vanish into the trees.

Roman stood near the Sergeant, his eyes drawn to the food being prepared in the makeshift camp. His stomach growled loudly, and he glanced around, wondering if anyone else had heard it.

"Knight Commander Dalf, if you aren't a sight for sore eyes," the Sergeant called out as the mounted commander approached, his men forming a disciplined line behind him.

"I'd bet," Dalf replied, dismounting with a fluid grace. "Was that the entire enemy force?"

"Yes, sir. We killed the separate branch they sent and held the bulk here until you arrived." The Sergeant's voice was filled with pride.

"With only fifty men? How is that possible? There had to be at least fifty thousand soldiers!" Dalf looked around, his disbelief clear.

"There were a hundred thousand initially, plus some beasts," the Sergeant corrected. "They started to retreat when they saw you on the horizon."

Dalf shook his head, incredulous. "I thought the stories about the Hydra Knights were exaggerated, but seeing this... It's unbelievable."

"I'd love to take all the credit, but a lot of this was thanks to this young man." The Sergeant gestured to Roman. "Knight Commander Dalf, meet Roman."

Dalf's gaze sharpened as he turned to Roman, a look of recognition in his eyes. "So, you're the one the King sent word about. He asked that we find and protect you. It seems, however, that you've been the one doing the protecting. You have my gratitude."

Roman shifted awkwardly, not used to such praise. "It wasn't just me. The Hydra Knights did most of the work. I just... ran fast and swung this glaive around."

"Fast enough to down at least eight hundred men!" The Sergeant interjected, his voice brimming with admiration. "And that's just what I saw before I got busy with my own fight. This man fought like ten of us combined."

Roman felt a flush creeping up his neck. "You're exaggerating, Sergeant. You and your men held the line. I just distracted them."

The Knight Commander laughed, clapping both men on the shoulders. "You're both incredible. I'll be sure to tell the King of your bravery."

A shout came from behind them. "Sir, the King's army has arrived! Commander Athel is with them!"

Dalf's eyes widened. "That was fast. He must have pushed them hard to get here so quickly."

Roman felt his heart sink at the mention of the King's army. The King... He wasn't sure he was ready to face him, not after everything that had happened. But he didn't have a choice.

"Roman," Dalf said, turning back to him, "the King has requested your presence in the capital. This man will escort you there." He gestured to a soldier holding a horse.

The Sergeant stepped forward; his expression serious. "We'll take care of things here. You go. The King needs to know what happened."

Roman nodded, his heart pounding. "Thank you." He turned to the soldier and took the reins, swinging up into the saddle.

"We'll keep fighting here, Sergeant," Dalf said, his voice carrying across the camp. "Push those bastards back, and don't stop until they're out of our land!"

The Sergeant saluted, and the men around him echoed the gesture, their eyes fierce with determination. Roman watched them for a moment, feeling a strange mix of pride and sorrow. He had fought with these men, shared their struggle. Now he was leaving them behind.

With a deep breath, he turned the horse and followed the portal man. The soldier moved his hands in a complex pattern, and a shimmering portal appeared before them.

Roman glanced back one last time, the battlefield now calm, the Hydra Knights standing tall amidst the wreckage. He took a deep breath, then spurred the horse forward and stepped through the portal, into the unknown.

Chapter 10

The Enemy King

The tent was dimly lit, the only source of light a series of candles arranged meticulously around a sprawling table covered in maps. The flickering flames cast eerie shadows over the parchment, giving the detailed lines of rivers, cities, and battle formations an almost sinister appearance. The man standing over them, their King, looked down with a cold, calculating gaze.

His hands, adorned with jeweled rings, moved with careful precision as he traced the lines on the map, his mind working through the logistics of his next move. He was tall and imposing, his presence suffused with a quiet menace that seemed to permeate the very air around him. His armor, blackened steel inlaid with gold, gleamed faintly in the candlelight.

"Eidon has fallen," he murmured to himself, his voice a low, dangerous rumble. "And soon, Meridia will follow."

He leaned closer, studying the map of the Northern Continent, his eyes lingering on the various symbols representing his troops and the cities they had already claimed. Eidon was just the beginning. He had grander plans, and each piece was falling into place perfectly.

Or so he thought.

"My lord," a nervous voice interrupted his thoughts, and the King turned, his gaze piercing the soldier who stood at the entrance of the tent. The man's face was pale, his eyes wide with fear.

"Speak," the King commanded, his voice sharp as a blade.

"The vanguard, my lord... they're retreating," the soldier stammered, his hands shaking as he held out a scroll. "The scouts reported a small contingent of Meridian troops, led by the Hydra Knights, engaging them. The bulk of our forces are falling back into the forest."

The King's eyes narrowed, a dangerous light flaring in their depths. He took the scroll, his fingers tightening around it as he read the hastily scrawled report. His expression darkened with each word.

"They're being routed by a mere fifty men and some child?" His voice was deadly quiet, but the soldier flinched as if struck. "How could this happen?"

"The reports... they mentioned a man, my lord. He moved with impossible speed, cutting through our ranks like a demon. The men are calling him a ghost."

"A ghost, you say?" The King's lips curled into a mocking smile, but his eyes were cold. "So, the ghost has come to haunt us, has he?"

He turned back to the maps, his mind racing. The Hydra Knights were formidable, but fifty men should not have been able to turn back an army of tens of thousands. This "ghost" must be something more. But no matter—he would deal with this annoyance personally.

The King's smile widened, his teeth glinting in the candlelight. "If they think they can hold Eidon with a handful of soldiers and a ghost, then they are gravely mistaken."

He turned, his voice a harsh bark. "Release the beasts."

The soldier's eyes widened in shock. "M-my lord? The beasts? But they are—"

"Unleash them," the King repeated, his voice brooking no argument. "Let them taste the blood of our enemies. If Meridia wants to play games with us, we will show them the true meaning of fear."

The soldier swallowed hard and bowed deeply before hurrying out of the tent. The King watched him go, his mind already shifting to the next move in his grand game. He could almost hear the screams of the Meridian soldiers as the beasts were unleashed upon them, their howls and roars filling the night air.

"Let the real battle begin," he whispered to himself, his eyes gleaming with anticipation.

Eidon: The Monster Invasion

The night air was filled with the sounds of battle, the clashing of swords and the cries of the wounded echoing across the plains. The Meridian soldiers, though outnumbered, had fought bravely, holding the line against the enemy forces. But now, as the first of the monstrous creatures appeared on the horizon, a sense of dread settled over the battlefield.

The beasts came in droves, their massive forms silhouetted against the darkening sky. Towering figures with thick, scaly hides and eyes that glowed like embers. Some were hulking brutes, all muscle and claw, while others slithered across the ground, their serpentine bodies covered in armored scales.

And leading them, like some twisted parody of a royal procession, was a drake—a monstrous, wingless dragon, its body covered in scars and chains that clinked ominously as it moved. Its eyes blazed with a savage intelligence, and when it opened its maw, the roar that escaped was deafening, shaking the very ground beneath the soldiers' feet.

"Fall back! Fall back to the city!" Sergeant Smithson's voice rang out over the chaos, his tone urgent but controlled. He swung his sword, cutting down an enemy soldier before turning to his men. "We can't fight these things out in the open!"

The Hydra Knights moved with precision, their retreat orderly even as the beasts closed in. Sergeant Smithson, fighting at the front, felt the ground tremble beneath him as one of the massive brutes charged. He dodged to the side, as he swung it in a wide arc, the blade biting deep into the creature's thick hide.

The beast howled in pain, its blood pouring from it, but it did not fall. Instead, it turned, its eyes locking onto Sergeant Smithson with a rage that was almost tangible. He grit his teeth, bracing himself for the next attack.

"Keep moving!" he shouted to the soldiers around him, his voice carrying above the din. "We can't hold them here!"

The soldiers rallied around him; their faces set with grim determination as they fought to keep the monsters at bay. The Sergeant moved among them, his sword a blur of silver and lightning, cutting down any creature that came too close.

But it wasn't enough. The monsters were relentless, their sheer numbers overwhelming. For everyone they brought down, two more took its place, their roars filling the night as they pressed forward.

"Fall back!" The Sergeant yelled again, his voice straining with the effort. "To the city walls! We'll make our stand there!"

The soldiers obeyed, their retreat turning into a desperate dash as the beasts closed in. Seargeant Smithson brought up the rear, his gaze sweeping over the battlefield. He could see the city walls of Eidon in the distance, the gates open and the archers on the battlements ready and waiting to start firing down at the approaching enemy once they got in range.

They reached the city and the gates slammed shut behind them just as the first of the monsters slammed into the outer defenses. The gates groaned under the impact, the wood splintering but holding.

The beasts roared in fury, their claws raking against the stone walls, their massive bodies crashing into the gates. The archers fired down on them, arrows raining from above, but it was like trying to kill an ocean with a bucket.

The Sergeant turned, his breath coming in harsh gasps. The soldiers around him were battered and bloodied, their faces pale but determined. They had made it to the city, but the real fight was only just beginning.

The Capital of Meridia

The atmosphere in the capital was tense, the usual hustle and bustle of the city replaced with a quiet, anxious energy. In the grand throne room, King Juelius sat on his throne, his expression unreadable as he listened to the reports of the ongoing conflict.

Beside him, Roman stood with Seth, Jessika, Z, and Lexi, the group huddled together as they waited for news. They had been summoned to the capital just after the battle in the forest, and the King had questioned Roman at length about his abilities and the events that had transpired.

A messenger burst into the room; his face flushed with urgency. "Your Majesty, news from the front!"

The King leaned forward; his eyes sharp. "Speak."

"The enemy has unleashed a hoard of beasts upon our forces. They've fallen back to the city of Eidon and are making a stand there. They are holding for now but the monsters are battering the defenses."

King Juelius' face darkened, his jaw tightening. "Damn them," he muttered under his breath, his gaze flicking to Roman and his friends. "We cannot let Eidon fall. If the beasts break through, they will ravage the countryside."

"I'll go," Roman said, stepping forward, his voice steady. "I can help."

The King shook his head. "You have done more than enough already. I will not send you back into that."

"With all due respect, Your Majesty," Seth interjected, his voice firm, "we need to help. This is our kingdom, our people. We can't just stand by."

"Seth," the King began, but his son cut him off.

"Father, please. I'm not a child anymore. I can fight. We all can." He gestured to his friends, each of them nodding in agreement. "If we don't do something now, more people will die."

The King's expression softened, a mixture of pride and fear in his eyes. He looked at his son, then at Roman, weighing his options. Finally, he sighed, a weary sound.

"Very well. But you go with my blessing and my orders. You are not to take any unnecessary risks. Do you understand me?"

"Yes, Your Majesty." Seth nodded seriously.

"Where are the troops we sent? Are they close?" The King turned and asked one of his Generals.

"Aye, Your Majesty. They should be arriving shortly." The general answered promptly.

"Good, do we have any portaleers who can get these kids, sorry, these young warriors back into the fight?" The King asked, correcting himself after looking at his son.

"Yes, your Majesty." One man said and stepped forward.

"Good, take them back and then report here with any news." The King said.

"Your Majesty." The man said and bowed.

"Good, take them back and then report here with any news," the King said. The portaleer stepped forward, ready to transport them into the battle.

Roman, however, hesitated, an idea forming in his mind. "Your Majesty, before we head to Eidon… there's something I need to check."

The King raised an eyebrow. "What is it?"

Roman turned to Seth and the others, then back to the King. "There are stones here in the capital—testing stones, right? For checking stats and skills?"

The King nodded slowly. "Yes, but you said the system doesn't grant you levels. You won't be able to read your stats like the others."

Roman's expression was determined. "I know. But I've been able to cultivate in a way that's… different. I think the stone might still reveal something about my progress. I'd like to see what I'm working with before I go back into battle."

Seth exchanged a glance with Jessika and then to one of the King's advisors who stood nearby, Lady Syrrin the Keeper of the Stones, who shrugged. "It's worth a shot," she said. "At least we'll know what we're dealing with."

The King sighed. "Very well. If this will help you, then, go to the testing chamber before you depart. But do not waste time—Eidon needs you all."

Roman bowed slightly in gratitude. "Thank you, Your Majesty."

The group was led through the palace to a large stone room, its walls lined with torches casting flickering shadows across the stone floor. In the center of the room stood a large obsidian stone, crackling faintly with magic. This was one of Meridia's ancient testing stones, a relic designed to read the stats and abilities of any who touched it. Seth, Jessika, Z, and Lexi had each used one when they came of age, marking their place in the kingdom's military forces. But this was Roman's first time facing one and the one he faced was nothing like what Jessika Z and Lexi faced. Seth used this same one but for the others...this stone was 5 times the size and gave off a much stronger hum of power.

"Well," Seth said with a smirk, "no time like the present."

Roman approached the stone, a strange mixture of anticipation and anxiety churning in his gut. He placed his hand on its cool surface, and immediately, the air around him hummed with energy. The stone lit up, swirling with vibrant colors as it assessed his strength.

At first, nothing appeared. The others exchanged confused glances. "I told you, Roman," Seth said, "if you're locked out of the system, it might not—"

Suddenly, the stone flared brightly, the light so intense that everyone shielded their eyes. Roman gritted his teeth as he felt a surge of energy run through him, the stone reacting wildly to something deep inside him. Then, glowing text began to appear in the air above the stone, shimmering for everyone to see.

Name: Roman
Race: Human
Title: [World Walker], [Exponential Growth], [Cultivator's Body]
Level: ERROR
Cultivation Rank: Empowered Core
Physical Strength: 350 (Exceeds Normal Human Limit)
Agility: 680 (Greatly Exceeds Normal Human Limit)
Potential Growth: Unlimited

The room fell into stunned silence. Seth's mouth hung open as he stared at the numbers displayed above the stone. "Three hundred and fifty...? That's more than double the average strength of a trained knight."

Jessika's eyes were wide. "His agility too... And what is this 'Cultivation Rank'? I've never seen that listed before."

Roman felt the weight of their stares, the astonishment in their eyes. He pulled his hand back from the stone, his heart pounding. He hadn't expected these kinds of results either. His strength and agility were far beyond what he'd thought possible, and even though the system still didn't grant him levels, it seemed his cultivation had advanced more than he realized.

"I've been training—cultivating," Roman said, still processing the numbers himself. "It's different from your system, but it's clearly making me stronger."

Seth shook his head in disbelief. "Stronger? You're a powerhouse! These stats... Roman, you could take on half an army by yourself."

Roman winced at all the attention. "I'm not sure about that, but it means I won't be a liability in this fight. I needed to know what I could bring to the table before heading into Eidon."

Lexi whistled softly. "Well, I'd say you've got plenty to bring."

Z remained quiet but nodded in approval. "Whatever path you're on, Roman, it's clearly working. And I think we're going to need every bit of it."

Seth's eyes shone with renewed determination. "If Roman's as strong as the stone says, we stand a real chance at turning the tide in Eidon. Let's get back to the King and head out. We don't have time to waste."

Back in the throne room, the King listened intently as Seth reported Roman's unexpected strength. The King's expression shifted from disbelief to a guarded sense of hope.

"I didn't expect this," King Juelius admitted, his gaze settling on Roman. "Perhaps you're more valuable to this kingdom than I originally thought."

Roman didn't flinch under the King's scrutiny. "I'll do whatever it takes to help, Your Majesty."

The King nodded slowly. "Then may your strength be enough to turn the tide. Be swift—and may fortune favor you in Eidon."

With that, the group moved to the portal, ready to be transported to the front lines. As the magical energy swirled around them, Roman's thoughts raced. His strength had been revealed, but this was just the beginning. He had to keep cultivating, keep pushing forward if he wanted to survive—and if he wanted to help the people of this world win the war that was coming.

The portal shimmered, and with a final glance at the capital, Roman and his friends vanished into the light.

■■

As Roman stepped through the portal and into Kenan, the first thing that struck him was the sheer scale of the city. It was massive, stretching far beyond what he had seen in Eidon. The streets were wider, lined with immaculate stone buildings, their surfaces gleaming in the sunlight. Unlike Eidon, where the scars of recent battles and destruction were fresh and raw, Kenan radiated a sense of order and prosperity.

The architecture was familiar—built from the same stone and wood—but everything in Kenan was cleaner, more polished. Towering spires loomed over the city, their intricate designs suggesting a wealth of resources and craftsmanship. Elegant carvings adorned the facades of important-looking buildings, and banners displaying the kingdom's crest fluttered proudly in the wind.

For a moment, Roman felt out of place. Kenan was clearly a city of wealth and influence, and it showed in every polished corner, every well-maintained road, and every building that gleamed with prosperity.

Despite its beauty, Roman couldn't shake the unease that crept in.

Roman took a deep breath and clenched his fists. Kenan might look perfect on the outside, but he knew better now. He knew that even a city this grand could fall, just like any other. Especially with the roaring monsters throwing themselves at the gates trying to get in.

Chapter 11

"I know we didn't really get much time to talk, but... are you guys okay?" Roman asked, glancing around the group, his gaze lingering on Jessika and Lexi.

"Yeah, we're okay. Thank you for saving us... but... why?" Lexi's voice was soft, unsure. Her hands fidgeted as she clutched them together. "Why did you leave us? Why did you run?"

Roman's heart sank. He had expected this question, but the weight of it still caught him off guard. After a long pause, he finally spoke, his voice low and honest. "I saw the fear in your eyes, Lexi. I thought... I thought you were terrified of me."

"What?! I wasn't scared of you!" Lexi's voice wavered, trembling at first, but quickly gained strength, the shyness beginning to crack.

"It sure looked like it," Roman said quietly, regret clouding his gaze. "When you looked at me after I... after I killed those men, you looked so scared, like I was a monster. I didn't know how to handle that. So, I ran. I didn't want to make things worse for you, or for any of you." He paused, guilt weighing heavily on each word. "I'm sorry for leaving you all alone... and vulnerable."

Lexi's hands balled into fists, her voice rising with a mix of anger and hurt. "I wasn't scared of you!" she shouted, the timid girl disappearing in the heat of the moment. "Yes, I was scared—but not of *you!* I was terrified of what was happening! The chaos, the blood, the killing—it was overwhelming! But *you*... you saved me, Roman. You didn't scare me... you protected me!"

Tears welled in her eyes as she stepped closer. Her voice softened, but her words carried no less conviction. "You're not a monster, Roman. I wasn't afraid *of* you... I was afraid *for* you. I was terrified that you'd gotten hurt."

Roman's chest tightened, the realization of how deeply he had misunderstood the situation washing over him like a cold wave. He opened his mouth, but for a moment, no words came out. He hadn't expected this—a truth so far from what he had believed.

"I'm sorry," he whispered, his voice barely audible. "I didn't know..."

Jessika, who had been silent until now, placed a comforting hand on Lexi's shoulder. "She's right, Roman. None of us were afraid of you. We were afraid of everything else, but *not* you. You've always been there for us."

Roman looked between them, his guilt replaced by something warmer. He had run, thinking he was sparing them from his darkness, but in truth, they had never seen him that way. They had seen him as their protector.

Lexi stepped even closer, gently grabbing his hand and holding it tightly in hers. She looked up into his eyes, her voice steady but her cheeks flushed. "From the moment you walked up to our fire, it felt like you belonged with us. Like you were the missing piece we didn't know we needed. And…" She smiled shyly, her voice becoming bold. "It doesn't hurt that you're crazy handsome."

Roman blinked, caught off guard by her forwardness, but he noticed the shy blush spreading across her face. He chuckled softly. "You're right. Nobody could be scared of my *devastating* good looks," he teased, smirking as Lexi tried to pull her hand away. He gripped it tighter, playfully refusing to let her retreat.

Seth, standing nearby, grinned and rolled his eyes dramatically. "Oh great, now he's going to be *completely* insufferable. We'll never hear the end of his 'devastating good looks.'"

Jessika chuckled softly, crossing her arms. "Well, I can't say she's wrong, Roman," she teased, raising an eyebrow. "But if you start acting like royalty, we'll have to bring you down a peg or two."

Roman grinned back. "Don't worry, there's only one prince here," he said, turning to Seth. "Speaking of which, you've got some explaining to do."

Still holding Lexi's hand, which now felt natural, Roman didn't think much about it. Seth shifted uncomfortably.

"Oh... uh... yeah," Seth stammered, scratching the back of his neck.

"That's all you've got?!" Jessika blurted, throwing her hands up. "I knew you were some kind of wealthy noble, but the *Crown Prince*?!"

"I'm sorry," Seth said, his voice apologetic. "I just needed you guys to focus on escaping, not treating me differently. And I didn't want you to think of me as 'the prince.'"

Jessika huffed. "Yeah, whatever. Between Roman's insane strength and your royal status... what's next? Lexi, are you secretly a princess or something?"

Lexi giggled. "Not that I know of."

The group fell into a comfortable silence, soft smiles playing on their faces. Z, who had been quietly observing the exchange, finally spoke up, his dry tone breaking the moment. "Roman, lucky for you that your fighting skills match your looks, or we'd have left you behind a long time ago."

Lexi, still blushing, tried once more to pull her hand free, but Roman held on tighter. She laughed nervously, her face flushed with warmth. "Don't get too cocky now, Roman."

"I wouldn't dream of it," Roman replied with a smirk, their eyes meeting. For the first time in what felt like forever, the group shared a moment of genuine levity—a brief reprieve from the chaos surrounding them.

Seth walked over, clapping Roman on the back. "In all seriousness, man, you're one of us. Don't forget that. We're in this together."

Roman's smirk softened into a genuine smile as he looked at his friends, the weight of their acceptance washing over him. For the first time since entering this world, he didn't feel like an outsider. He felt like he had a place—among people who had his back, no matter how tough things got.

"Thanks, guys," Roman said, looking around at each of them. "I won't let you down."

Jessika nodded with a grin. "We know you won't. Now, let's go kill some monsters and level up! I'm this close to hitting level 20 and getting my class upgrade!"

"Oh right! I don't think I ever asked—what levels are you guys? Like, are you average, or on the stronger side?" Roman asked.

Z answered first. "We're on the upper side for adventurers, but still weak compared to the top fighters in the kingdom. I'm level 18."

"Same here," Seth added.

"Sixteen," Lexi said, a little embarrassed.

"And I'm 19, almost 20!" Jessika said excitedly before turning to Lexi. "I'm sorry, Lex."

"No, it's fine. I started later than you guys, but I'm catching up!" Lexi smiled, cheering herself up.

"Right!" Jessika agreed.

Roman looked thoughtful. "That's awesome. I wonder what my level would be if my system worked."

Seth chuckled. "Uh, probably like level 90, based on the stats we saw."

"What?! That high?" Roman asked, surprised.

Seth shrugged. "Maybe not that high, but one of the top royal guards is level 80, and your strength is higher than his. But levels aren't all about two stats, so who knows. I didn't see many skills either, so I'd guess you've got crazy stats but low skill level. You'd have unlocked more if you were higher level."

Roman frowned in thought. "So, you get skills from leveling up your class... but what if you don't have a class?"

Z chimed in. "I have no idea. Everyone I know has a class—even homeless people in the slums have the peasant class. You've gotta be an odd case."

Roman's mind raced as he considered this. He had unlocked a few skills on his own, like flash step and elemental damage for his glaive, but he had done it through sheer effort, not by leveling up.

Then the thought appeared to him...

Do I just need to create my own skills?

Chapter 12

"Sergeant! We meet again!" Roman called out as they climbed to the top of the walls. All around them, soldiers moved frantically, hurling rocks and cauldrons of boiling oil onto the creatures below, while archers launched a volley of arrows, trying in vain to pierce the thick armor of the monstrous horde.

The Sergeant turned, his grizzled face cracking into a brief smile. "Roman. Welcome back to the party." He nodded toward the chaos below. "Honestly, I was just thinking how useful it would've been if you'd stuck around. These arrows aren't doing a damn thing to those armored bastards."

"Aww, you missed me!" Roman replied with a broad grin. "Well, don't worry. I'm here now, and I brought some friends." He gestured to the others, who stood ready by his side.

"Good to see you all again," Smithson nodded toward the group, his eyes lingering on Seth for a second.

Jessika stepped forward, frowning. " Good to see you too Sergeant but let me get this straight—you're planning on going *out there*? Into the middle of *that*? Wouldn't it be safer to stay up here and keep hitting them from behind the walls?"

"Normally, yeah," Smithson replied, motioning for her to watch. Arrows rained down on the creatures below, bouncing off their armored hides like raindrops. The oil, while more effective, wasn't slowing the horde enough to make a difference. "But as you can see, we're not doing much damage. Those arrows are useless, and the oil isn't enough to stop them. We've got to meet them head-on."

Jessika's eyes scanned the walls. "What about magic? I don't see any mages. Can't they help us hold the line?"

Smithson shook his head. "Mage units were sent north to deal with the orc invasion. We're running on reserves here. No mages to back us up this time."

"Orc invasion?" Roman interrupted, surprise clear in his voice.

"Yeah," Smithson replied, his tone heavy with the weight of the situation. "The kingdom's dealing with a full-scale orc invasion from the north. Most of the army's already deployed there. These are just our reserve forces. The Hydra Knights, me included, were returning from a previous mission when we heard rumors of this mess. So, we came to investigate… and that's when we found you."

Roman glanced at his group, understanding the stakes had just gotten a lot higher. "So, the kingdom's split between two fronts," he muttered. "No mages, and only reserve troops holding this position."

Smithson nodded grimly. "That's the long and short of it. But we can't afford to let these beasts break through the walls, or we'll lose everything behind us. If they breach Kenan, the countryside will be overrun and there's nothing to stop them for a hundred miles till they reach the capital."

Jessika glanced at Roman. "Looks like we don't have much of a choice, then."

Roman gripped the handle of his glaive, his expression resolute. "We'll handle it. Let's get out there and push them back before it's too late."

Smithson smirked, a glint of respect in his eyes. "I knew you had guts, Roman. Let's see if you've got the strength to back it up. The gates will open on my command."

Roman's heart pounded in anticipation as the group prepared to face the horde head-on. This wasn't just about survival anymore—it was about protecting everything that lay beyond Eidon. And now, with the stakes higher than ever, Roman knew he'd need every ounce of his power to turn the tide.

"No need." He said, smirked at his friends and dropped from the walls. He felt alive, a rush of power surging through him as he prepared for this battle and he started pulling at his power and prepared a couple skills he'd never used.

Kinetic Absorption then he pushed out a Lightning Burst out in a massive cone in front of him. The wall was a lot higher than he thought which works to his benefit here because of Kinetic Absorption. I'm gonna push it even more. He thought and then stepped hard against the wall.

Flash Step

The ground seemed to appear before him in no more than a blink. He barely had time to twist so he would land feet first instead of flat on his face but then his boots made contact with the ground in between two giant beetle-like creatures who started to bite at him but his flash step through off their timing.

BOOM! He crashed into the ground and a huge cloud of smoke rose up all around. He lifted his head, tryin to get his bearings about him and smiled as he felt the new power surging from him because of Kinetic Absorption. This is awesome! He thought and stood tall with his glaive in his right hand.

He pushed off with his new strength and speed and swung quickly at the beetle to his left, swinging horizontally to cut through it and a good bunch behind it like he did with the soldiers.

CLANG! The blade bounced off the monster and the vibrations tore through his body; he ended up dropping the glaive as well as his whole-body shook.

Ahh!" He shook the weird feeling from his arm and had to step jump back to dodge the beetles' mandibles coming at his face. He felt the wall not too far behind him so he had to push out.

Slash damage doesn't work on these huh…He ran back through his gaming memories…when slash didn't work blunt damage was usually the next option.

"But my beautiful hands though!" He fussed as he ducked into another swing. Out of the corner of his eye he saw a couple huge fireballs falling at the monsters and the explosion tore through monsters, and then the new monsters that touched the area also caught fire. Magic? My initial strike did hella damage so let's try going all in.

He gathered a small amount of power and shot out a small lightning burst at the beetle and it dropped instantly.

"Oh word?! I didn't think that little amount of power would take them out!" He looked around and focused on around 10 monsters around him and *pushed* bursts of lightning at each out them and creating a clearing. As soon as there was enough room, he heard a loud thud next to him.

"Now you can see the true skills of a Guardian Knight." Z said proudly bringing his shield up and slamming it down hard. A shimmering blue bubble shield appeared in the clearing and the monsters rammed against it but it made no difference.

"My protector!" Roman swooned and Z laughed hard.

"Yall are having a little too much fun out here." Seth materialized next to Roman who jumped in surprise.

"Um my good sir! Please announce yourself next time before you get a fist through your face!" He exclaimed.

"Nah it's so much better this way." He chuckled. "So how about a little competition?"

"Say less! What's the bet?" Roman asked.

"'Say less'?" Seth asked.

"Sorry it's a saying from home…but uh…"

"Most kills get bragging rights…I don't think anything financial would be worth it with the amount of gold we'll be making after this anyway." Z answered.

"What gold?"

"Oh, there is a bounty out for these creatures, Count Kenan has agreed to pay 1 gold coin for each monster killed. How about for our bet I double it if y'all beat me but if I win then...Roman you tell me about your cultivation trick." Seth offered. So, he thinks it's some unique trick of the system or something?

"Ok deal. I'll take the middle since I've already started there." He nodded towards the destruction he had already caused there.

"Sounds good to me." Z said and turned to the right leaving the left for Seth.

"May the odds be ever in your favor!" Roman announced with a chuckle but the others just looked at him confused. He ignored them and burst forth out of the bubble of protection.

It's time to learn this system. Maybe I will make some attack skills on the go. So many questions needing to be answered...like just because lightning is the element I chose is it the only one I can use? His mind shot back to the carnage those fireballs caused. He did the same thing he did for lightning burst but instead of lightning he imagined an inferno bursting forth.

Chapter 13

"You've gotta be kidding me!" Jessika shouted, her voice carrying over the chaos of the battlefield. Without hesitation, she leapt from the walls, twin streams of fire blazing from her hands to slow her descent. As she landed next to Roman, flames still flickering from her palms, she whipped around to face him.

"How did you just do that?!" she demanded, her expression a mixture of shock and disbelief.

Roman blinked, confused, as he kicked away a small insectoid creature that had scuttled too close. "Huh? Do what?"

"That *huge* firestorm spell!" Jessika's arms gestured wildly as if trying to grasp the magnitude of what had just happened.

"Oh!" Roman said with a casual shrug. "I saw how effective your fireballs were and figured fire would work better than the lightning I was using. So I just... imagined the lightning as fire and, well, it did that." He said it so nonchalantly, as though casting a mastery-level spell on instinct was the most normal thing in the world.

Jessika's eyes widened, her frustration boiling over. "It took me *six months* of nonstop training to learn *Fireball*! And you just used the *mastery* version of it like it was nothing?!"

She punctuated her outburst by sending a massive fireball into an oncoming beetle, incinerating it instantly.

"I... I'm sorry?" Roman stammered, realizing too late how much he had unintentionally insulted her efforts. He glanced at the battlefield, noticing more monsters surging forward. "But I can't really chat right now—we've got a bet going on who can kill the most of these things." With that, he jumped away, disappearing into the fray before Jessika could shout at him further.

Jessika clenched her fists, flames sputtering from her fingertips as she fumed silently. She propelled herself back up onto the walls, using her flames to boost her jump, trying to keep her focus on the battle and not Roman's absurd talent.

"You okay, Jessika?" Lexi asked, her voice full of concern as she watched her friend land beside her.

"No!" Jessika snapped, then quickly saw the shock on Lexi's face and softened. "Sorry. It's just Roman. I don't know whether to be amazed or furious."

Lexi raised an eyebrow, curious. "What did he do now?"

Jessika quickly explained what had just happened, how Roman had seemingly mastered an advanced fire spell after just watching her. Sergeant Smithson, who had been standing nearby, listened in as well.

Lexi's eyes widened as Jessika finished her story. "Wait, so he just *thought* about fire magic, and it worked? Is he some kind of magical genius or something?"

Smithson chuckled, shaking his head. "Not just magic. I watched him earlier when our quartermaster handed him a glaive—a weapon he said he'd never used before. Within ten minutes, he was carving through the enemy like a seasoned warrior. I've never seen anything like it. Whoever Roman is, I'm glad he's on our side."

Lexi nodded; her brows furrowed in thought. "It's like he's able to pick up new skills instantly, whether it's magic or weapons. It's almost... unnatural."

Jessika crossed her arms, staring down at the battlefield where Roman was still fighting, his magic flaring brightly with each strike. "That's what worries me. He's powerful, but he doesn't even seem to realize how dangerous he is—or how easily he's surpassing everyone around him."

Smithson grunted; his tone serious. "Dangerous, yes, but I've seen plenty of powerful men lose themselves to their own strength. Roman... seems different. He fights for all of you. That's a good sign."

Jessika sighed, some of her frustration ebbing away. "Maybe you're right. But it doesn't make it any less frustrating when he casually pulls off something that took me months to learn."

Lexi chuckled softly. "Don't worry, Jess. We'll make him work for it next time. Maybe teach him that some things *do* take time."

Jessika couldn't help but smile at that. "Yeah, maybe."

Smithson, still watching Roman down below, grinned. "Until then, let's just hope he keeps killing more of those things before they overrun us."

The sound of Roman's laughter carried faintly on the wind as another explosion of fire erupted around him, scattering the monsters once more. Jessika shook her head, exasperated but unable to suppress the small, begrudging admiration creeping into her voice.

"Yeah," she muttered. "Let's hope."

"I wonder if he can teach us as fast as he learns…like if his ability to just learn stuff insanely fast would translate to teaching someone else…you think or am I just being too hopeful?" Jessika asked after a bit.

"Might be too hopeful." Lexi chuckled. "But hey let's make sure he sticks around for a while and find out…I have a few things I want him to teach me too."

"Oh? Like what?" Jessika asked, her voice raising in suspicion and her eyebrows lifting.

"like…what? What do you mean?" Lexi stuttered and then turned back to the wall. "Look at the size of that monster approaching!"

"Yeah, no. that's not gonna work. What do you want him to teach you Lexi?" Jessika pushed making suggestive faces and sounds as she leaned into the archer.

"N-nothing! I meant like stealth! You saw how he moved with Seth and we didn't hear anything! I've always struggled with Stealth!" Lexi argued.

"Mmhmm, If you say so. I've seen the way your eyes linger on him when he isn't looking. You're not tricking me! But hey go for it! Stake your claim now because after this battle he is going to be famous and every lady in a hundred miles is going to be clamoring for him! Especially after the King rewards us all with titles!" Jessika said which made Lexi blush hard.

***

Roman was having the time of his life. He was just playing around with fire...which, given the circumstances, felt both exhilarating and ironic. Each time he unleashed another burst of flames, it felt like the power inside him was growing, evolving, feeding off the chaos around him. The monsters didn't stand a chance as he swept through them, his fiery blasts reducing the beetles and insectoids to smoldering husks.

This is insane, he thought, launching another cone of flame. *How is this even happening?* He couldn't quite explain it, but somehow, it felt *right*—like he was tapping into something deeper than just raw power. Maybe it was the world itself or something about the way the magic worked here. But whatever it was, Roman couldn't stop the grin that stretched across his face as the monsters scattered in fear of his next attack.

He summoned another firestorm with a simple gesture, watching as the fiery vortex obliterated everything in its path. *I could do this all day,* he thought, feeling almost giddy with the power coursing through him.

Then, suddenly, the ground beneath him shook violently, the force sending him staggering back a few steps. A deep, guttural roar echoed across the battlefield. Roman looked up just in time to see something massive lumbering out from the heart of the horde—a creature unlike anything he had faced before.

It was enormous, towering over the other monsters, its body encased in thick, shimmering armor. Its multiple legs dug into the earth as it moved with terrifying speed. A massive, spiked tail whipped behind it, smashing through the ruins and leaving destruction in its wake. It resembled a giant, armored scorpion, but with a twisted, almost nightmarish quality to its features.

Okay… that's new.

The smaller monsters seemed to rally behind the creature, as if emboldened by its presence. Roman felt his adrenaline spike again, but this time there was a flicker of uncertainty in his gut. This thing was far bigger, far stronger, and far more dangerous than the rest of the horde.

"Alright, let's see what you've got," Roman muttered to himself, his fingers sparking with electricity as he prepared for a different approach. Fire had worked wonders so far, but something told him he'd need more than that for this beast.

He squared his shoulders, focusing on the monster as it barreled toward him. He quickly scanned its movements, searching for any weaknesses in its armor, any openings he could exploit. The creature's front pincers clicked menacingly as it closed in, and Roman could feel the weight of its power pressing against him like a physical force.

The scorpion-like creature lunged at him, its tail arcing through the air, aiming to crush him. Roman's reflexes kicked in, and with a quick *Flash Step*, he vanished from its path, reappearing several feet away. But he could feel the raw energy of the beast—its presence was overwhelming, almost suffocating.

This thing is on a whole different level. Roman could see that brute force wouldn't be enough here. He needed to be smarter, more tactical.

His mind raced, thinking of a way to hurt this beast then his mind landed on *Kinetic Absorption*. That ability had helped him earlier when he entered the fight, and now he needed to push it even further. *Absorb the impact… then hit back harder with a touch of lightning as flavor.*

As the beast turned, charging at him once more, Roman braced himself, letting the monster come closer. He watched as its massive tail swung down again, the force behind it enough to crush a house. But Roman stood his ground.

Now!

At the last second, he activated *Kinetic Absorption*, allowing the immense energy from the strike to flow into his body. It hit him like a freight train, the shockwave rippling through and rattling his bones, but instead of being thrown back, Roman absorbed the power, his muscles buzzing with the stored energy.

The beast reared back, confused, but Roman grinned, his body now humming with potential. He clenched his fists, feeling the raw energy pulsing inside him trying to go to his strength and speed like usual but he stopped it and pushed it all to his fist, and then released it all at once.

Lightning Burst!

A massive explosion of electrical energy shot out from Roman's fist as he swung at its nose, amplified by the kinetic energy he had absorbed. The blast hit the creature dead-on, sending waves of electricity crackling across its armored body. The beast screeched in pain as the force of the strike rocked it back, its armor sizzling and smoking under the onslaught.

Roman panted, watching as the creature stumbled and there was a literal dent in its face, but it wasn't done yet. It let out a roar, angrier now, and charged once again.

"Alright," Roman muttered, gritting his teeth as he prepared for the next round. "Let's see who breaks first."

Chapter 14

The throne room in Eidon's captured keep was dimly lit, the stone walls casting long, cold shadows across the room. Seated on a blackened iron throne that was recently placed atop the previous city ruler's meager chair, was King Varnok, the man responsible for the terror that had swept across the land. His eyes, dark and calculating, gleamed with a hatred so deep it seemed to radiate from his very core. Around him stood his generals—men hardened by years of battle; their loyalty bound not by honor but by fear.

King Varnok leaned forward, his gauntleted fingers tapping against the armrest of his throne as his lips curled into a sneer. His voice, low and venomous, cut through the silence like a blade. "Our forces are advancing, but it's not enough. I want this city reduced to ashes. I want the screams of the dying to echo through the streets."

One of the generals, a grizzled veteran with a jagged scar across his face, hesitated. "Sire, the resistance has been... stronger than anticipated. Their reinforcements have arrived, and—"

"Stronger?" Varnok's voice rose, a dangerous edge creeping into his tone. He stood abruptly, his black cloak billowing behind him. "Do not speak to me of strength, General. They are vermin, nothing more." His eyes gleamed with malice. "We control the beasts, and soon, we will control *everything*."

There was a collective intake of breath among the generals. Some shifted uncomfortably, but none dared to speak. They all knew what their king was capable of, the depths of his cruelty, and the power he had over them.

Varnok began to pace, his heavy boots thudding against the stone floor. "The orc horde will ravage the north, as I've commanded. Their brutish strength will serve me well as a distraction. While they tear through the kingdom's armies, we'll continue to advance from the south. By the time they realize what's happening, it will be too late."

One of the younger generals, braver than the rest, cleared his throat. "Sire, what of the... *other* plan? The one we've been keeping hidden?"

Varnok paused, a twisted grin slowly spreading across his face. "Ah, yes. The *other* plan." His voice dropped to a chilling whisper. "Soon, that will be revealed as well. When the orcs have done their part, and the kingdom lies in ruin, our final weapon will be unleashed. Not even the capital will stand against it."

The general's face paled. He had heard rumors, whispers of something far worse than the orcs. But Varnok was a master of manipulation, and he had learned long ago that the king's thirst for power knew no bounds.

Varnok turned back to his generals, his eyes burning with malevolent intent. "Remember, this isn't about conquest. This is about domination. The people of this land will kneel before me, or they will burn. There is no middle ground. We leave nothing standing."

His generals nodded; their fear palpable. None dared to question him further.

Varnok strode back to his throne, sitting down with a look of dark satisfaction. "Now, let's watch as our enemies fall, one by one."

Roman's Battle Continues

Meanwhile, outside the walls of Eidon, Roman was fighting for his life. His earlier confidence had been replaced with the grinding weight of exhaustion. His body ached, his muscles screaming with every movement as he faced down the monstrous creature before him. The initial thrill of battle had worn off, replaced by the harsh reality of fatigue.

He punched out with a lightning burst again, but his strikes were slower now, less precise and a whole lot weaker. The hulking scorpion-like creature in front of him was relentless, its spiked tail lashing out with deadly precision. Roman barely managed to dodge, the tail striking the ground where he had been standing moments before, shattering the stone beneath it.

"I can't keep this up, Roman thought, his breath ragged. His magic reserves were nearly depleted, he could feel it, the energy that was bursting from him earlier was now fading from his body. Each movement felt heavier than the last, as though the weight of the battle was dragging him down.

The beast charged at him again, its pincers snapping dangerously close to his chest. Roman rolled to the side, narrowly avoiding the attack, but the strain was evident. His legs burned with every step, and his arms felt like lead as he raised his glaive to block the next strike.

Come on... Roman growled to himself, forcing his body to keep moving. He had fought so hard, pushed his limits further than ever before. But the fight wasn't over, and the monstrous creature was still coming at him, relentless and unyielding.

He tried to summon another burst of magic, but the energy flickered weakly, the flames sputtering out before they could fully form. Roman cursed under his breath, realizing he was tapped out on power.

The scorpion-like beast lunged again, and this time, Roman couldn't dodge in time. The massive tail struck him square in the chest, the force of the blow sending him flying backward. He crashed into the ground, pain shooting through his body as he gasped for air.

Get up. Get up, he told himself, his vision swimming. The beast was closing in, its pincers clacking ominously as it prepared for the final blow.

Roman's heart pounded in his chest, his mind racing. *I need more power. I can't let this thing win.*

But there was nothing left. His body was drained, his magic all but spent. He struggled to his feet, wobbling slightly as he tried to steady himself. The beast was right in front of him now, its massive form towering over him.

Just as the creature's tail swung down for the killing strike, Roman's mind flashed to *Kinetic Absorption* once again. He had used it before, but now, in his weakened state, it was his only hope.

With the last of his strength, Roman planted his feet and braced for impact. The tail slammed into him, and for a split second, Roman felt like he was going to be crushed under the force of it. But then, the energy from the blow surged into him, filling his body with a sudden rush of power.

Now!

Roman unleashed the stored energy in one final, desperate attack. His body crackled with electricity as he pushed out a massive *Lightning Burst*, the power amplified by the kinetic energy he had absorbed. The blast hit the creature point-blank in the dent he had caused earlier and had been targeting this whole fight, the force of the electricity tearing through its armored hide and sending it reeling backward with a deafening screech.

Roman collapsed to his knees, gasping for breath, watching as the beast shuddered and then fell, its massive body crashing to the ground in a smoking heap.

For a moment, Roman could barely believe it. The battle wasn't over—there were still more monsters to fight—but for now, he had survived. And as he stood shakily, preparing to face whatever came next, he knew one thing for certain:

He beat the brakes of that scorpion. He chuckled and started to lose consciousness when a soft warm hand grabbed his, he looked to his left and saw Lexi smiling up at him and in that moment, he had never seen anything so beautiful.

"Wow, So beautiful." He whispered and passed out, his head landing on her shoulder as she twisted to support his weight.

"I got you." Lexi said, her face shining a bright red after hearing his words. He gripped him then tugged the rope she repelled down on and they were slowly lifted back to the top of the walls.

"Thank you." He muttered, regaining his senses barely.

"Of course, we're a party." She smiled down at him.

"I wish we could be more than that…but I know it's too fast since we just met but being with you feels right." He said and leaned up and kissed her. She didn't move a muscle, stayed completely still until he slouched back into her arms. Her mind raced in a thousand directions and none at the same time. *He kissed me! He said he wanted to be with me!*

"LEXI!!!" A scream in her ear snapped her back with a shock.

"Huh? Why are you yelling?!" She shot back at Jessika.

"I have been calling you and talking to you for the past thirty seconds!" Jessika shot back; she was leaning on the rail for support after using all of her magic to keep the monsters away to give her time to retrieve the boys. Everyone was now back on the walls and completely wiped.

"O-oh sorry. I was thinking and didn't hear you." Lexi answered shyly.

"Thinking about what that your ears turned off?" Jessika pushed.

"N-Nothing. Are the guys, ok?" she asked and tried to walk past Jessika who wouldn't budge.

"Yeah, they're fine, don't try to change the subject! What were you lost in thought and blushing so hard for?"

"Blushing? I wasn't blushing." Lexi answered.

"I could have probably seen that blush from the capital." Sergeant Smithson said with a chuckle which made her blush more.

"There you go again! Why were you blushing? Did Roman say something to you or just holding him in your arms filled your heart with the warm and fuzzies?" Jessika chuckled.

"And?! What about you and Z!" She yelled and Z's head snapped up.

"Come again?" He said and looked between them. Now Jessika was the one blushing and trying to change the subject but before she could even start speaking about the thing she was pointing out, Lexi kept going.

"Yeah, you're always on my case because I like Roman but you've been drooling after Z from the time we've met and never said a thing! I just met Roman two days ago so had a reason to take some time as we got to know each other but what about you!" Lexi asked and a again Z looked shocked.

"Come again?!" He said again, mouth still hanging open in shock.

"Yes, Z, Jessika is in love with you and has been throwing you hints for months and you've ignored them all...she basically thought you weren't interested which is why she has been so miserable lately." Lexi said and walked away with Roman still in her arms towards one of the medical tents before Jessika or Z could get a word in while Sergeant Smithson just chuckled.

"Can I get someone to check on him please." She asked as she entered the tent.

"Sure, right this way please." They spread him down on the hard wood surface and Lexi stepped back so they could examine him.

"Lexi!" An older grizzled voice called out to her from one side of the tent and Lexi smiled as her old master approached and her friends stepped back out of the tent to give them space.

"Master Wong!" She called out. He was her instructor most of her life, finally leaving her father's service to get back on the road when she turned 16, saying she was all set and would have to develop her own fighting style from here. That was when she fell in love with the bow.

"Look at you! I have been following you guys as much as I can but you know gossip can be so unreliable. I heard you were out here fighting with the army and couldn't believe it so made my way down here and here you are!" He exclaimed.

Before she could answer, Roman started coughing so she stopped and looked at him but since medical team didn't look alerted, she relaxed and tuned back to Master Wong but now he looked nervous.

Chapter 15

"Is this your friend Alexis?" He asked and she got immediately on high alert because he called her full name instead of just Lexi like everyone called her.

"Yes, why? What's wrong?"

"I have never seen anything like this! He made a Mana core but with Chi instead...that is unheard of. Impossible." Master Wong kept going on about how impossible it was for a while before calming down and stepping closer and reaching a handout to examine Roman closer.

"What are you talking about?"

"Have you seen him fight? Does he use magic or is he a physical fighter?" he asked.

"Both. Initially he was only physical but during this fight since these monsters' armor stopped his blade, he switched tactics and rained magic down on them all day."

"How long was he fighting and were the attacks powerful?" He asked.

"All day I said...we got back here sometime this morning and the sun is going down...he's been fighting since we got here. And each attack was clearing out a good chunk of them...I would say each hit wiped out 3 or 4 at least of the bigger ones...the small ones didn't stand a chance and were demolished by the 10s or 20s." Lexi answered.

"Impossible." Master Wong whispered as he looked closer at Roman's solar plexus.

"What is! You haven't explained anything."

"So, you know how I taught you to create a mana core?'

"Yes."

"And remember how I told you that since mana wasn't your strong suit you should focus on building your internal Chi energy instead?"

"Yes?"

"So, he used chi energy and built a core...with Chi and not mana!"

"Is that possible? I've never heard of that."

"No, it's not!" Master Wong was so excited and in awe he started losing control of his volume and one of the nurses came over to silence him.

"My apologies." He said calmly before turning back to Roman.

"So would the Chi core make one stronger then?" Lexi asked.

"I don't know! Mana comes from the earth around you, everything has mana but chi...while everything has chi supposedly, you can't absorb it you have to cycle it. There's a set amount of

Chi in your body and you use the energy in some of it then cycle it back to get recharged so to speak. But with his core….it is constantly cycling so there's never a down period. Technically, he could use his power endlessly…but then I guess there is always fatigued to deal with, while his core can take it, his body has to manage pushing the power through and after a while it wears down." Master Wong explained in awe.

"Wow. Is that possible for another person to do or is that special to just him?" Lexi asked.

"I have no clue…I've never heard of anything like this before, I didn't think something like this was possible." Master Wong said and was about to keep going when they heard Roman mumble something and fidget a little.

"He must be dreaming, he'll be ok." Lexi said with a smile then that smile started to drop when she saw the sweat forming on his head and how fast his eyes flashed back and forth. He was having a nightmare. "Roman, wake up! It's just a dream, wake up Roman. Its ok"

■■

Roman

As Roman's body twitched and writhed under the hospital bed, his mind was back home. Golden light cascading through the sheer curtains casting a soft glow throughout the cozy apartment. He walked into the kitchen where he could hear quiet singing but more importantly the smell of bacon. He turned the corner to see her standing there before the oven as she flipped over the omelet with one hand and turning the oven off with the other. He smiled as he watched the sun kiss off her shoulders and form a small angelic aura around her small frame.

She was about 5 foot 5, soft caramel colored skin that was absolutely flawless, not even one blemish as if she'd been in a protective bubble lined with baby oil her entire life. Her hair was currently a dirty blonde but she was born a brunette, He didn't care which, either way she was the most beautiful woman he had ever seen but she didn't like her natural color. He stood there admiring the woman that had finally agreed to be his wife, the woman he had waited 14 years before working up the nerve to ask her out. The woman that made every other woman in the world seem like nothing but third rate…besides his mom of course…Then she bent to open the oven door and he jumped into action sliding up behind her and wrapping his hands around her waist. She jumped in shock and let out an adorable squeak of fear before relaxing into his arms.

"You scared me!" She laughed and smacked his arm before laying her head on his shoulder. "Mmm…Good morning." She sighed.

"Good morning my love." He squeezed tight, her back in his chest and his chin now resting on the top of her head. He tilted and kissed her head before going back to how he was. She turned her head and started nibbling on his arm.

"Ah! You're such an animal!" He fake-complained before nibbling on her ear which caused her to giggle and try to squirm away.

"You're gonna make me burn the eggs." She exclaimed and reached out.

"Ok Ima walk closer but I'm gonna be your backpack for a while." He grinned and shuffled forward so she could get closer to the stove.

He blinked and then they were in the park in the afternoon. He smiled as he remembered this. This was the day he asked her to be his girlfriend. The sun was shining brightly and she was twirling as her dress swirled around her as she kept her hands around mid-thigh so the dress didn't rise too high. After spinning for a bit she got dizzy and giggling like crazy she rammed right into him and they both went down laughing as he pretended to wrestle her and she got on top and kissing him. He pushed her hair out of her face and behind one ear before kissing her again.

"Jaimee, I gotta ask you something." He said and paused as she sobered and looked him in the eye.

"What's wrong?" She asked him.

"Nothing…I just…I know it took me a while to build up the nerve to ask you out…do you…do you regret it?" he asked nervously.

"What? No! Well yeah, I regret that it took you 14 years and that I listened to my friends instead of asking you out myself!" She huffed. "Why the hell did it take you so long anyway?!"

"What do you mean?! Look at you! I didn't think I ever had a chance with you, it was such an honor that you even wanted to be my friend so I didn't want to risk that."

"Lame! You gotta have more confidence than that!" she said and laughed as she shook her head.

"Ok well I'm tryna do better so, will you be my girlfriend?" He rushed out before his fear could stall him again. She looked at him in confusion.

"I already am your girlfriend dumbass." She said and he sagged in relief.

"Oh yeah?" He said and kissed her.

"Yeah! What did you think we were this whole time?" She asked.

"I saw you as that but we never talked about it…and I heard from your cousin, JJ, that you went out with some dude last week…I waited but you never mentioned it so I thought…"

"You thought I was cheating on you and didn't say anything?"

"Well, I justified it in my head that you never said we were exclusive so I couldn't be mad at you."

"No, you idiot! We were exclusive from the moment I agreed to go on the first date with you. There was no one else! The guy I went to see was about getting this as a gift for you it wasn't a date!" She said and pulled a thick gold ring with a flat black part on top and a golden cross in the middle. She put it on his finger and kissed it.

"You got me this?" he asked, looking down at the ring.

"Yeah, I know how much your faith means to you and you lost your chain…I couldn't find a chain but did find this that had the same colors as the chain.

"Thank you, babe!" he said and kissed. "I don't have a ring for you but can we use this as an engagement ring? Will you marry me?"

"Uh no you better get me a ring outta that dollarstore or something first! You not gone use my gift to you to ask me that!" She said and smacked his shoulder.

He jumped up and ran as she laughed behind him.

He looked back at Jaimee with a smile but she wasn't there...the park wasn't there anymore, he was now in a grimy alley.

"No, no, no." He started muttering as he recognized the place. He heard Jaime scream and tried to run to her but his body wouldn't move. He could see her a few feet away from him but he couldn't budge, not even a muscle would respond to his pleas. "JAIMEE!!!" He screamed but no sound exited his mouth.

"Roman, wake up!" He heard but didn't know where it came from and kept screaming as Jaimee screamed.

"Roman, wake up! Its just a dream, wake up Roman."

"JAIMEE!!! NO LET HER GO!! NO PLEASE+!" He screamed as the thug lifted the gun.

"NOOO!!! JAIMEE!!!" He screamed at the same time as he heard. "ROMAN!!!!"

Chapter 16

Roman shot upright in his hospital bed, a guttural scream tearing from his throat.

"Jaimee!"

The name echoed in the sterile room, his voice hoarse and filled with anguish. His chest heaved as he fought to pull air into his lungs, the terror of the dream gripping him like iron chains. His eyes darted around wildly, that night still fresh in his mind—the deafening bang of the gun, Jaimee's scream, the blinding pain. It all felt so real.

Before he could spiral further, a pair of arms wrapped around him, strong but gentle. Lexi. She pulled him close, her warmth cutting through the cold panic that gripped him. "Shh, Roman, you're safe. I'm here," she whispered softly, her voice steady despite her concern.

His body trembled, and he buried his face in her chest, the sobs escaping in ragged gasps. He was shaking uncontrollably now, the memories too much to bear. Jaimee's smile, her laughter, all of it slipping away from him in that single horrific moment.

Lexi held him tighter, her hand cradling the back of his head as he wept. "It's okay, Roman," she whispered, her fingers threading gently through his hair. "It's okay. I've got you."

He clung to her as if she were his lifeline, the floodgates opening as the pain and guilt he had held onto for so long poured out. His tears soaked into her shirt, but she didn't mind. She just rocked him softly, humming under her breath, her voice a low, soothing melody in the dark.

"I'm here," she repeated, her breath warm against his ear. "You're not alone."

Roman's sobs began to slow, his body still shaking but less violently now. Lexi continued to hold him, her heartbeat steady beneath his cheek. For the first time in what felt like forever, he allowed himself to let go.

And for a moment, even in his grief, he felt a flicker of something—maybe it was peace, or maybe just exhaustion—but wrapped in Lexi's arms, he found a brief respite from the storm. He felt comfort not just from her but from the One he had been ignoring whenever things suited him. He felt the warm embrace that had gotten him through every other tough time in his life that ever since coming to this world he just kept forgetting about for some reason!

Wait…Lexi's arms? His eyes popped opened and his body stiffened, his breath catching in his throat as the realization hit him. Lexi's arms—*Lexi's*—were still wrapped around him, holding him close. Her warmth, her gentle presence, all of it had been so soothing in the midst of his breakdown. But now that the haze of emotion had lifted, the weight of the situation started to settle in, and he felt like he'd just crossed a line he hadn't even seen coming.

His eyes popped open, staring at the stark white hospital wall in front of him, but his thoughts were everywhere else. His pulse quickened—not with panic, but with something else entirely. He was suddenly hyper-aware of every small detail: the way her fingers were still lightly stroking the back of his head, the steady rise and fall of her chest beneath his cheek, and the soft, rhythmic sound of her breathing.

He hadn't realized how tightly he'd been holding onto her, and now, he didn't know what to do with his hands. Should he pull back? Say something? Anything? But what would he even say? *Thanks for letting me sob all over you—also, sorry I didn't realize you were right there?* It sounded ridiculous, even in his head.

Lexi hadn't said anything either. She just kept holding him, her touch still as gentle as it had been when she'd first pulled him into her arms. Maybe she hadn't noticed the shift in him, or maybe she had, but either way, her presence felt natural—too natural, in fact. Roman's throat tightened, and the room suddenly felt smaller.

He swallowed hard, his mind racing. *How did we even get here?* Sure, they'd fought alongside each other, survived battles together—but this? This was different. They had shared moments, yes, but nothing like this.

He shifted slightly, trying not to disturb her too much, but his body betrayed him. The muscles in his back tensed, and his heart felt like it was beating too loudly, thudding in his ears. His hand twitched, as if it couldn't decide whether to stay where it was or to find somewhere—anywhere—else to be.

Lexi must have felt the change in him, because her arms loosened around him just slightly, her hand stilling where it rested against his hair. She didn't pull away completely, though. Instead, she tilted her head to look down at him, her voice soft in the quiet room. "Roman?"

His name hung in the air between them, and for a split second, he didn't know if he could answer. He tried to clear his throat, but it only made him more aware of how close they were. "Yeah?" he finally managed, though it came out more like a croak.

Lexi's hand hesitated before it fell gently to her lap. "You okay?" she asked, her tone filled with that same calm concern, but now there was something more there—something quieter, something almost... uncertain.

He nodded quickly, too quickly, and awkwardly shifted again, sitting up just enough to put a little distance between them. "Yeah, yeah. I'm good. Thanks for..." His words trailed off as he scratched the back of his neck, unsure how to even finish the sentence. *Thanks for comforting me? Thanks for holding me while I had a breakdown?*

Lexi didn't push, didn't ask for more. She just smiled softly, pulling her legs up onto the bed as she sat back a bit, giving him space. "I'm glad," she said, her voice still as gentle as it had been the entire time. But there was something in her eyes—something that made Roman's chest tighten again.

Silence settled between them, but this time it felt different. Roman didn't know what to do with it, and the longer it stretched, the more he could feel the awkwardness creeping in. He wanted to say something, anything, to break the tension he'd just imagined into existence. But all he could think about was how close they'd been a moment ago, how natural it had felt to be in her arms, and how unnatural it suddenly felt now that they weren't.

His hand hovered awkwardly in his lap, and for the first time, Roman wasn't sure if he should be relieved or nervous that Lexi had been the one to step back. The yearning to get up and take her into his arms kept building and it was baffling. Lexi had always been there and of course he had had thoughts of her…she's gorgeous but…it was more like a quick oh she cute, he never really had time to think anything more about it so why was his mind now acting like he had had a crush on her for years?

Wait! Is this emotional maturity? Am I finally stopping to think about how I feel instead of just acting on stuff? He thought to himself with a chuckle which made Lexi tilt her head in confusion.

"S-sorry, I was just thinking about something and I think I finally reached a level of emotional maturity. Was just feeling proud of myself but thank you so much Lexi. I really needed that." He said sincerely.

"Oh ok, You're welcome Roman." She smiled softly. "Do you want to talk about it?" She asked.

"I do but…. I can't right now, I don't have the energy. I feel too raw right now." He replied.

"Ok no rush. I'm here whenever you're ready."

"Thank you, I really mean that. Thanks." He said, grabbing hold of her hand and looking into her eyes. Before that could start getting awkward again someone cleared their throat to roman's left and he turned to look.

Master Wong moved with slow, deliberate steps; his hands clasped behind his back as he walked. On the surface, he looked every bit the old, frail man—his skin weathered, his silver hair tied back into a neat knot at the base of his neck, and his posture slightly hunched. His face was etched with deep lines, evidence of a life lived long and hard. His faded, loose robes fluttered lightly in the breeze, making him seem almost weightless as he moved across the ground.

To any casual observer, he would have appeared weak, perhaps even fragile, the kind of man who might struggle to lift a wooden staff. But Roman... Roman knew better.

The moment Master Wong came into view, Roman felt it—a dense, overwhelming presence, like the air itself had thickened around the man. There was a stillness to Master Wong, an unshakable calm, but beneath that serene exterior, Roman could sense an ocean of power, vast and unyielding. It radiated from the old man in waves, though nothing in his outward appearance gave it away.

Roman's muscles tensed instinctively, every fiber of his being alert. It wasn't just power—*it was mastery.* He had felt strong people before, fought warriors whose skills far exceeded his own, but this was different. This was like standing in front of a mountain that could shift at any moment. Roman couldn't tell if he could win in a fight against him. In fact, he wasn't even sure if he would survive one.

Master Wong's eyes, sharp and piercing despite their age, briefly met Roman's. In that fleeting moment, Roman felt as though the old man could see through him, past the physical, right into his soul. There was no malice in Wong's gaze—just an ancient, calm knowing, as if the man had seen a thousand battles and come out of each one unscathed. Roman swallowed hard, his body refusing to relax, even as Master Wong's expression softened into a faint, almost amused smile.

Roman blinked, trying to shake the uneasy feeling gnawing at him, but the sheer weight of Wong's presence was impossible to ignore. He had never felt so small in front of someone who looked so unassuming. It was as if Master Wong had complete control over every aspect of the world around him, yet he walked as if it were nothing more than a leisurely stroll.

The contrast between the man's appearance and the power that Roman could sense was unsettling. He wasn't sure if he would ever be able to gauge Wong's limits—if there were any.

"Oh, Roman this is my Master that trained me to fight, Master Wong, this is my new friend Roman. He's super strong and took on most of those monsters out there on his own."Lexi said proudly introducing the two.

"It is nice to meet you Sir." Roman said respectfully.

"You as well, young Roman. I do have a few questions for you if you'd allow me to skip the pleasantries." Master Wong said, still looking deep into Roman's eyes.

"Of course. What would you like to know?" Roman asked, while knowing he wouldn't win against this man...he still felt no fear of him.

"Who taught you to form that core?" He came right out and said it. Roman paused for a sec not sure what he was asking then it clicked.

"Uh...nobody. I taught myself." Roman said.

"Mmhmm. In the world you come from was there magic?" He asked and Roman's blood went cold. He froze and looked around. "Relax. No one else knows but its not something that you need to hide either. We have had some people from another world here before, not sure if it's the same world you're from though. Are you from Earth?"

"U-uh..." Roman wasn't sure what to say. How did this man know so much?

Master Wong's piercing gaze never wavered as he waited for Roman's response, his eyes betraying no surprise at Roman's hesitation. It was as if he had already pieced together the truth before Roman even arrived. There was no pressure in his tone, no malice—just a deep, unshakable curiosity, like a man who had seen too much of the world to be fazed by any revelation.

Roman cleared his throat, trying to compose himself. "Y-yeah. I'm from Earth." The words felt strange coming out, as if saying them aloud somehow made his situation even more surreal.

Master Wong nodded slowly, a faint smile playing on his lips. "I see. So, the veil between worlds is thinning again." His voice was soft, contemplative, as though he were speaking more to himself than to Roman.

Roman's mind raced. *People from Earth have been here before?* His thoughts spiraled for a moment, but he forced himself to stay focused. "Wait—what do you mean by 'again'? Has this happened before?"

Wong clasped his hands behind his back and began to pace slowly, his movements deliberate and calm. "Indeed. You are not the first, nor will you be the last, I suspect. Travelers from your world have crossed into ours many times, though it is a rare occurrence. Some come here by accident, others by design." He paused, turning back to face Roman.

Master Wong's gaze softened as he watched Roman, his hands still clasped behind his back. "People from other worlds have always fascinated this realm," he began. "You see, the power you possess is not unusual for those like you. In fact, people from other worlds thrive here. You and others like you are sought after by kingdoms, empires—anyone who understands the true value of your potential."

Roman blinked, his confusion only deepening. "Sought after? Why?"

Master Wong's expression remained calm, but there was a spark of something in his eyes—knowledge that few others possessed. "Because your kind—the travelers from other worlds—are the reason this world has magic at all. And from what I've read, anyone in your party or that fights alongside you gets exponentially stronger at an astounding rate."

Roman's heart skipped a beat. "What do you mean?"

Wong smiled faintly, his voice taking on a more reflective tone. "Long ago, when the veil between worlds first broke, it unleashed a flood of magic and mana into this realm. Before that event, there was no magic here, no leveling system, no abilities like the ones you've discovered. The arrival of people from other worlds—people like you—changed the very fabric of this reality. Mana pooled from your presence, and the world adapted to it, forming the monsters you've been fighting and then strengthening humans and forming the magical system we rely on today."

Roman felt his breath catch in his throat as he processed what Wong was saying. The very world he had been thrust into—its magic, its leveling system—existed because of people like him. "So… I'm part of the reason why this world is the way it is?"

Master Wong nodded. "Exactly. That first influx of mana reshaped the world, and now every traveler that comes here brings their own potential, their own spark. Some kingdoms even prepare for the arrival of such individuals, knowing that they often possess powers that far exceed those born here. Those from other worlds often grow stronger and faster, adapting to magic like it's second nature. You've already demonstrated that yourself."

Roman thought back to how quickly he'd learned magic, how his body seemed to just *know* what to do. It had felt instinctual, but now, it made sense. He wasn't just learning; he was *unlocking* something deep within himself, something tied to the very essence of this world's magic.

"You and others like you are a gift to this realm," Wong continued. "You bring new energy, new life to a world that once had none. The leveling system, the magic you see—it is all a reflection of your kind's influence. But with that power comes great responsibility. Those who learn to wield it wisely thrive, as you have. But without guidance, that power can consume even the best of people."

Roman swallowed hard, understanding the gravity of what Master Wong was telling him. "So... I'm not just some anomaly?"

Wong shook his head. "No, Roman. You are the continuation of a legacy—one that has shaped this world into what it is today. And your potential, much like the others who came before you, can change the course of this world's future."

Roman took a deep breath, feeling a strange mix of awe and responsibility settle over him. The revelation that he and others like him were the catalysts for this world's magic was staggering, but it also made sense of so many things. His rapid growth, his ability to adapt—it wasn't random. It was part of something much larger.

Lexi, who had been quietly listening, spoke up, her eyes wide with wonder. "So... travelers from other worlds are why we have magic at all?"

Master Wong nodded. "Yes. And it is why you, Roman, possess such incredible potential. Your connection to the mana in this world is different from ours. You can shape it, bend it to your will, faster than anyone born here. That is why kingdoms seek out people like you—to harness that power."

Roman looked down at his hands, still processing everything. "But... I didn't even know what I was doing half the time."

Wong chuckled softly. "That's what makes you dangerous, Roman. You don't even realize the full extent of what you're capable of yet."

Roman's heart raced as he met Wong's gaze. He didn't know how to feel—whether it was fear, excitement, or something in between. But one thing was clear: he wasn't just a visitor in this world. He was a part of its story, its magic, and its future.

Chapter 17

"Okay, so I've got a bunch of questions I need to ask you real quick before I head back out there," Roman said hurriedly, as a loud crash reverberated through the room—another monster slamming against the wall. For a moment, he had forgotten about the ongoing battle outside.

"Of course," Master Wong chuckled softly, clearly amused by Roman's eager thirst for knowledge.

"When I woke up in front of Eidon, I figured out how to open my status screen, and it showed I had the title of *World Walker*... but it said the title was broken. I can't access levels or skills. Do you know how to fix that?" Roman asked hopefully, holding his breath, almost afraid of the answer.

Master Wong's eyes brightened with curiosity. "Fascinating. So, you can see your status at any time? That's quite impressive." One hand stroked his beard thoughtfully.

"Yeah, but can you fix it? I mean, it really sucks not being able to gain levels or skills, aside from weapon abilities," Roman said, the frustration evident in his voice.

"Wait—you're *this* strong without being able to level up?" Lexi exclaimed, her eyes wide with surprise.

"Well, I'm pretty sure you *have* been leveling up," Master Wong corrected, his tone serious. "You just don't have access to it and can't see it." He paused, thinking deeply. "But to answer your question... no, I don't know how to fix it. However…" His voice trailed off.

Roman's hope flickered. "But?" he asked, leaning forward.

"I do know someone who might be able to help. He's a reclusive man living in the Dragon Fang Mountains."

Roman turned to Lexi, who seemed to deflate at the mention of the remote location. "Where's that?"

"Our kingdom is surrounded by mountains on three sides—that's what's kept us safe and difficult to invade… until now," Master Wong explained. "The Dragon Fang Mountains are to the southeast. Honestly, they're not that far from here."

"And it works out perfectly because the King is sending us there to train once we handle this invasion," Seth said, walking into the room with the others. For the first time since waking up, Roman really took in his surroundings. Nurses moved around, tending to the injured, but the place was mostly deserted. Roman realized he was on the first bed near the entrance, so those deeper inside couldn't hear their conversation. But Seth and the others, now close by, had overheard everything.

Roman shook his head, smirking. "You shadow users… always sneaking around, eavesdropping on people's conversations."

Seth chuckled and patted Roman on the shoulder. "Hey, I always get the juiciest gossip."

Roman laughed, but his thoughts quickly returned to what Seth had said. "So, the King is sending us to the mountains to train? Why there? What's so special about them?"

"There's a new dungeon we recently discovered in the area," Jessika answered, sitting next to Lexi at the foot of Roman's bed.

"A dungeon?" Roman's voice betrayed a spark of hope, though he tried to temper his excitement, worried it might not be what he was thinking.

"Yes," Master Wong said, nodding. "It's a space where a magic core has transformed its entire environment. Dungeons are unlike anything else in the world, except perhaps the Beast Plains. Monsters within the dungeons respawn after a set time, and they drop items—what you might call 'loot.'"

Roman blinked. "Respawn? Loot?" He repeated the words, confused that they were using terms he knew from games back on Earth.

"Oh yes," Master Wong said, smiling. "Some of the earliest Otherworlder used these terms a lot, so they stuck. It's part of our vocabulary now."

Roman shook his head, mentally kicking himself. *Of course*, he thought. *I should have known that.*

"Ok next question, do you know what cultivation is?" He asked and watched Master Wong for any sign of shock or surprise but saw none.

"Yes, I have been taught this by my master. He learned from an Otherworlder and created an Academy but none of us were able to improve our bodies so the school changed to just the martial arts he taught and not the cultivation side." Master Wong answered honestly.

"Ok so it's not a foreign concept to you then. That is how I am this strong. I have been cultivating since I arrived. The first monster I killed I felt this energy fill me and I got scared and didn't know what to do with it." Roman said and trailed off as he remembered that first fight.

"Yes, every monster you kill releases energy like that, we call it experience, or XP." Seth answered.

"What do you do with that energy? Does the XP fill your body?" Roman asked.

"No, we sort of breath it in and then the system banks it, after receiving a certain amount of XP we level up." Seth answered again.

"Ok…so that's different from what I did. I breathed it in but then it sat in my chest and was uncomfortable then I remembered about another title I have and about cultivation from my world so started compressing the energy into a ball, then the system said I formed a broken core. Later on I fixed the core by changing the shape more into a tree…which is what felt right to me at the time, I don't know why. After I made that change it was like…power I had never known rushing through me. I was faster, stronger, I could even heal myself almost immediately." Roman answered, it felt good to lay all his cards out there for the first time.

"Ok couple questions but first, another title?" Lexi asked.

"Yeah, I've been itching to ask you ever since we did the scan in the capital but things kept happening, but you have three titles?!" Jessika asked excitedly.

"Oh yeah, I wish there was a way I could show you my status screen how I see it." He mused and then started trying some things and it worked on the first one. "Share Status Screen." He thought and visualized what he wanted. He smiled when everyone jumped in surprise.

Status:

Name: Roman
Race: Human
Age: 19

Title: [World Walker] (Incomplete) – *World Walker* is a title earned by traversing the cosmos to arrive on another world capable of sustaining life and with access to the System. This title is currently incomplete; the user has only the lite version. Levels and stats are unavailable.

Title: [Exponential Growth] – The user's growth in all areas increases exponentially. All activities completed by the user are influenced by this title until the body can no longer sustain it. Once this limit is reached, the user must improve their body's constitution and vigor for continued growth.

Title: [Cultivator's Body] – The user has the ability to enhance bodily functions through cultivation. Energy from the environment and defeated enemies is absorbed and stored directly into the body for self-enhancement, bypassing the System.

Core: Empowered Core

Skills and Proficiency:

- **Sword Mastery:** Lvl 10 (Mastered)
- **Glaive Mastery:** Lvl 10 (Mastered)
- **Enhanced Agility:** Lvl 10 (Mastered)
- **Athleticism:** Lvl 10 (Mastered)
- **Elemental Weapon Mastery - Lightning:** Lvl 9
- **Weapon Proficiency - All Weapons:** Lvl 8
- **Enhanced Strength:** Lvl 8
- **Healing Acceleration:** Lvl 6
- **Split Focus:** Lvl 5
- **Battle Instincts:** Lvl 7
- **Combat Awareness:** Lvl 8
- **Energy Manipulation:** Lvl 6
    - **Elemental Energy creation**
- **Spiritual Connection:** Lvl 8
- **Leadership Presence:** Lvl 6
- **ETC>**

"Wow this is amazing!" Master Wong exclaimed. "So, you can keep growing skills as long as you cultivate and make your body strong enough to handle it?! So, what if a skill gets out of hand and passes your cultivation level? And are the ones that say mastered your current level?" The questions spewed out of him so fast, Roman couldn't keep up.

"I-I don't know." He muttered.

"So, you don't use mana at all you use…what, Chi?" Lexi asked, looking to Master Wong to see if she said that word right.

"I think so. What does mana feel like?"

Jessika closed her eyes for a moment, feeling the familiar warmth of mana flowing through her. "Mana… it's like this constant hum beneath the surface. It's everywhere, in the air, in the ground, in the very core of everything around us. When I draw on it, it feels light, like water or wind brushing against my skin. There's this gentle pull when you focus, like it's just waiting to be shaped, molded into whatever spell or ability you need.

"Once you start using it, it's like a river flowing through you—warm, but not overwhelming. It's… responsive. You give it shape, as you say the spells it gives it form and rules. It bends easily, like clay in your hands."

She smiled slightly. "But it's fleeting. Once the spell is cast, the mana dissipates back into the world, like mist. I can draw it in again, but it never stays long."

Roman, listening to Jessika, paused before offering his own perspective. "Chi... it's different from what you're describing. For me, chi isn't just in the world around us, though it exists there too—it's in me. It's personal, like a pulse or a heartbeat. When I'm cultivating, the energy feels... denser. Heavier. It's not something that flows as easily as you describe mana. It's more like I have to pull and push it around. I can feel its always there and at first I thought the energy I was absorbing was it until talking to Master Wong...now I know that energy was probably just XP initially and then some mana that I forced to act like Chi...now that I know about the different things when I focus inward I can see two different types of energy and I've been using them the same which is wrong. I have some mana in me and Its just been getting pushed around along with the Chi. Chi doesn't just pass through me like a river. It stays. It lingers, building up pressure if I don't handle it right. It's raw, powerful, and wild. I have to compress it, shape it, and refine it constantly, like taking a wild storm and forcing it into a bottle. Luckily my core spins it for me so its a lot easier, I don't even have to think about it much anymore, just will it and it does what I'm imagining most times...When I use it, it's not like casting a spell where you release it—it's like pushing that stored energy into action. Every punch, every movement is powered by that internal force."

He chuckled, scratching the back of his neck. "So yeah, I guess it's a lot more intense. Chi feels like lava—once it's there, it doesn't just fade. It can burn you up if you're not careful."

Master Wong listened attentively to Roman's explanation, his expression calm but thoughtful. "Yes,

Roman, that aligns with the core principles of chi manipulation. Chi is an internal force, a life energy that, once harnessed, becomes a permanent part of you. It doesn't fade away like mana—it stays with you, strengthens you. But it's also volatile, which is why cultivation is so important. Without proper control, chi can easily overwhelm the body."

Roman nodded as Wong spoke, realizing just how similar their understandings of chi were, even though Roman had discovered it on his own.

Wong smiled. "You've done remarkably well for someone who's been navigating it blindly. You have even come to some of the same discoveries that were taught to my master."

Roman suddenly popped up from the bed, energy and excitement flashing across his face. "I have to try something." His sudden movement startled everyone, but there was no stopping the flood of thoughts and ideas racing through his mind.

"What are you trying now?" Jessika asked, bemused by Roman's enthusiasm.

Roman turned to her, his eyes wide with anticipation. "I want to try using mana—just mana. I think I've been confusing it with chi this whole time, forcing it into something it's not. I need to learn how to use them separately."

Master Wong tilted his head with interest. "That would be wise, Roman. If you can distinguish between the two energies, you could expand your abilities greatly. But mana requires a different kind of discipline than chi."

Jessika stood up, brushing off her clothes and headed out of the tent walking into a clearing far away from anything flammable. "Alright, I'll help you with that. Mana isn't something you just brute force into a shape. You have to guide it. Let me show you how I cast spells." She paused for a moment, looking thoughtful as the rest of the group followed behind her. "When I cast, I usually chant in my mind. Some people have to say the incantation out loud, but I've gotten good enough that I only need to think the words to tell the mana what to do."

Roman looked intrigued. "So, it's all about directing the mana through thought?"

"Pretty much," Jessika confirmed. "You give it shape, form, and purpose. It responds to intention, but you still need to be specific, or the spell can fizzle out or go wrong."

Roman nodded, soaking in her words. "Okay. Can you teach me how to cast a basic spell, like fireball?"

"Alright, first close your eyes and try to sense the mana around you."

Roman obeyed, taking a deep breath and focusing inward. For the first time, he tried to separate the sensation of chi from the other energy he'd been ignoring mana. It was subtle, but he could feel it now lighter, more fluid, like a breeze compared to the dense, heavy pulse of his chi. He hadn't noticed the difference before because he was used to forcing them both into the same mold.

"I can feel it," Roman said softly, his eyes still closed. "It's... different from chi. It feels more like what you said—like a river flowing around me."

"Good," Jessika encouraged him. "Now, imagine reaching out to it. Don't try to grab it like you would with chi—just gently guide it. Let it respond to you. Then, in your mind, start the chant. 'Fireball.' Visualize it. See the flames forming in your hand."

Roman followed her instructions carefully. He didn't pull at the mana like he would with chi; instead, he allowed it to gather slowly, like swirling air currents, responding to his mental command. He imagined the word 'fireball,' picturing flames in his palm.

To his amazement, he felt warmth begin to bloom in his hand. His eyes shot open in surprise, and there, hovering above his palm, was a small, flickering fireball.

"Whoa," Roman whispered, staring at the flames.

Jessika grinned, clearly pleased with herself. "See? You just needed to stop forcing it. Mana wants to work with you—you just have to guide it."

Roman's focus shifted back to the flame, marveling at how different this felt compared to when he had been using chi to create elemental energy. The fire was much lighter, more flexible, like it was alive in a way his chi-enhanced attacks never were. Chi was like brute force, raw and intense, but this—this was delicate, like holding a wisp of flame that could vanish at any moment.

"So, this is mana," Roman muttered, more to himself than to anyone else. "It feels... easy, but hard at the same time. It's not as intense as chi, but I have to be careful with it, or it might slip away."

"Exactly," Jessika confirmed. "Mana doesn't stick around. Once you use it, it's gone until you draw more. That's why it's important to be efficient with your spells. If you try to use too much at once, you'll burn through it fast and tire yourself out."

Roman nodded, still staring at the fireball. He flicked his wrist, and the flame dissipated into a wisp of smoke. "That was... incredible. I've been pushing the mana around with my chi this whole time, and I didn't even realize I was doing it wrong."

Master Wong stepped forward, nodding in approval. "It seems you've taken your first step toward understanding the difference. The ability to manipulate both chi and mana separately will make you far more versatile. The things your predecessors were able to do was astonishing. The power they wielded enough to shape the entire world on a whim. And Some of them did just that! These mountains for instance! These were made by a man who just got sick of the monsters for the Monster Plains leaking into the small town he chose to call home…it kind of got out of hand and stretched all the way and completely closed us in on all sides though."

"The Scorched lands too! Its now a permanent desert nothing can grow out there and there's not an ounce of water even though a giant river runs not too far from it!" Z spoke up for the first time in a while.

Roman smiled, feeling a surge of excitement. "So, if I can combine what I know about chi with this new understanding of mana, I'll be even stronger."

Master Wong raised an eyebrow. "That's the idea, but don't get too cocky. Mana and chi are different beasts. It's not about mixing them together recklessly—you have to respect how they work individually. Otherwise, you'll lose control."

Roman's grin softened, acknowledging her point. "Got it. Step by step."

Seth, who had been watching the entire time, finally spoke up. "So, not only are you ridiculously strong with your chi stuff, but now you're going to master mana too? You're really going for the 'overpowered protagonist' title, huh?"

Roman laughed. "Hey, I'm just trying to keep up with this crazy world. Wait how do you even know about…" He paused and then thought about it. "One of my predecessors used to say stuff like that a lot right?"

Seth just grinned.

Master Wong folded his arms, smiling wisely. "It seems Roman's journey is only just beginning. The ability to understand and master multiple energies—chi and mana—sets him apart, but it also places a great responsibility on him. Roman, you must remember that true strength comes not from raw power but from balance and control. While yes you can unleash devastating blasts like I saw you doing earlier, with balance and control you can create the most devastating and battle changing attacks."

Roman nodded seriously. "I understand, Master Wong. I'll work hard to get it right."

"Good," Wong said, his tone gentle but firm. "Then let us continue. There's much more to learn."

With a renewed sense of purpose, Roman felt more ready than ever to face whatever challenges lay ahead. Whether it was mastering his chi or learning the subtleties of mana, he was determined to rise to the occasion. There was no turning back now.

"One more thing I want to tell you as I can see you're itching to get out there. The people like you, your predecessors were not humans according to the system. They all carried a different title and race name. Sons of God. I noticed that your race still says Human, I would suggest hurrying up with this battle so you can seek out help in those mountains and find out how you attain your true race. I am sure the power you attain then would make the strongest human now seem like a toddler with a stick. I do not remember seeing anything about what they needed to do to gain the title but I remember there was something."

"Thank you." Roman answered and then his mind went back to the words. "Sons of God huh?"

"Those words mean something to you?" Seth asked.

"Yes...uh, are you guys religious?" He asked and looked around.

"There are a few religions in the Kingdom but the major one these days follows the goddess Athena, goddess of Wisdom and War. I'm not too religious though." Seth answered. Roman looked at him in shock.

"Athena?! Is there Zeus, Poseidon, Hades as well?" Roman asked.

"Yes, you know of them?" Jessika asked excitedly. "I follow Athena myself."

"Yes, they are part of what is called the Greek gods in my world. Greek Mythology." He said. "They were forgotten after a while and other religions rose and fell but one that carried through time, the one I follow is called Christianity and I serve the one true and living God."

Chapter 18

A hush fell over the group as Roman mentioned Christianity, the weight of his words hanging in the air. He could tell that the names of gods like Athena and Zeus sparked recognition, but the concept of a single "true and living God" seemed foreign to his friends. Jessika, for instance paused at the word true making it seem like her goddess wasn't true. That thought honestly made her very angry but she held her tongue.

Master Wong was the first to break the silence, his eyes narrowing in contemplation. "It's fascinating how different worlds can carry the echoes of the same deities yet interpret them so differently. I've heard many travelers from other worlds mention similar gods, but this... Christianity you speak of sounds unique."

Roman nodded slowly. "Yeah, it is. In my world, Christianity teaches that God is the creator of everything. It's not a pantheon of gods, but one all-powerful, all-knowing God. I can't say I've been the best at following His teachings lately, but I still hold onto my faith."

Lexi, who had been silent, finally spoke up, her voice soft but curious. "So… in your world, you follow one God, but here we have many. Do you think your God is here too?"

Roman smiled warmly at her. "Yes, I know for a fact He is. From the moment I got here, I could hear and feel His presence. It's the only way I've made it through. It's how I knew I could trust you guys with my secrets and my life. Sometimes I hear a calm, still voice guiding me, but most of the time it's just a feeling of warmth blooming in my heart, and I just *know*..." He trailed off, searching for the right words. "I'm sorry, I don't know how else to describe it."

Lexi's expression softened as she listened, her curiosity mingling with a quiet respect for Roman's faith. "That sounds... comforting," she said. "I've never experienced anything like that before."

"It is," Roman agreed, a gentle smile on his face. "It gives me peace, even in the middle of all this craziness. I may not fully understand why I was brought here, but I know I'm not alone."

Master Wong watched Roman carefully, his expression contemplative. "Faith is a powerful thing, Roman. And it seems that your faith, much like your abilities, has guided you through unimaginable challenges. But faith also requires balance, much like the power you are learning to wield."

Roman nodded, appreciating the wisdom in Wong's words. "Yeah, I get that. Just like with my chi and mana, I need to find balance in everything."

Seth broke the thoughtful silence with a chuckle. "You know, all this talk of gods and balance is making my head spin. You're strong, man, and whether that's because of your God or because you're just a beast, I'm glad we've got you on our side."

Roman laughed, feeling the tension ease. "Thanks, Seth. But I still have a lot to learn."

Master Wong folded his arms and smiled knowingly. "Indeed, Roman. The journey ahead will test you in ways you have not yet imagined. The ability to balance your faith, chi, and mana will make you formidable—but it will also carry great responsibility."

Roman took a deep breath, the weight of that responsibility settling on him. "I understand, Master Wong. I'll do my best."

"Good," Wong said, his tone both gentle and firm.

"Well if we're done talking…" Roman said and starts to hop from foot to foot like a boxer…or his favorite anime protagonist. "I'm itching to fight and I saw a few gigantic monsters out there. Hey who won the bet by the way?" he asked Seth

"You did." Seth grumbled but answered honestly.

"Wanna go double or nothing and I will only fight using magic? No weapons." Roman goaded.

"No! I've already seen that your magic is the only thing that is effective against them and now its gotten stronger! Do you think I'm dumb?!" Seth yelled and Roman chuckled.

"I had to try." He grinned loving the feeling he got when he was able to joke around with these guys. It felt right. "Hey! That feeling I was telling you about is back. So, I guess its confirmed that I'm supposed to be part of this party. And if I remember correctly, master Wong didn't you say that people in my party get exponentially stronger?"

"Indeed. But that might be after you ascend to your true power... I am not sure." Master Wong answered.

"Well either way those monsters have to die before we can go get the answers, we need so...let's get to it." He said and pushed off his right foot with everything he had, practically teleporting from his spot and over the wall. His momentum took him a good hundred feet away from the wall before his body started feeling gravity's effects and he started to plummet to the ground. He activated Kinetic Absorption and grinned when he crashed into the ground causing another crater. He jumped from the hole and pictured himself as a firebender as he shot bursts and torrents of flames with each punch and kick. Each move caused the fire to spread farther and farther out as he focused on pushing more mana into it. One trick he had discovered while Jessika was teaching him about mana that he didn't want to rub in her face. Mana was everywhere and in everything so once she taught him to find and feel it, he could automatically attune his core to pull it into himself as it cycled his qi. As his qi moved, it pulled substantial amounts of mana with it.

He chuckled to himself. "I'm such a cheat code!"

He continued fighting, pushing himself and his mana use, trying new ideas of how to use the mana. Can I create an Ultimate Skill?! He thought to himself and gasped. One of those monster skills that drank all remaining mana and could only be used once per day type of thing... He pictured what that would be. Most games for fire it would be like a huge fire tornado or like meteors falling to devastate everything...meteors! Let me ask Jessika if that's a thing first.

He jumped and pushed off with two twin jets of flames behind him as he flew to the walls where Jessika was hurling attacks down.

"Jessika!" He called out when he was close enough.

"What?!" She yelled.

"Are there such things as Ultimate Skills? Like a skill so big and devastating it can only be used once?" He asked.

"Yeah, but you have to reach Mastery rank in your element to unlock it. But then again you're a freak so I guess you could just create one." She spat to him in what he thought was fake envy which made him laugh but was really residual anger from his earlier statement but his laughter got to her after a few seconds. She grinned too, her earlier anger melting away.

"So, I'm gonna do it…Is there anyway to confirm that there is nobody out there that is friendly? I'll try to aim it as far away as I can so I don't hit the walls by accident."

"What are you about to do?!" Jessika asked in panic.

"Meteor Shower." He grinned.

"What?! What even is that?"

"Yall don't know what meteors are? Have you ever had huge burning rocks fall from the sky?" he asked.

"I have heard of that happening once." Master Wong said. "They called it a falling star."

"That's weird how could…meteors are like space debris but when they get into the atmosphere of a planet, they start falling down at incredible speeds which causes them to be coated in flames. When they impact, they could destroy entire cities…continents if its big enough."

"Oh, they come from space, then that is why we haven't seen them. There is a barrier that was placed by Athena around the world that keep the World Eater monsters away." Jessika answered.

"World Eater or most commonly called Void Beasts. They are huge beasts that exit in the darkness of space. We were attacked a few times by them, and each time Otherworlders like yourself rose to protect us and defeated them…maybe…maybe that is why you are here now?" Master Wong asked in awe.

"You think one of those things might be coming and that is why I was brought to this world?" Roman asked, half scared and half excited at the thought of fighting a space monster.

"Yes! From what I can remember each time we learned of an Otherworlder a Void Beast appeared within their lifetime…the reason it hasn't stuck out is because some of them lived hundreds of years!" Master Wong practically shouted.

"Oh, that's crazy!" Jessika gasped.

"Is there anything you can check to confirm that? Like yall have any records?" Roman asked.

"Yes! I will go confirm it!" He said and ran off, a lot faster than his old body should allow…a lot faster actually. Roman thought as he looked on in shock as the man moved like the Cheetah.

"Ok back to my ultimate skill." He grinned.

"Please don't overdo it!" Jessika pleaded. "Just remember that your power is insane so dial it all the way back!"

"Ok I'll only do about 60 percent?" He asked.

"Maybe 30." Lexi offered as she approached. Roman smiled at her.

"Ok I'll do it at only 25 percent first shot ok?" He asked and she smiled back.

"Ugh, so now you two shared a bed and were all cuddly this is gonna be a regular occurrence?!" Jessika spat in disgust. Both Roman and Lexi blushed and turned to deny her but she already jumped off the wall to fight.

Roman just turned back and lifted his hands, too embarrassed to say anything. He pictured three meteors evenly spaced and falling out into the opening almost to the rear of the monsters which was probably a good mile away. He pushed as much mana as he could to make it work, hands and lips trembling at the sheer effort it took to hold the mental picture. It was as if the more he tried to hold it it slipped from his hands like an oiled fish. After a while of struggling, he finally felt it, it felt right like he had the right amount of mana and focus to make it work. He took sort of a mental picture for next time and lowered his hands and internally shouted 'Meteor Shower" to initiate the attack. The sky immediately darkened and he heard screams of terror from behind him as the soldiers saw what was happening.

"Shoulda probably warned them too huh?" He mumbled and Lexi standing behind him chuckled.

"You think?" She laughed.

The sky was now brightening due to the flames now coating the giant boulders falling from the sky until it started to look like there were three suns. Even the monsters were scared and tried to scatter but there had been so many of them and all pushing in the same direction that there wasn't much they could do now. Roman focused on the first meteor to see if there was anything he could do to affect them now of if it was a cast and forget type of spell. He focused on it and pushed to make it go faster and soon it doubled the distance between it and the nearest one. And finally, it hit the ground, the boom and shockwave not reaching them for a few seconds but when it did, it almost knocked them all off their feet. A huge explosion that looked like a bomb went off erupted and flames shot out in all directions along with molten rock like shrapnel. Then…the next two hit.

"Ok yeah that's too much." Roman said when he was able to speak again a good 30 seconds after the third shockwave hit him. He looked down at the devastation and had trouble making anything out because of the dust and smoke but he knew for sure that one attack took out maybe 70 percent of the monsters in one go and the rest didn't look like spring chickens.

"T-that was only 25%?" Jessika asked in astonishment.

"Might have been closer to 35, I had a lot of trouble pulling the mana back once it started." Roman explained.

"Yeah, next time how bout we stick to about 5%?" Lexi said and patted him on the arm.

"Yeah, I think you're right."

Chapter 19

Roman stood in the aftermath of his ultimate skill, the ground still smoldering from the meteor impact that had decimated the battlefield. The air was thick with the scent of charred earth and smoke, and as he took in the sight, he couldn't help but feel the weight of what he had just done. Seventy percent of the monstrous horde had been wiped out in one fell swoop, and the survivors were fleeing in every direction.

Turning back, Roman searched for Sergeant Smithson or anyone in command. His eyes landed on the Sergeant, standing near a tent, frozen in place. The man's face was a mixture of awe and disbelief, his wide eyes locked on the destruction Roman had unleashed.

"Hey Sergeant, sorry about all that," Roman called out as he approached, his voice hesitant. He ducked his head, feeling an awkward shame creeping over him. "I tried to hold back."

"S-so that was you," Sergeant Smithson ground out, his voice barely above a whisper.

Roman winced, the guilt twisting in his chest. He had intended to help, to protect the city, but the sheer magnitude of the destruction he had caused left him feeling uneasy. The power he had unleashed was far beyond anything he had expected. He glanced at the scorched landscape, the once-mighty monsters reduced to ash and rubble.

"I didn't mean for it to be... this much," Roman admitted, his voice quieter now, more subdued. He shifted uncomfortably under the Sergeant's intense gaze. "I was just trying to push them back, not... you know, obliterate the battlefield."

The Sergeant blinked slowly, as if struggling to process what he had witnessed. His mouth opened and closed a few times before he finally managed to find his words. "Roman... I've seen a lot in my years on the front lines, but I've never seen anything like that." His voice was still low, but there was no anger in it—just shock. "You wiped out an entire army of monsters. With one attack."

Roman sighed, rubbing the back of his neck, still unsure of how to feel. "Yeah, but I wasn't really in control. I just... let go. It wasn't supposed to be that destructive."

Smithson finally tore his eyes away from the battlefield and looked directly at Roman. The shock on his face gave way to something else—respect, maybe, or even fear. "You're telling me that *wasn't* you going all out?"

Roman shook his head. "No. I've been working on balancing my chi and mana, but that—" he gestured toward the destruction, "—was an accident. I wasn't trying to destroy everything."

The Sergeant let out a low whistle, his hands resting on his hips as he surveyed the damage once more. "Well, Roman, you've definitely made an impression."

Roman chuckled nervously. "Not exactly the impression I was hoping for."

At that moment, Jessika made it back to him with Z and Seth in tow. Lexi had walked over to the Sergeant with him and he didn't even realize, when he saw the others, he looked confused for a second when he didn't see her and started looking around. She touched his arm knowing what was going on in his head. He smiled at her and turned back to the Sergeant.

"So I hope you guys have got it from here. We've gotta run." He said and grinned to the rest of his friends.

"Y-yeah you took out the hard-shelled monsters when you three went down there…everything else was a piece of cake…just a whole lot of them but they were hard to fight…you just went a little…" The Sargeant trailed off as his eyes went back to the carnage. As if the wind was trying to make a point, it shifted and the smell hit them.

"Ah!" Jessika shrieked and she covered her nose. The smell of charred meat and smoke mixed with sulfur and something else, not a good mixture and it had her struggling not to throw up. The rest of the crew wasn't any better off.

"Jess!" Roman shouted between coughs. "Do you have any wind spells to push this smell away?"

"I'm a fire girl, you're the one that can use any element!" She shot back. Just then they heard a deep and guttural grunt followed by a earthshaking stomp. Roman's head shot up and he saw Master Wong twist his body and push off hard from the foot he just stomped down, before clapping his hands together. Hurricane level winds erupted from his hands and shot over their heads and towards the craters, extinguishing the lingering fires down there as it went, the force just too much for the flames to survive.

Roman watched in awe as Master Wong's powerful gust of wind cleared the battlefield of the suffocating stench and the smoldering fires. The elderly man landed gracefully, his robes settling around him like he hadn't just unleashed the force of a hurricane with a single stomp. Roman still couldn't believe how effortlessly Wong could manipulate the elements, even though his appearance suggested otherwise.

Jessika, Z, Seth, and Lexi all stared in amazement, with Jessika muttering, "Well, guess we didn't need a wind spell after all…"

Master Wong approached the group, his expression calm but serious. "Now that this battle is behind us, we need to return to the Kingdom," he said, his voice firm but measured. "There is little time to waste. You all fought bravely, but you're not ready for what lies ahead. The Dragon Fang Mountains hold many dangers—especially the dungeon we spoke of."

Roman straightened, his exhaustion momentarily forgotten. "You think we should hit the dungeon first? What about the hermit who might be able to fix my title? Wouldn't that help us out more?"

Master Wong shook his head. "The hermit will be important, yes, but your friends aren't ready for the trials they'll face in the mountains as they are now. The dungeon is a chance to grow, to strengthen yourselves. Right now, Roman, your power is growing exponentially. But your comrades will need to level up significantly if they are to survive the journey ahead. The dungeon will allow you all to gain experience, skills, and even wealth to fund your future endeavors. After you've proven your strength there, you'll be better prepared for the hermit's guidance."

Seth crossed his arms with a smirk. "So, we're dungeon crawling before visiting the wise old hermit, huh? Sounds like fun."

Z glanced at Roman. "I don't know much about dungeons, but if it means we can level up faster, I'm in. I've seen how fast you've been growing, Roman. The rest of us need to catch up."

Jessika nodded in agreement. "The last battle showed me just how far behind I am. If there's a way to gain new skills and boost our power, I'm all for it. We'll need everything we can get for whatever's waiting for us in those mountains."

Lexi, who had remained quiet through the discussion, finally spoke up, her eyes focused on Roman. "Master Wong's right. We need to get stronger, and the dungeon sounds like the best way to do that. But... just promise me you won't try to carry all the weight on your own, Roman. We're a team. Let's make sure we do this together."

Roman smiled at her words, grateful for the support. "I wouldn't have it any other way. And yeah, the dungeon sounds like the perfect opportunity to help you guys catch up. I mean, if I can power level myself, why not help you all do the same? I will only act as a kite, drawing enemies."

Master Wong smiled slightly. "Indeed. The monsters within dungeons respawn, offering ample opportunity for training. The loot will allow you to arm yourselves better, and the experience you gain will be vital for the trials to come."

Roman's excitement began to build as the idea of dungeon diving and power leveling his friends sank in. The thought of getting stronger while gaining wealth and loot wasn't just practical—it was downright thrilling. "Alright then, it's settled. We'll head back to the Kingdom, regroup, and hit the dungeon first."

Sergeant Smithson, who had remained quiet through the conversation, finally spoke up, his eyes lingering on the still-smoking craters. "You've done more than enough here. We'll take care of the aftermath and ensure the city's defenses are reinforced. I wish you and your friends luck in whatever you face next." He extended a hand to Roman, his respect clear in his tone.

Roman took the Sergeant's hand firmly. "Thanks, Sergeant. We'll be back once we've powered up." He smiled, but there was a determination in his eyes. He wasn't just saying it to sound confident—he believed it.

Smithson gave a curt nod before addressing the rest of the group. "You've all fought well. The city owes you its thanks. Stay safe out there."

As Roman and his friends began to gather their things, Master Wong moved to the side, beckoning Roman over for a private word. Once out of earshot of the others, Wong spoke quietly. "Roman, you need to be careful with how fast you're growing. Power can be a dangerous thing, especially when it grows unchecked. Your chi, your mana—they're becoming difficult to balance. The dungeon will give you a controlled environment to test your limits. Do not take this lightly."

Roman nodded seriously, the weight of Wong's words sinking in. "I understand, Master. I'm not taking this lightly. I'll work hard to control it. I know I need to."

Wong placed a hand on Roman's shoulder. "Good. I've watched many warriors lose themselves to their power. Do not be one of them."

Roman gave a firm nod. "I won't."

With that, Wong stepped back, letting Roman rejoin his group. Roman looked at his friends—his team—and felt the excitement bubbling up again. A dungeon, loot, power leveling, and new challenges? He couldn't wait.

"Alright," Roman said with a grin, "let's head back to the Kingdom and get ready for our next adventure."

The group gathered their belongings, then Roman paused and turned to face everybody else.

"Hey…uh.. You said we're surrounded on three sides by mountains, right?" Roman asked.

"Yes, last side is the Ocean." Seth answer.

"Right, and Fairen shares a border with us that is unpassable mountains, right? So…" Roman trailed off looking between his friends as the light bulbs went off.

"How did they get their army here?" Lexi whispered.

"Are we even sure that army is from Fairen? I was just fighting because the Sergeant said they were the enemy but I don't know nothing about yall's politics." Roman said and turned to Smithson.

"Those were Fairen colors and flags, yes. We had been in fight mode this whole time so I didn't even think about how they got here but the only thing would be portals…there's no passing through those mountains let alone leading all those monsters through." Sergeant Smithson answered.

"Good point." Z said. They all looked at each other to see if anyone had any idea.

"They would need an army of just portaleers the size that we fought to bring those beasts here." Smithson offered.

"Well, what if they didn't bring these monsters? What if these were monsters from the forest and mountains and they just herded them?" Roman asked.

"That is a possibility. Also makes sense why there weren't as many monster as we expected when training." Jessika said.

"Yeah, but no offense, that doesn't really help us right now. The monsters might be gone but we still have the troops to deal with." Lexi said.

"Well, those troops aren't that tough. We're not really worried about them. Smithson and a squad of 50 held them off and didn't even lose one person!" Roman exclaimed proudly.

"Well…that's because they're the Hydra Knights. The strongest fighters in our kingdom. The rest of the soldiers wouldn't be able to compete." Z said.

"Not even close." Seth agreed.

"OK, well…how about for now we just go to the dungeon and get stronger and trust these men to hold until we can get back and clean things up if needed." Roman asked.

"Sounds like a plan." Seth agreed again.

"We won't need you but yeah go ahead. I'll get you a port-" Sergeant Smithson's mouth snapped shut as the words died in his mouth.

"That won't be necessary." A deep voice said into Roman's ear but loud enough for the rest of them to hear. Roman was gasping in pain and struggling to catch his breath. *What is going on?! What is this? Who is this? Where did he come from?!*

Chapter 20

Roman gritted his teeth, his body convulsing in agony as the blade twisted deeper into his side. Blood gushed from the wound, soaking the ground beneath him. His vision blurred, and the pain clouded his mind as he tried to summon his power, but it was no use. Whatever weapon had been used against him, it was more than just physical—it was suppressing his very ability to heal, blocking the flow of chi and mana alike.

"Don't move, or I'll make sure your leader here bleeds out before your very eyes," the voice growled, cold and mocking. The man standing over Roman was calm, methodical, and terrifyingly precise in his actions. He knew exactly what he was doing.

Z stepped forward, his fists clenched, but the assassin twisted the blade again, drawing another pained scream from Roman. Z froze in place, his entire body shaking with frustration and helplessness.

"Good," the attacker sneered, his eyes gleaming with dark amusement. "I've been watching all of you for quite some time now. I have to say, you're an impressive group, a rare mix of power and potential." His gaze swept over Jessika, Z, Seth, and Lexi. "But none of that matters now. You see, I've studied each of you. I know how you fight, how you think, and how to make you all useless."

The man yanked the blade free from Roman's side, and Roman collapsed to the ground, clutching the wound as blood poured out. His vision was darkening, the pain nearly unbearable. He could feel his strength slipping away with every passing second.

Jessika rushed forward, her hand already lighting with fire, but before she could cast a spell, the assassin moved with lightning speed. In an instant, he closed the gap between them and clasped a strange metal collar around her throat. The artifact latched onto her skin, glowing faintly as Jessika gasped, her magic fizzling out completely.

"What the—" Jessika's eyes widened in horror as she tried to summon her power, but nothing happened. The flames she'd called upon moments before were gone, smothered by the device around her neck.

The assassin smirked. "This little trinket disables any magic user it touches. Thought I'd make sure you wouldn't be able to burn me alive."

Jessika struggled to rip the collar off, her hands trembling, but it was useless. Her connection to mana had been severed completely.

Before anyone could react, the assassin moved again, this time targeting Lexi. He was a blur, darting toward her with such speed that she barely had time to raise her bow. But he was already too close. With a swift motion, he knocked the bow from her hands and shoved her to the ground, pinning her down.

"Too slow," he sneered. "A bow is worthless if you can't get the distance you need."

Lexi kicked and struggled, but the assassin's grip was unyielding. He easily kept her subdued, rendering her unable to use her weapon. Roman, still gasping for air on the ground, tried to push himself up, but his body refused to obey. The wound was too deep, the blood loss too great. He could barely stay conscious, let alone stand.

The assassin finally turned his attention to Z, who stood seething with rage but couldn't make a move without risking Roman's life.

"You," the assassin said, smirking at Z. "The brute with all the strength. Too bad you can't reach me from over there, can you?"

Z growled low in his throat and charged at him. The assassin stepped back, keeping a careful distance, knowing that Z's strength was useless unless he could close the gap. He had planned this meticulously, exploiting each of their weaknesses. He threw three small blades, targeting the gaps in Z's armor, two struck home and Z dropped to the ground like a sack of potatoes and slid to a stop. He lay there groaning in pain, unable to get up as those blades were coated in some type of toxin, he assumed. It was the only thing that made sense.

Satisfied with how easily he had neutralized them, the assassin returned his attention to Roman, who was still struggling to breathe. He crouched beside Roman, his voice dropping to a menacing whisper. "You, Roman, are the most interesting of all. So much power... but you're still just a boy playing with forces you don't understand."

Roman tried to speak, but only a weak gurgle came out. His chest heaved as he fought against the darkness closing in around him.

The assassin raised his blade again, this time aiming for Roman's throat. "I could end this now," he mused. "But where's the fun in that?"

Before Roman could even register the next movement, the assassin drove his foot into Roman's side, right where the wound was deepest. Roman's body jerked violently, a hoarse scream tearing from his throat as another wave of agony shot through him. He could feel his consciousness slipping away, his vision dimming.

The assassin rose and turned his attention back to the group, walking toward the soldiers who had been standing guard, their faces pale with shock and fear. "Now," he said with an eerie calmness, "let's make sure no one interferes."

In a blur of movement, the assassin unleashed a devastating barrage of attacks on the remaining soldiers. His blade cut through them like they were nothing, and within moments, the camp was littered with bodies. Sergeant Smithson tried to rally his men, but the assassin was too fast, too lethal. He was a whirlwind of destruction, tearing through the ranks like a force of nature.

Roman's friends could only watch in horror, helpless to stop the carnage. Z struggled to contain his fury, but he couldn't move without risking Roman's life. Jessika clawed at the collar around her neck, tears of frustration welling in her eyes as she failed to summon even a flicker of magic. Lexi, still pinned beneath the assassin's foot, could only watch as more and more soldiers fell to the ground.

The assassin finally turned back to Roman, who lay barely conscious on the ground, blood pooling beneath him. He crouched down once more, grabbing Roman's hair and lifting his head just enough to make him look at the destruction around him.

"See that?" the assassin whispered. "This is what happens when you think you're invincible."

Roman's vision blurred, the world fading in and out as he struggled to stay awake. He used the last of his strength to spit at the assassin. "You think you're so tough, you attacked a camp full of nobody but exhausted and wounded soldiers. Why didn't you attack when the Hydra Knights and the rest of the soldiers were still here? You Coward."

"I'm not here to prove anything to anyone." He grinned evilly.

The pain was overwhelming, his body screaming for rest, for an end to the torment. He could barely hear the assassin's words, but they cut through the fog in his mind like a knife.

"I've been sent to break you, Roman," the assassin continued, his voice dripping with malice. "And when I'm done, you'll wish you had never set foot in this world."

The last thing Roman saw before darkness claimed him was the assassin's cold, cruel smile.

Capital

The King's face twisted with fury as he listened to Sergeant Smithson's report. His hand gripped the arm of his throne so tightly that the wood creaked under the pressure. The room, once buzzing with the sounds of strategy and discussions about the war, fell into an eerie silence as every eye turned toward the King, waiting for his response.

"*An assassin?*" The King growled, his voice low and dangerous. "Who dares to lay a hand on my son? Who dares to attack my kingdom's finest without consequence?"

Smithson, still kneeling, shook his head weakly. "Sire, I don't know. He wore no insignia, no markings. He was fast, precise, and... he knew us. He had been watching us for a long time, anticipating our every move. There was nothing we could do."

The King stood, his dark robes billowing out behind him as his fury radiated through the room. "I will not stand for this. My son... Seth... He will not be left to the mercy of some shadow in the night."

The generals around the room exchanged nervous glances. One of them, General Torken, stepped forward cautiously. "Your Majesty, if this assassin is as skilled and prepared as Smithson says, we must be careful. We don't know who sent him or what his goal was beyond incapacitating Seth's group. It could be a prelude to a larger attack."

Before the King could respond, the massive doors to the throne room burst open, and a group of royal guards rushed in. Their faces were pale, their eyes wide with fear.

"Your Majesty!" one of the guards shouted, "The palace is under attack! We're surrounded by a small army!"

The King's eyes widened with shock, but before he could react, the air in the throne room grew cold. A chill swept through the chamber, unnatural and unsettling, and the flickering flames of the nearby torches dimmed. The shadows around the room seemed to grow darker, as if they were stretching and shifting.

Suddenly, the throne room erupted into chaos.

Black-clad figures materialized from the shadows, their movements swift and deadly. There were at least half a dozen of them, each moving with an assassin's grace, blades gleaming in the dim light. The guards barely had time to react before the first assassin was upon them.

The clash of steel rang out through the hall as the royal guards fought back. The King, his face a mask of rage, reached for the sword at his side. The leader of the King's Guard stepped in front of the King. "Protect the throne!" he bellowed, his voice echoing through the stone walls.

Sergeant Smithson, despite his injuries, struggled to his feet, drawing his own sword. His body was weakened, but he would fight to the last breath if it meant protecting the King. "Your Majesty, stay back! We'll handle them!"

But the assassins were relentless. They moved like shadows, darting between the guards with terrifying precision. One of the assassins lunged at the King, his blade aimed for the monarch's heart. But just as the blade descended, a flash of steel intercepted the strike—General Torken, his own sword drawn, parried the blow.

"You'll have to do better than that," Torken growled, forcing the assassin back.

The King's eyes flickered with fury as he unsheathed his sword. "You dare attack me in my own throne room? You will pay for this."

He swung his sword with deadly accuracy, but the assassins were quick, slipping in and out of the shadows like wraiths. One assassin managed to get behind a guard and slit his throat before vanishing again into the dark corners of the room. Another guard was thrown across the hall, his armor clattering as he crashed into the stone wall.

Smithson gritted his teeth, his grip on his sword weakening, but he refused to back down. His vision blurred, the blood loss from his earlier wounds taking its toll. He swung at one of the attackers, but his blade met only air.

The assassins were playing with them, toying with the guards as if this were a game.

But then, amidst the chaos, one assassin made a fatal error. He lunged too quickly, aiming for the King's unprotected side, but the King, moving with a warrior's instinct, spun and struck. His sword cut through the assassin's midsection, sending him crumpling to the ground in a pool of blood.

The other assassins hesitated for a brief moment, but that was all the guards needed. Torken and the remaining soldiers pressed the advantage, forcing the attackers back.

Suddenly, the lead assassin stepped forward, his eyes cold and calculating beneath his mask. He raised a hand, and the other assassins immediately stopped, retreating into the shadows.

"You've proven to be a formidable opponent, Your Majesty," the assassin said, his voice smooth and unnervingly calm. "But this is not the end. My mission is not yet complete."

The King glared at him, sword raised. "Who sent you?"

The assassin tilted his head slightly, his eyes gleaming with amusement. "All in good time, King Juelius."

With a swift motion, the assassin dropped a small, glass vial onto the ground. It shattered upon impact, and a thick, black smoke filled the room. The guards coughed and stumbled back, momentarily blinded by the sudden cloud.

When the smoke cleared, the King and the assassins were gone.

The throne room was left in disarray, bodies of the fallen guards strewn across the floor. The King's Guard stood at the center, swords still gripped tightly in their hands, eyes scanning the room for any sign of the attackers.

But they had vanished.

General Torken rushed to the Throne. "Where is his Majesty?" He called out.

"They took him." Smithson answered weakly. Nobody knew what to do, everything just froze for a second until the General moved.

"Ok men, The King has been kidnapped! Alert the guard, gather all available units, send out a general call to any able-bodied men who are ready to fight.

Send it out to the Adventurer's Guild as well, post it there and you bet every last one of those money hungry mercenaries will be out searching." The General said.

"I don't think we should pull any other soldiers here. Remember we're getting attacked from two fronts right now, we can't afford to pull men from either." Smithson argued.

"Sergeant, I understand all you have done for us in your service but shut your mouth. You are out of your pay grade now." The General spat and stomped off. Everybody in the room bursting into motion.

As everyone hurried to carry out his orders, the General stood in the wreckage of the throne room, his mind racing. This wasn't just a random attack. Someone had orchestrated this carefully, knowing exactly how to strike at the heart of the kingdom.

Whoever this enemy was, they had just made a deadly mistake.

Chapter 21

Roman's eyes flickered open, his vision blurry as he struggled to make sense of his surroundings. The rough jolting of the ground told him he was lying on a moving surface—a wagon, its wooden planks digging into his back with each bump along the road. As his vision cleared, he noticed the chains clamped around his wrists and ankles, the cold iron biting into his skin.

A faint groan slipped from his lips as he tried to shift, pain shooting through his side where the assassin had stabbed him. He felt incredibly weak, and when he instinctively reached inward for his Chi, cautiously channeling the energy through his body. Relief flooded him as he felt the familiar warmth of his chi respond, albeit sluggishly. He tried once again to heal his wound and this time Chi responded, maybe because the blade was no longer inside him...no diddy.

He tried to reach for mana and felt nothing but dead silence in a vast box of nothingness. Even though he only just learned to use and connect to mana, it became part of him so not finding anything was messing with his brain. Like he was missing a limb or something.

Then he noticed it—a metal collar clasped tightly around his neck, much like the one he'd seen the assassin use on Jessika during the ambush. So they'd managed to disable his magic.

His chi wasn't completely cut off though, just weakened…maybe because of his exhaustion… and for now, he decided it would have to be enough. He would bide his time and strike when the moment was right. He would just focus on healing and cycling his chi to rebuild strength.

He glanced around the wagon, finding his friends beside him, each of them bound in chains. Seth, Z, Jessika, and Lexi lay nearby, their eyes closed, faces etched with exhaustion and strain. They looked battered but alive. He felt his chest tighten as he looked at Lexi, her face pale as she shifted uncomfortably, her breathing shallow but steady.

The rough laughter of the guards at the front of the wagon broke through his thoughts.

"Did you see the look on that fool King's face?" one of the guards sneered, his voice carrying through the night. "He really thought he'd scare us off with his little sword tricks. I'll never forget the way he went down on his knees, begging before we cut his head clean off."

Roman's stomach twisted with anger, his blood boiling at their words. He forced himself to remain still, his face impassive as he listened. He needed to know more. To his right, Seth's head slowly turned, his eyes widening with horror as the guards continued.

"Yeah, I saw it," another guard added, snickering. "The crown didn't do him any good in the end. After all his threats, he ended up just like the rest of 'em—another trophy. And now the King's head's been paraded through the camps, like a prize for all the lads to see. Guess he won't be giving any more orders from up high!"

Roman's heart sank as he watched Seth, whose face had gone deathly pale. Seth's body stiffened as he realized what they were saying, and Roman could see the disbelief, the raw pain, and rage flickering in his friend's eyes.

The guards kept talking, oblivious to the devastation their words were causing. "Kenan and Eidon fell quick enough. Without that powerhouse Roman and his crew, they were easy pickings. And the capital?" One of the guards scoffed. "Once we got through the walls, it was a slaughter. Could barely tell who was fighting back with all the bodies piling up."

Beside him, Jessika stirred, her eyes blinking open as she took in the guards' words. Horror filled her gaze as she met Roman's eyes, and he could see the pain reflected back at him. He wanted to reassure her, but there was nothing he could say—not yet.

A soft groan to his left told him Lexi was waking as well. Roman quickly shifted his hand toward hers, subtly brushing his fingers against hers to let her know he was there, that he hadn't given up. She didn't respond at first, her face twisting with pain as she struggled to make sense of her surroundings, but when her eyes finally found his, he gave her a faint, reassuring nod.

"Everyone... hold on," he murmured quietly, his voice barely audible over the sound of the wagon. "We're going to get through this."

Seth's fists clenched, his knuckles white as he glared at the guards, every muscle in his body tense with barely contained rage. Roman knew that Seth's instinct would be to fight back, to take revenge on the men who had killed his father. But in his current state, weakened and chained, Seth would only get himself killed. Roman caught his eye, giving him a look that said, *Not yet. Wait.*

Seth's jaw tightened, his eyes dark with fury, but he gave a small nod, reluctantly accepting Roman's silent command.

One of the guards sneered, oblivious to the tension in the wagon. "And don't get me started on those heroes," he said with a laugh, jerking a thumb back at the prisoners. "They fought hard, sure, but look at them now. All chained up, just like the rest of the fools who thought they could stand against us."

The other guard chuckled in agreement. "I was so excited when we got cart duty. The King was offering a nice bounty for Roman's head specifically but I bet he'll pay us even more for him alive and the rest of his group! Plus, maybe we'll keep him around for some fun first. I'd like to see what he's capable of with all those fancy powers gone."

Roman forced himself to remain calm, ignoring the surge of anger and helplessness bubbling within him. They didn't know he still had access to his chi, and he intended to keep it that way for as long as possible. If they underestimated him, it could be the only advantage he had left.

Lexi's hand trembled beneath his touch, and he tightened his fingers around hers gently, hoping to give her a bit of strength. When she looked at him again, he mouthed, *We'll make it out.* She gave a small nod, the determination in her gaze returning as she took a deep, steadying breath.

The guards continued their bragging as the wagon rattled along the mountain path, each jibe and boast, stoking the fire of Roman's anger. But he forced himself to wait, to stay focused. If he was going to protect his friends, he needed a plan. The guards' arrogance would be their downfall—he just had to wait for the right moment to strike.

The King is dead? How did they get to the capital so fast? Roman's mind raced. Their army couldn't have moved that quickly... unless they had used a portal, like how they entered the kingdom in the first place. But even then, something didn't sit right.

And where's the Commander with the bulk of the army? Roman thought, frowning. *He should have arrived by now.*

He paused his racing thoughts, shifting his focus back to his body. The blade lodged deep in his side was slowly pushing out as he healed. Roman gritted his teeth, making sure the weapon didn't fall and alert the guards. A sigh of relief escaped him as the wound fully closed, though the damage still left him feeling weak. Now, his priority was regaining strength.

He spun his chi faster and faster, cycling it through his body, pulling the fatigue from his muscles with each breath, and drawing in new energy, revitalizing his body. Though the collar around his neck suppressed his mana, his chi was still accessible flowing freely now, slowly bringing him back to full capacity.

The wagon jolted as it moved along the rough trail, and Roman's thoughts returned to the situation. The enemy had been too fast, too coordinated. The assassin who attacked them had been precise, surgical, and now the capital had fallen. *But how? None of this makes sense.*

He needed more information. First, though, he needed a way to detect anyone stealthy moving around him. His chi might be perfect for this since it seemed that no one else in this world could use it. *There must be chi in everyone, human or monster,* Roman reasoned.

Closing his eyes, he focused on his chi, pulling it outward until he could sense it outside of his body. The process was slow and painstaking—like trying to push his head through a narrow opening—but eventually, he broke through. What he saw made him gasp.

The world around him glowed in ethereal light, almost spiritual. The wagon, once dull and nondescript, was now illuminated with a faint aura. His friends shone brightly with untapped power—especially Lexi. Her glow was almost blinding, so intense that Roman had to shield his eyes.

He pushed his chi further, extending his perception past the two guards. They glowed faintly but were weak, insignificant compared to his friends. His awareness stretched farther and farther until it reached around 100 feet in all directions.

Then, something shifted. Roman tensed. There were about twenty small orbs of light sprinting toward them at an incredible speed. He couldn't tell what they were, only that they were fast and approaching quickly.

Blinking away the chi vision, Roman glanced at his companions. Each was still reeling from the news of the King's death. Seth sat beside him, his expression hard and stony, eyes burning with anger and grief. Roman could see his fists clenching, muscles taut, ready to snap the chains that bound them. He wanted to say something comforting, but there were no words that could soften the blow of losing his father.

Jessika, pale and shaken, kept reaching for the collar around her neck. Her fingers brushed the cold metal repeatedly, as if still in disbelief that her magic had been cut off. She looked utterly lost, stripped of the very essence that had always made her powerful.

Z sat silently; his massive frame slumped in defeat. Lexi, beside him, seemed just as stunned, her hand still gripping Roman's for reassurance, her eyes unfocused as she tried to process everything.

Roman grit his teeth, forcing himself to stay calm. The guards were still laughing, still boasting about their victories, completely unaware that Roman was steadily regaining his strength.

In a low whisper, he called out to his friends. "Guys."

They stiffened at the sound of his voice, but when the guards didn't react, Roman continued. "Something's coming... about twenty somethings. Brace yourselves."

They exchanged quick glances of confusion but understood his meaning. Silently, they began adjusting themselves as best they could, preparing for whatever was approaching. Each of them was bound in chains, their hands behind their backs, and all were lying in different positions—Roman on his stomach, Z on his side. Slowly, they shifted, easing into positions that would allow them to burst to their feet if necessary.

Roman quietly slid one knee under himself, focusing his chi on the joint in the chain binding his wrists. With steady pressure, he pushed against the weak point until, with a soft crack, the chain broke. He quickly covered the sound with a cough.

For a tense moment, Roman froze as one of the guards turned back, his eyes narrowing. The man grinned wickedly as he looked over at them, clearly satisfied with their helpless state. "Comfortable back there, heroes?"

Roman kept his head low, hiding the fire burning in his eyes. He couldn't afford to draw attention to himself, not yet. Instead, he continued to breathe steadily, his chi cycling through his body faster and faster, slowly restoring his strength.

Then, the wagon came to a stop. The sound of one of the guards' boots crunching on the gravel echoed as the man approached. Roman tensed, doing his best to stay still for just a little longer.

The guard stopped beside Roman, leering down at him. "What's the matter, big guy? Not so tough now, are you?" He kicked Roman's leg, but Roman didn't react, keeping his body limp and his head low. The time to strike hadn't come yet.

The guard spat on the ground and turned to walk back to the front of the wagon when a deafening howl split the air, much closer than expected.

Wolves.

Roman's pulse quickened as a grin tugged at his lips. The guard, now tense and visibly unsettled, whipped his head around. His swagger vanished as he eyed the dark tree line on both sides of the narrow mountain trail. The forest loomed close by to the south, its thick trees and underbrush casting shadows over the trail. Roman recognized it immediately—it was the forest where all of this had started. He assumed they had passed through it while unconscious.

The guard took a nervous step back, his eyes scanning for the source of the howl. But before he could retreat any further, Roman acted. With lightning speed, he kicked both legs into the back of the guard's knee, a satisfying crack echoing as the man's leg gave way. The guard tumbled from the wagon with a heavy thud, screaming as he hit the ground. His cries, however, were soon swallowed by a chorus of low growls that reverberated through the trees.

Roman activated his chi vision, the ethereal glow revealing the scene beyond. Wolves were moving in from all sides, their lean, muscular bodies slipping through the darkness with predatory grace. Their eyes glinted with deadly intent as they closed in on the guards, ripping into them with brutal efficiency.

Roman's heart raced, but not from fear. The wolves were tearing through the enemy like paper. Ahead of the wagon, another group of soldiers—likely a reinforcement squad—was being attacked just as savagely. Wolves leapt from the shadows, their fangs flashing, limbs moving in perfect sync with one another. Within minutes, the guards were decimated.

Then, Roman heard the sound of heavy paws landing on the wagon behind him. He froze, heart pounding. Slowly, he turned, propping himself up on one elbow. A large grey wolf, bigger than any of the others, stood over him. Its fur was thick and matted, and a long scar ran over its left eye, giving it a weathered, battle-hardened look. Its massive chest expanded and contracted with each breath, and as it loomed over Roman, it lowered its muzzle to sniff at him.

You, Roman thought, recognizing the wolf from before. The same one he had spared.

The wolf lowered its head further, gently gripping the chains that bound Roman's legs with its powerful jaws. With a sharp twist of its head, the chains snapped like brittle twigs.

"Thank you, buddy," Roman murmured, his voice low. The wolf's golden eyes locked onto his, and it nodded—an almost human gesture that sent a shiver of disbelief down Roman's spine. Still, he approached cautiously, unsure of how much trust he could place in the creature. Just because it freed him didn't mean they were friends.

The wolf's head dipped slightly, and it nudged Roman's hand with its nose. Slowly, Roman reached out, placing his hand on the wolf's thick fur. The beast leaned into his touch, a low, rumbling growl of approval vibrating from its chest. Roman scratched behind its ears, marveling at the connection between them.

"Alright," Roman said, standing to his feet. "You're the hero today, but let's free the others first."

The wolf padded toward Lexi, using the same precise bite to free her from her chains, while Roman moved down the line, tearing apart the restraints with his chi-powered hands. The others slowly stood, rubbing their sore wrists and exchanging glances as the pack of wolves formed a protective barrier around them.

The forest, once ominous and filled with enemies, now seemed eerily peaceful. The moonlight filtering through the trees cast long shadows across the blood-stained trail. Roman looked out over the carnage, wolves prowling silently through the fallen bodies of the guards.

But not all of them were dead.

As Roman finished freeing the last of his companions, his eyes caught movement near the edge of the trail. One of the guards was still alive, groaning and clutching his side. Roman strode over, his expression hardening as he crouched beside the injured man.

The guard flinched, trying to crawl away, but Roman grabbed him by the collar and yanked him back, his grip tight. "Where were you taking us?"

The guard's eyes were wide with terror as he glanced around at the wolves pacing nearby, their teeth bared and low growls rumbling in their throats. "P-please," he stammered. "I was just following orders. We—we were supposed to deliver you to the fortress in the north… as prisoners."

"Fortress?" Roman's voice was cold, his patience thin. "Who gave the order?"

The man's lip trembled, his gaze darting between Roman and the wolves. "I—I don't know his name. Just some noble. Said we had to keep you alive... for now. He wanted you brought to him."

Roman narrowed his eyes. "And what happens when we get there?"

The guard swallowed hard, clearly realizing there was no way out of this. "Interrogation," he muttered, barely audible. "They... they want information. About your powers, your titles."

Roman's eyes darkened. "And the King? How did they take the capital so quickly?"

"They used... they used a portal. The same one they opened to invade Eidon. They—they moved their troops fast. It was over before anyone knew what hit them. The King... the King didn't stand a chance." The guard's voice cracked as he finished, his face pale with fear.

Roman's grip tightened for a moment before he released the man, shoving him back into the dirt. The wolves immediately moved in, but Roman raised a hand. "Leave him," he commanded softly, and the wolves stopped, their golden eyes gleaming in the moonlight as they awaited his orders.

Roman stood, his mind racing as he pieced together what he had learned. He glanced at the large grey wolf, which had been watching him closely throughout the interrogation.

"How did you find me?" Roman asked, and the wolf dipped its head, taking in a loud sniff of the air.

"You followed my scent?" Roman asked, surprised. The wolf nodded, its tail swaying slightly.

Roman smiled in disbelief. "You really understand me, don't you?"

The wolf nodded again; its eyes gleaming with intelligence. Roman knelt down, scratching the wolf under its chin. "Thank you for saving us. I owe you my life."

The wolf shook its head and gently tapped Roman's chest with its paw, a firm, almost insistent gesture.

Roman frowned. "No? You're saying… you owe *me* your life?"

The wolf nodded once more, its gaze unwavering.

Roman let out a quiet laugh. "How about we call it even? We both saved each other's lives."

But the wolf shook its head again, more adamant this time. It tapped its own chest, then Roman's, before lifting its head with a sense of finality.

Roman blinked, taken aback. "You're saying… you'll stay with me? For life?"

The wolf nodded.

Roman glanced at the rest of the pack. "And what about them?"

As if answering his unspoken question, the other wolves bowed their heads, lowering themselves to the ground in a gesture of submission. Roman stared at them in awe.

"Well… I guess I've got a pack of wolves now." Roman grinned. "That's… pretty awesome."

Chapter 22

After the interrogation, Roman and his companions moved quickly to gather supplies from the fallen guards and wagons. Armor, weapons, anything useful—there wasn't much, but enough to get them through the journey ahead. Roman kept a close eye on his friends, especially Lexi, who still looked shaken from the ordeal.

As they worked, Roman turned to the large grey wolf that had saved them. "We need to head back to Kenan. Can you lead us there?"

The wolf's ears perked up, and it tilted its head slightly, as if considering Roman's request. Then, with a low growl, it shook its head. The wolf padded over to the edge of the trail and sniffed the air, glancing back at Roman.

"Not safe?" Roman asked, frowning. The wolf gave a short nod of confirmation and then turned its head to the north, gesturing with a nudge of its snout.

"North, through the forest," Roman murmured, following the wolf's gaze. He turned to the others. "We'll avoid Kenan. The wolf says it's not safe. We go north through the forest until we reach the plains."

Seth nodded in agreement; his expression still grim from the news of his father's death. "Makes sense. We don't know how many enemy troops are still near Kenan. If they've already taken it, we'd be walking straight into a trap."

Lexi, still standing close to Roman, glanced toward the distant horizon. "But what about Eidon? We'll be near it if we follow the river. If they've taken the capital and Kenan, they could've reinforced Eidon too."

Roman looked in the direction of Eidon and could already see fires burning in the distance. Columns of smoke rose into the sky, and even from where they stood, they could see faint figures patrolling the walls. The city was heavily guarded.

"We won't get too close," Roman said, his voice firm as he visualized the map he saw in Sergeant Smithson's tent. "We'll make a wide berth around it and follow the river north, toward the capital. It's safer than going straight through enemy territory…then again, we have to be cautious and assume everything is enemy territory since we have no clue what's waiting for us out there."

"We stick to the forest for as long as we can, move quietly, and we'll be fine," Z rumbled, adjusting the gear he had scavenged from one of the wagons. His massive frame exuded confidence, though the fatigue of their capture was still evident.

With the plan in place, Roman gestured for the wolf to lead the way, and the pack began their journey north through the dense forest. The trees loomed overhead, casting long shadows as they moved deeper into the woods, away from the city.

The wolf led them through the thick underbrush, its movements graceful and silent. Roman followed closely, his senses heightened, always on the lookout for any signs of danger. He kept his chi flowing, scanning the area around them for any hidden threats, though it was clear the wolves were doing much of the heavy lifting when it came to keeping them safe.

Hours passed, the group moving cautiously, avoiding any open spaces that could leave them exposed. The sound of distant patrols echoed occasionally through the trees, but they stayed far enough away from Eidon to avoid detection. As the sun began to set, they reached the river that would guide them north toward the capital. The wolf stopped and looked at him.

"You can't keep going with us can you?" He kneeled and asked the large gray wolf. The wolf looked back the few hundred feet behind where the rest of the wolf pack had stopped and were still waiting.

"Ok, I won't keep you. But…thank you." He said and scratched the wolf's head again. The wolf lifted its head in the direction they had been headed and nodded, then sniffed to the east, towards Eidon, and shook its head and stomped the ground.

"Ok so we're good to stay this way for a while but not that way?" Another nod.

"Thank you again!" Roman called out as the wolf ran off back towards its pack.

The night air was cool, the river's gentle current providing a soft backdrop to their silent trek. Roman's thoughts kept drifting back to the assault on the capital, and what had happened to Seth's father. The weight of it hung over all of them, but none more so than Seth. The young man hadn't spoken much since they had fled the ambush, but Roman knew the grief was eating away at him.

It was near dawn when they came across a small encampment nestled a few miles north of Eidon. Roman's sharp eyes caught the glint of armor and the low glow of campfires. Instinctively, he signaled for the group to stop. He squinted into the distance, using his chi vision to get a clearer look at the men gathered around the fires.

"It's the Commander," Roman whispered to Seth, his tone a mixture of relief and urgency. "He's made camp here."

Seth's eyes brightened for the first time since they had escaped. "Let's go."

They approached the camp cautiously, making sure not to startle the guards. As they neared the encampment, one of the sentries spotted them and raised his hand.

"Halt! Who goes there?" the guard demanded, his spear at the ready.

Seth stepped forward, holding up his hands. "We're with the royal army! We need to speak to Commander Vellis immediately."

The guard hesitated, eyeing them warily, before signaling to one of the men behind him. Moments later, Commander Vellis emerged from a large tent, his expression grim. His battle-worn armor was covered in dirt and blood, but his eyes were sharp as ever.

"Seth?" Vellis asked, his voice filled with both relief and surprise. "You're alive."

Seth nodded stiffly. "Barely. We were captured after pushing back the monster horde. There was an assassin. He... he knew exactly how to take us down." He clenched his fists, his voice growing thick with emotion. "We just found out that my father's dead, Commander."

Vellis' face fell, and for a moment, the hard lines of the commander's face softened with sorrow. "I'm sorry, Seth. We... we heard about the capital. But I had no idea..." His voice trailed off, unable to find the right words.

Roman stepped forward. "We need to know everything, Commander. What happened after we pushed back the monsters? How did the enemy move so fast?"

Vellis let out a deep breath. "It was the portals. They moved their entire army in a matter of hours, overwhelmed our defenses before we even had time to regroup. We were stretched too thin, and they hit us where it hurt the most. We didn't stand a chance."

Roman's heart sank. "What about Kenan? Is it lost?"

Vellis shook his head. "We don't know yet. We've had no word from the city. We sent scouts, but none have returned. It's possible they've already taken it."

A heavy silence settled over the group as the gravity of the situation set in. The capital was in enemy hands, Kenan was likely lost, and they were running out of options.

Seth looked up, his jaw set with determination. "Then we need to strike back. We can't just sit here and do nothing."

Vellis frowned. "I agree, but we can't rush in blindly. We need a plan. The enemy is expecting us to retaliate, and they'll be prepared for it."

Roman nodded slowly, his mind already working through the possibilities. "Then we'll have to hit them where they don't expect. And before we do anything, we need to regroup and build our strength."

The others nodded in agreement, their expressions hardening with resolve. The battle wasn't over yet—not by a long shot.

And Roman knew that the time would come for them to strike back. But first, they needed to survive—and that meant finding allies, building their strength, and waiting for the perfect moment to turn the tide.

"They are spreading false rumors through every city and town, as if they are trying to get the people on their side. So far it hasn't worked from what I've seen but who knows. What I need you guys to do is lay low for a bit, where I know you'll be and go undetected by the enemy. Can you do that?" Vellis asked and looked each in the eye.

"Yes." They answered in unison.

"Good. So I am going to keep moving through the lands in secret and gather back our army that's probably hiding and laying low themselves. When we heard the news and I saw what was happening I split them up and had them scatter and blend in. We need more men if we are going to fight back. So, here's the plan. The enemy is doing sweeps through every town and city but it doesn't look like they plan to do it twice. There's a town close to the capital that I want you to go to and hunker down. Blend in, get jobs, be townsfolk until I give the signal." Vellis said.

"OK what will the signal be? What are we supposed to look for? And what are we supposed to be doing in the meantime, farm?!" Seth asked.

"You'll know the signal when you see it…as far as what you need to do, keep your eyes and ears open for enemy troops and plans. Stay alive until the time is right for us to strike back! For the new King to take the throne." He said sadly and looked at Seth who bit down hard trying to control his emotions.

"Now's not the time. Keep heading north along the river but when you see the capital turn to give it a wide berth and when you hit Sky Lake you're there. The village I am from is there, where the Slynn River finally meets Sky Lake. Anyone there would take you in and I know for sure that the enemy has already cleared over there." Vellis said. "Keep your head down, train and prepare for the war that's coming."

This whole time he had been talking to them as soldiers, just spitting his orders as rough and stern as usual but Seth noticed something that was different. He was giving them a lot more info than he usually does and he's talking a lot…so he must feel really awful about what happened to Father. Seth thought.

"Vellis, here." Roman said and stepped toward him holding out what appeared to be a rag. He wiped his forehead with it and held his hand out to the Commander.

"Boy-" but before the Commander could start, Roman explained.

"I saved a wolf's life in the forest and it along with its pack helped us get here so figured if you smelled like me when you ran into them it might help you out." He said and the Commander finally relented.

Chapter 23

The group had been walking for about an hour after leaving the Commander and his camp. They had been pretty silent the whole time, each lost in their own thoughts. Roman had been thinking about how to try to teach the others to use chi...or like how to force it on them. He figured if he couldn't teach it to them, he could put a little bit of his chi in them and command it to build and follow the host's orders...but that seemed weird and impossible but then again so was almost everything he's been doing so far. Roman glanced at Lexi as they walked, the thought of sharing his chi bouncing around his mind. It was risky and untested, but it could make a difference. He took a breath, slowing his pace until they were walking side by side, slightly apart from the rest of the group.

"Lexi," he said softly, drawing her attention. She turned, eyes filled with curiosity and a hint of weariness. "I want to try something, but it's... unconventional."

She furrowed her brow. "What is it?"

"I think I can share a small part of my chi with you," Roman explained. "If it works, you'll be able to harness it, use it for strength, maybe even start cultivating your own power."

Lexi's eyes widened, her surprise giving way to determination. "I trust you. What do I need to do?"

Roman slowed a bit but kept walking and gestured for her to do the same. Roman gently grabbed Lexi's hand, her tiny hand lost in his much bigger one, feeling the coolness of her skin. He closed his eyes and summoned a small thread of chi, guiding it carefully from his core to hers.

"Focus on this," he whispered, nudging the glowing energy forward. Lexi's eyes shut tightly, and her breathing became shallow as she felt the pulse of warmth begin to spread through her. The chi moved sluggishly, as though unsure of its new home.

"I feel it... but it's slipping," Lexi said, her voice tight with concentration.

"Don't fight it. Guide it gently for now, it's a lot more physical than mana but it doesn't recognize you yet," Roman encouraged. He kept his hand steady, using his own chi to push and stabilize the thread as Lexi struggled to take hold. The glow between them flickered, and beads of sweat formed on her brow. Time seemed to slow as they stood there, locked in silent focus.

Behind them, Seth, Jessika, and Z noticed their unusual stance and stopped walking. They exchanged glances but remained quiet, their curiosity evident as they watched Roman and Lexi work in unison.

Finally, after what felt like an eternity, Lexi's expression shifted. A small smile curled at her lips, and her eyes opened, shimmering with an inner light. The seed of chi had settled within her, its pulse steady and warm spinning gently as Roman set it.

"I can feel it now," she said, her voice soft with wonder. "It's... different, but it's there."

Roman's shoulders relaxed, a relieved smile spreading across his face. "Good. Now, you need to focus on shaping that energy, building it into a core. Once you have that, you can start cultivating it on your own, spinning your chi to cleanse it, and maybe you can even absorb it and add to your own like I can...not sure the extents of this."

Before he could say anything more, a sudden alert blinked across Roman's vision:

<System Alert: Permanent Party Formed. All party members gain benefits from party leader's titles.>

He blinked, a rush of realization washing over him. Lexi had just gained access to the benefits of his titles, which meant she would grow stronger and faster leveling at his speed. He glanced at her, the subtle glow in her eyes already hinting at the changes taking place.

"What just happened?" she asked, noticing his shift in expression.

"We're a party now," Roman said, still processing the implications. "You'll gain the benefits of my titles. You're going to grow stronger, faster than before."

Lexi's eyes widened, and then a determined gleam settled in them. "Then we need to do this for the others."

Roman turned to Seth, Jessika, and Z, who had stepped closer. They must have heard, their expressions filled with anticipation.

"Your turn," Roman said with a grin. One by one, he implanted a small seed of his chi into each of them, guiding it until it settled and their eyes reflected the newfound energy within. Each time, the system alert repeated, solidifying their bonds as a permanent party.

The group continued their journey north, the renewed sense of power and unity palpable. The forest began to thin, giving way to open plains where the town awaited. Rows of farmland stretched out before them, dotted with crops and grazing livestock. The air carried the familiar scent of earth and hay, a stark contrast to the dense forest they had just left behind.

Roman took a deep breath as they approached, the sight of simple life in the town a welcome change after days of hardship. But they all knew this moment of peace was just a brief reprieve. The true test was still ahead.

As they stood on the edge of the open plains, a sudden shimmer of blue crossed Roman's vision again:

<System Alert: Permanent Party Details Party Members:

- Roman (Leader)
- Lexi
- Seth
- Jessika
- Z
- Grey Wolf (Unnamed)

Party Benefits:

- Party members gain shared benefits from the party leader's titles.

- The more party members cultivate their cores, the greater the benefits and accelerated growth they gain.

- Cultivation progress will dictate individual leveling speed and effectiveness of shared benefits.>

Roman's eyes widened as he read the new alert. He turned to the group, who were still basking in the afterglow of their newfound power, and took a moment to let the significance sink in.

"Oh cool." Roman said, glancing between each of them "The more you cultivate, the more you'll benefit from my titles. It means your cultivation will directly affect how quickly you grow stronger."

Lexi's eyes shone with determination. "So, if we cultivate like you do, we'll level up as fast as you?"

Roman nodded, a smile breaking through the seriousness of the moment. "Exactly. It's not just about gaining power; it's about how we shape it. The better we are at cultivating, the faster we can take back what we've lost."

Z clenched his fists, his massive hands tightening with newfound resolve. "Then we have no time to waste." They started walking again. Eager to try things out as they moved or better yet get to the town already so they can settle down and really get to it.

...

The town ahead stood bathed in the warm glow of the setting sun, surrounded by golden fields of wheat and patches of vibrant green crops. The peaceful sight was a stark contrast to the chaos they had left behind. And Roman knew this wasn't time to relax in the peaceful town—it was time for preparation, time to get stronger.

"Let's move," Roman said, looking at the party around him. "We've got a lot to learn, and even more to fight for."

They stepped into the open, the farm fields crunching beneath their boots, ready to face whatever lay ahead. The battle wasn't over—it was only just beginning.

As they approached the edge of the fields, a tall, wiry man stood upright in the golden sea of wheat, a scythe in his hands glinting faintly in the sunlight. He shaded his eyes with one hand and called out, his voice carrying over the rustling stalks.

"Hey there! You folks have business in the town?"

His shout drew the attention of others nearby. Five more heads popped up from the wheat, their faces wary but curious as they glanced in Roman's direction. Each of them appeared to have been hard at work harvesting, their tools momentarily idle as they waited for a response.

Roman slowed his pace and raised a hand in greeting. "Yes, sir! We're travelers passing through and looking for a place to rest!" he called back. As they closed the distance and his voice could carry more easily, Roman added with a casual tone, "We've been out of touch for months—exploring that new dungeon everyone was buzzing about—and we have no idea what's going on. Things seem... different now." He feigned curiosity, watching the man's reaction closely to gauge the tension in the area.

The man spat onto the ground, his face twisting with anger. "You got that right—things are different! We were attacked!"

Roman furrowed his brow, mimicking shock. "Attacked? By who?" he asked, injecting a note of incredulity.

"They never confirmed it," the man growled, his voice rough with rage, "but it *has* to be those Fairennian scum!" He spat again, his disgust palpable. "They've been prowling around those mountains for generations, lookin' for a way to strike. My daddy used to warn about it all the time, but did anyone listen? No! He used to say, 'If only we had a King more interested in the safety of the whole Kingdom than just his precious capital!' And he was right. We should've been combing through those mountains ourselves, but the King ignored it. And now look at us—doomed!"

His voice cracked, the bitterness raw. "The army tore through here, took everything that wasn't bolted down. Livestock, supplies, tools—you name it. All we've got left is this harvest, and God help us if we lose that too."

Roman nodded solemnly, his face painted with concern while his mind churned through the new information. "I'm so sorry to hear that," he said earnestly. Seth stepped forward, his shoulders tense.

Roman glanced at him, wondering if the talk about an absent King had struck a nerve.

"Well," Seth began, his voice calm but firm, "do you mind if we stay awhile? We can help out with the harvest if you show us what to do. We're also good hunters, so we can bring in fresh meat if needed."

The farmer nearest the stone wall leaned on it, his face weathered but his eyes sharp. "We'd welcome the help, of course," he said, wiping his hands on a ragged cloth. "But hunting's not what we need. Ever since that bastard army passed through, the monsters they brought with them escaped and have been terrorizing the area. If you can deal with those, we wouldn't have to stand guard all night just to sleep a little before working all day."

Roman nodded eagerly. "Monsters? Consider it done. Just show us where to settle down, and then point us in their direction."

One of the older men stepped forward, his gait slow but steady, his voice carrying the weight of experience. "The Markenson family fled before the army came through, but word is they were attacked on the road and didn't make it. Their farm's empty now—unused and abandoned. You can stay there. We'd been trying to figure out how to handle their harvest along with ours, but maybe this'll solve both problems. We've lost too many hands since the attack. Most of the younger folk fled to the coastline, hoping to reach family and safety." He sighed, shaking his head. "But enough of my rambling. Follow me—I'll show you where to put your feet up."

The man turned, leading them down a narrow dirt path that soon widened into a cobblestone road. Roman's gaze wandered over the vast fields of wheat on either side, golden stalks swaying in the breeze. The farmhouses were scattered across the land, some looking well-kept while others bore signs of abandonment—broken windows, overgrown yards, and roofs that sagged with neglect.

As they walked, other farmers raised their heads and offered wary nods or half-hearted waves, their weariness clear. Roman returned their greetings, offering smiles where he could. The tension in the air was palpable, the kind of unspoken fear that lingers long after devastation.

"We'll help them," Roman murmured under his breath, his voice firm with resolve. His companions glanced at him and nodded. The destruction left behind by the army—and the abandonment that followed—reminded him of Eidon, and the thought of doing nothing while these people struggled was unbearable.

The old farmer finally stopped in front of a modest farmhouse with a faded red door. The surrounding fields were still intact, but the farm itself bore the marks of neglect. "Here it is," the man said, gesturing to the house. "It's not much, but it's yours to use. I'll come by later to tell you about those monsters and where they've been spotted. For now, settle in and rest up. You'll need it."

Roman nodded, stepping forward to take in their temporary home. "Thank you. We'll make sure this place is put to good use."

The farmer tipped his hat, a ghost of a smile crossing his lips before he turned and shuffled back toward the fields. Roman stood there for a moment, the weight of the situation sinking in. He wasn't sure what kind of monsters they'd face or what they'd find in this worn-down farm, but one thing was certain: they'd fight, not just for themselves, but for the people who were left to pick up the pieces.

"Let's get to work," he said, turning to his friends. "We've got a lot to do."

And with that, they stepped into the farmhouse, ready to face whatever came next.

Chapter 24

The farmhouse was eerily silent, broken only by the faint creak of the wooden floorboards as Roman and his companions stepped inside. Dust lingered in the air, swirling lazily in the dim shafts of sunlight filtering through the grimy windows. The room was sparse—overturned chairs, a scarred table with deep scratches etched into its surface, and a fireplace blackened with soot that hadn't seen use in years. Despite the disrepair, the sturdy bones of the structure promised it would serve as their base for now.

"This'll do," Seth said, his voice steady though his gaze drifted, distant and thoughtful. He ran a hand over the back of a dusty chair, brushing off a thick layer of grime. "We'll clean it up and make it livable."

Jessika wasted no time, already pulling supplies from her pack. "First things first—Mr. Magicman, why don't you blow all this dust out of here before we choke to death?"

"Good idea," Lexi agreed, already stepping outside. "I'll wait out here until it's safe. No way I'm inhaling centuries of filth."

Roman chuckled as the others followed her, leaving him alone in the dim interior. He took a deep breath, planting his feet firmly on the uneven floor as he focused. He called upon his mana, envisioning it swirling into currents of wind, and began directing the energy through the house. At first, it was a gentle breeze, enough to shift the dust, but not enough to clear it.

"Alright, let's turn it up," Roman muttered. He pushed harder, channeling more energy. The wind strengthened into a vortex that roared through the room, lifting chairs, papers, and even a few scattered utensils into the air. He barely ducked in time as a chair spun toward his head. When it came back around, he snatched it out of the air and guided the whirlwind toward the back window. The glass rattled but held as the vortex shot outside in an explosive gust.

Satisfied, Roman repeated the process, opening all the windows to let the sunlight flood in. By the time he finished, the room was dust-free, though most of the furniture was in complete disarray. Still, nothing had broken.

"Is it safe?" Z's voice called nervously from the doorway.

Roman smirked. "Yep. All clear."

The group filtered back inside, Seth shaking his head at the toppled furniture while Jessika lit the fireplace. "Now let's get the fire going. It's going to be a cold night," she said, her voice pragmatic.

But Roman wasn't paying attention. He was already moving toward the door, his gaze scanning the distant tree line. The farmers' words echoed in his mind: *Monsters have been terrorizing the area.* He flexed his fingers, his palms itching to grip his glaive.

"We don't have time to settle in," Roman said sharply, his tone leaving no room for argument. "People are counting on us to deal with those monsters. I'll scout ahead and see what we're dealing with."

Seth stepped forward, frowning. "Roman, you've been pushing yourself too hard. Let's plan this out. Rushing in blind isn't going to help anyone."

"We don't have the luxury of time," Roman shot back, his voice softening as he glanced at them. "I'll be careful. I just need to know what we're up against."

Lexi crossed her arms, her expression skeptical. "I know this might be asking a lot, but maybe—just *maybe*—don't do anything reckless. If it looks too dangerous for even a crazy person, come back and let us know."

Roman smirked faintly. "No promises."

He stepped out into the sunlight, his confidence steady, but inside, his thoughts were anything but calm. *If I were a monster, where would I be?* he mused, scanning the horizon. His body fell into a natural rhythm as he jogged toward the outskirts of the farmland, letting his enhanced senses take over. Seth's words gnawed at him, though, and as much as he hated to admit it, they were right. He had been pushing himself to the brink—physically, mentally, emotionally. Since waking up in this strange world, he'd been on a relentless march from one fight to the next, barely stopping to breathe, let alone process anything.

Why? The question whispered in his mind, unbidden. *Why do I care so much? Why am I so desperate to protect these people?*

The thought hit him mid-stride, making him stumble slightly as he weaved through the scattered remnants of the town. He tried to shove the question away, but it refused to be silenced, swirling in his mind like an echo in an empty hall. *Why do I trust them so easily? Why do I even consider them my friends?*

His feet faltered, but the answer came to him, clear and resounding like a bell tolling in his soul: *Faith.*

The realization steadied him. This world might be new. His memories might be fractured. But his faith—that constant, unshakable foundation—remained. It was the first thing he remembered when he woke up in this foreign land. It was the only thing that had never abandoned him. And that same faith had made it easy to trust, to find a connection even when everything else felt alien. It wasn't blind trust. It was trust forged by decades of miracles, moments of grace.

A small smile tugged at his lips, but he quickly shook it off, forcing his focus back to the present. *This isn't the time for reminiscing,* he told himself firmly. He pushed the swirling thoughts aside and homed in on the task at hand. *You've got a job to do. Let's get to hunting.*

With renewed determination, Roman activated his new **Chi Vision** skill, scanning the area with heightened clarity. The world around him shifted, glowing faintly as energy signatures came into view. He sprinted toward the tree line, weaving through the remnants of the abandoned village. His enhanced perception picked up faint tracks—deep claw marks in the dirt, faint vibrations in the air where creatures had passed recently.

Roman's lips curled into a focused grin. He was close. His doubts quieted as his mind sharpened with a single goal: find the monsters, protect the people, and keep moving forward. Whatever came next, he was ready.

Roman ran tirelessly, his breath steady and his strides smooth as he circled the town repeatedly, widening his search with each lap. The world around him blurred into a haze of trees, fields, and scattered ruins as he ventured farther and farther out. His **Chi Vision** pulsed faintly, highlighting the life around him—ordinary creatures, both prey and predator, moving through the wilderness. Deer grazed quietly in the shadows of the forest, while a lone wolf padded silently along a distant ridge. None of them were what he was looking for.

He avoided any unnecessary interactions, instead mentally marking promising hunting spots. The townsfolk would need food and knowing where to find it might save them later. Despite the normalcy of what he found, a strange sense of foreboding lingered in the back of his mind. He couldn't shake the feeling that something was out here—waiting.

After nearly an hour of searching, his **Chi Vision** suddenly pulsed harder, pinging a dense cluster of energy signatures to the north. Roman slowed, his instincts taking over as he moved with careful precision. He crouched low, his steps nearly silent as he followed the energy to its source.

As he approached, the terrain shifted—a large crater opened up before him, its jagged edges cutting sharply into the earth. Roman climbed to higher ground, keeping to the cover of the trees as he surveyed the area. His enhanced vision pierced the shadows, and what he saw made his jaw tighten.

Inside the crater, a huge group of monsters wandered aimlessly, their movements erratic. Some paced in circles, their claws dragging grooves into the dirt, while others snapped at each other, their guttural growls carrying faintly through the air.

At one end of the crater, the slope was barricaded by tall iron gates reinforced with thick wooden beams. Roman's eyes narrowed as he focused his vision past the barricade. A smaller group of humans and monsters was moving toward the crater, their pace unhurried. The humans wore mismatched armor, and the monsters—smaller but no less disturbing—followed obediently behind them, as if under their control.

Roman flattened himself against the ground, his heart pounding as he watched the group approach. He held his breath, every muscle tense.

The humans stopped just outside the gates, their muffled voices carrying faintly on the wind. Roman couldn't make out the words, but the tone was sharp and commanding. Moments later, the gates groaned as they were pushed open, revealing two massive men clad in full plate armor. Each held a long spear, the polished steel gleaming even in the muted light. The gatekeepers braced themselves, their boots digging into the dirt as they held the gates open wide.

Roman's gaze snapped back to the smaller group. The humans barked an order, and the monsters following them began to move forward. They hesitated briefly at the edge of the slope, their snarls growing louder, but another shout drove them on. Roman's hands tightened into fists as he watched the creatures stumble into the crater, their movements growing wilder as they approached the larger group already inside.

The moment the last monster crossed the threshold, the gatekeepers moved in perfect unison, slamming the gates shut with a deafening *clang.* The iron groaned as the locks clicked back into place, sealing the creatures within.

What the hell is this? Roman thought, his mind racing. He had seen monsters before—fought them even—but this was something different. This wasn't random. It was organized, deliberate.

He pushed his **Chi Vision** farther, letting the glowing energy signatures illuminate the scene in sharper detail. The smaller group of humans lingered for a moment, speaking briefly to the gatekeepers before turning back the way they had come. Roman followed their movements, his jaw tightening as they walked out of his range. Roman's gaze flicked back to the crater. The creatures inside were growing more agitated, their snarls rising in volume. He watched as one particularly large beast, its body that appeared to be a gigantic lion clad in thick fur, lunged at a smaller monster, its claws raking across the other's side. The smaller creature yelped and recoiled, the wound pouring blood that drew the attention of the others but one snarl from the lion silenced the rest and lunch time began.

Roman's stomach turned. He needed to report this back to the others. But he hesitated, his eyes narrowing as he tried to count the monsters one more time. At least 10 almost the size of the huge lion but the smaller ones? 100, maybe more. If they broke free, the town wouldn't stand a chance. He glanced back toward the humans retreating into the distance. He could track them, follow them to see where they were coming from—but the thought of leaving the monsters unchecked left a sour taste in his mouth.

He dropped back down behind the ridge, his mind racing. *One step at a time,* he told himself. He needed to regroup with his friends, lay out what he'd seen, and figure out how to handle this.

But one thing was clear: this wasn't random chaos. Someone was orchestrating it, and Roman was determined to find out who—and why.

Roman turned back toward the town, his breath steady as he sprinted with everything he had, burning the location of the crater into his memory. He would need to find his way back later to show the others. The tree line blurred past him, the wind rushing in his ears, when suddenly he caught sight of movement ahead. As he broke through the edge of the forest, he skidded to a halt.

A group of soldiers stood in the middle of the town, confronting the farmers.

"Crap! Did they find us already?" Roman muttered under his breath. His pulse quickened as he dropped to the ground, crawling low to remain unseen. From his current position, he couldn't tell if the soldiers were friend or foe, but the scene was tense. The soldiers seemed to be barking orders, and the farmers were arguing back. Roman crouched and moved as quickly and silently as he could, weaving through the underbrush to get closer. His enhanced hearing and vision kicked in as he drew within range, catching snippets of their heated exchange.

"Old man, if you'd just give us water and food, we'll be on our way. Why are you making this harder than it needs to be?" one of the soldiers barked, his voice sharp and impatient.

"Because you bastards already took everything we had! We have nothing left to give!" the old man shouted back, his voice steady and unwavering despite the threat before him. Roman recognized him as the farmer they had spoken to earlier—the same man who had stood so tall, despite his bitterness and exhaustion.

The soldier sneered, clearly unimpressed. "I'm getting real tired of this nonsense," he muttered, turning to his men. "Take everything. Kill them if they resist."

The command was cold and final, and Roman's heart sank as the soldier turned and strode back toward a carriage parked at the rear of the group. The other soldiers sprang into action, drawing weapons and advancing on the townsfolk. Some of the farmers stood their ground, makeshift tools raised defiantly, but others screamed and scrambled to hide behind the few remaining structures.

Roman's jaw tightened as his eyes darted across the scene. *If I fight, they'll know we're here. Whoever sent these soldiers will expect them to return, and when they don't, they'll come with reinforcements.* He grimaced, his mind racing. *But if the townsfolk fight alone, even if they somehow win, those same reinforcements will come back anyway, and there's no way these people can handle a second attack.*

His fists clenched, nails biting into his palms as his choice became clear. *I can't let that happen. I won't.*

Roman rose to a crouch, pulling his glaive from inventory and gripping it tightly. The weapon felt solid in his hands, humming faintly with latent energy, as if it, too, was waiting for his decision. He locked eyes on the soldier commanding the group, still strolling casually toward the carriage as if he had already won.

"Not on my watch," Roman muttered, pushing off the ground. In an instant, he was running, a blur of movement across the edge of the clearing. He moved like a shadow, the soldiers too focused on the townsfolk to notice his approach. He didn't need to decide anymore. His body moved with purpose; his path clear.

It was time to even the odds.

Chapter 25

As Roman charged forward, ready to swing his glaive and take the first soldier's head, a sharp shout rang out behind him. Reflexively, he stepped back just as a volley of arrows, shimmering with glowing blue mana, rained down from the sky. The soldiers barely had time to react before the arrows struck, tearing through them like a storm. The battlefield fell silent in seconds, the enemy reduced to lifeless forms scattered across the ground. The ethereal arrows dissipated as quickly as they had appeared, vanishing into the air.

Roman turned, his heart still racing, and spotted Lexi kneeling a short distance away, her bow still pointed toward the sky. Her eyes were locked on the soldiers' remains, her expression cool and focused as if ready to fire another volley if needed. Once satisfied the threat was gone, she lowered her bow and stood, walking over to Roman with an air of quiet confidence.

"That was incredible. New skill?" Roman asked, his breath still uneven as he glanced at the aftermath.

Lexi nodded, brushing stray strands of hair from her face. "Yeah. I've been experimenting with combining mana into my shots, trying to mimic something I saw Jessika do with fire. After a lot of trial and error, I finally got it. Seems like it works."

"That's more than 'works.' That was insane!" Roman grinned, his admiration clear. "Super powerful, too."

Lexi blushed faintly, her usual composure slipping for a moment. She looked away, pretending to adjust her quiver as Roman turned his attention to the retreating figure of the soldiers' leader. The man had abandoned his carriage, stumbling as he ran, still shouting over his shoulder. His cries of indignation echoed across the field.

"How dare you! You'll pay for this!" he bellowed, his voice wavering with fear as he fled.

Roman chuckled, "That guy's really committed to being a stereotype, huh?" he muttered.

Lexi, already walking toward the townsfolk who had been cowering behind their leader, glanced back with a raised brow. Without hesitation, she nocked a single arrow, took aim, and loosed it with precise elegance. Without even a second glance, Lexi turned her attention back to the townsfolk.

Roman smirked when the arrow hit right through the back of the guy's neck and stuck out the other side, his respect for her marksmanship growing by the second. *She's scary when she wants to be.* He then chuckled as the turnaround shot reminded him of a certain Chef and his signature no-look shot.

Lexi's tone softened as she addressed the townsfolk. "I'm sorry for the commotion," she began, her voice calm but firm. "We couldn't let them start killing everyone. I know this is going to bring more trouble your way. You have a choice to make. If you're willing to stay and fight, we'll stand by you and protect whoever stays. But if you're afraid—and I wouldn't blame you if you are—it might be safer to leave now."

Her words hung in the air as the villagers exchanged uneasy glances. Some stared at her with newfound resolve, while others avoided her gaze, their fear still evident.

The old man who had stood up to the soldiers earlier stepped forward, his voice clear and resolute. "I'll stay and fight. Those bastards will not take anything else from me and mine!" he declared.

His defiance seemed to ignite something in the others. A few more villagers nodded and stepped forward, their expressions hardening with determination. Others muttered their agreement, though their fear hadn't entirely vanished.

Lexi nodded, offering a small but encouraging smile. "Good. Let's prepare. We'll need to fortify this place and make sure everyone who's staying knows what they're up against."

Roman joined her, resting the glaive on his shoulder as he surveyed the villagers. "This might not be easy, but it's better than waiting for the next wave to roll over you. Together, we've got a chance."

The old man looked between Roman and Lexi, his weary face softening with a flicker of hope. "Thank you," he said simply, his voice trembling with emotion. "For not leaving us to face this alone."

Roman exchanged a glance with Lexi, a heavy sense of responsibility settling on his shoulders. They had made their stand, but the path ahead was far from clear. Now they had to follow through.

Roman cleared his throat, turning to face the group of villagers who were still gathering their courage. "We have another problem," he began, his voice steady but grim. His eyes scanned the area until he spotted Seth, Jessika, and Z standing off to one side. He waved them over, motioning for them to join the discussion.

Once the group had assembled, Roman addressed them all, his tone measured but urgent. "While I was scouting earlier, I found something. The monster problem—it's not natural. There's a group of people collecting monsters in a huge crater a few miles in that direction." He gestured toward the northern horizon.

The murmurs among the townsfolk grew louder, and one of them gasped audibly. "World's End?" a voice asked, prompting a ripple of muttering.

Roman frowned, his gaze shifting to the speaker. "What's World's End?" he asked.

"That's what we call the crater," the old man—the leader—explained, his voice tinged with unease. "It's a massive pit left over from some ancient battle. No one goes near it anymore. You're saying there are people there? With monsters?"

Roman nodded. "I don't think they're attacking here directly. From what I saw, they're holding the monsters there for something bigger—maybe to target the kingdom. But some of the monsters must have gotten loose, and that's why they've been attacking you."

The old man's jaw clenched, his hands curling into fists. "So, they're storing up monsters like weapons, ready to unleash them when it suits them?"

Seth folded his arms, his sharp gaze fixed on Roman. "What if they're doing it deliberately? Releasing a few at a time to keep these people scared and compliant, so they can keep taking their supplies without resistance?"

Roman paused, considering Seth's point. He hadn't thought of that. "That's... possible," he admitted. His eyes scanned the villagers, their faces marked with fear and anger. "If that's the case, it's even more urgent we do something about it."

A heavy silence settled over the group, the weight of the revelation pressing down on them. Jessika broke the quiet, her voice calm but firm. "Then we have two priorities: protect the town and figure out what's really happening at that crater."

"Agreed," Lexi said, her tone resolute. She turned to the villagers. "For now, we'll help fortify the area and keep watch. But we need to know—do any of you have experience with the crater? Anything we can use?"

An older man stepped forward, his face deeply lined and his eyes shadowed with memories. "I've hunted near the edge of World's End a few times. It's dangerous, even without these people you mentioned. The terrain is rough, and there are caves that run deeper than anyone's dared to explore. If there are people there, they'd have plenty of places to hide."

"That's good to know," Seth said, nodding thoughtfully. "It means we'll need a solid plan before heading out. But for now, we focus on protecting the town. Let's start setting up defenses."

"You're forgetting I can scout them out. They can't hide from me." Roman smirked over to Seth who grinned when it clicked.

The old man—the leader—raised his chin, determination hardening his features. "If they think they can keep us under their thumb, they've got another thing coming. We'll fight. We'll stand together."

A murmur of agreement passed through the crowd, the fear in their eyes giving way to a spark of hope. Roman caught Seth's gaze and nodded, his resolve firm.

This town wasn't just a random stop anymore. It was a stand—a line drawn in the dirt against those who preyed on the weak. And Roman intended to hold it.

"Archers with me!" Lexi yelled out as she started walking towards the makeshift archery station they built using bay hales they painted to act as targets. A few folks followed her with bows and arrows in their hands that they made themselves after she taught them.

"Mages here." Jessika yelled and a much smaller group followed. She searched each person for mana capacity and only found a few that could work so she took them to the side to train.

"Fighters!" Z yelled and the majority of the men of the town shouted in unison in response which made Z smirk at the others.

"Alright that leaves the scouts for us." Seth said looking over at Roman.

"Well, for you. I'm just here as like a supervisor." Roman said.

"A what?" Seth asked.

"Uh…like an overseer?"

"Oh wow." Seth exclaimed and tried to push Roman but he easily dodged which made the group of about 6 young men laugh.

"So, you guys are all used to the woods around here right? Are any of you good at stealth? Any fighting experience?" Seth asked.

"Yes sir!" They all answered.

"Which parts? All?"

"Yes Sir!" They all answered and then one stepped forward and continued. "We were all training to be town guards so have been fighting monsters in the area for the past two years. We learned stealth skills first from the town hunter. He's out now though. We haven't seen him in a while. But the 6 of us always fought and trained together."

"Ok, names?" Seth asked.

"Nah that would be too confusing don't you think? Give them numbers, nicknames to go by which also serve as rank so they follow the hierarchy as well as keeping their info secret." Roman said thinking back on some of the cool anime that did that.

"Uh…alright?" Seth said, not totally convinced but lacking any reason to refute it so he went along. "Well since you spoke up first, you'll be 1, you rank the rest based on skill level." Seth said.

1 went through and named each one by number based on skill level and some of them grumbled about their rank but they all accepted it and quieted down quickly.

"If you want to improve you rank that is entirely possible, we can hold tournaments where you go at it and can challenge the rank above you to try to improve. Only rank 1 can't be challenged...or it takes more to challenge the rank since he will become the decision maker so that rank needs more than just fighting skills, you need courage and instincts and a sharp mind too. Either way, we'll get all of that worked out in the future, for now let's get you all trained up."

Roman stepped away from the town and looked back at the buzz of activity. Some of the townsfolk that didn't feel comfortable fighting volunteered to handle the fortifications. That is where Roman decided to apply himself. He figured he could speed that process up by a lot with his physical strength but also his magic.

Some men were chopping down trees for spikes to go into a ditch some others were digging. Roman looked at both groups and figured he could chop trees faster than dig so he'd move the current choppers to dig and he'd take over.

"How many trees do we need felled and where would you like me to leave them?" Roman went up to the man coordinating everything and asked.

"We need this whole section of trees down, not just for spikes but to ensure they have nowhere to sneak up on us. You can leave about 12 of them over there and another 12 over there." He pointed out the spots and Roman nodded.

"Ok cool, you can move all the choppers here to the ditches and I'll handle all the cutting and moving the trees myself." Roman answered and stretched.

"Uh…you sure?" he asked, a second of doubt flashed and Roman grinned.

He turned around drawing his scythe as he turned and swung the blade about waist high. Swoosh!

Roman grinned as five trees fell in a cone around him, he actually had to punch one of the trees to the side because it was falling in their direction.

Chapter 26

After three grueling days of peace punctuated by intense training, Roman and the group finally allowed themselves a day of rest. During those days, Roman had thrown himself into preparation with relentless focus. Cutting down trees took hours, but he managed to fell enough to lay the foundation for simple defenses. He dug and set traps, with the guidance of a local villager who showed him how to craft rudimentary but effective snares. By the time he was done, the surrounding land was a minefield of deadly ingenuity. Roman made sure everyone in the group could spot the traps while ensuring they were subtle enough to confuse any intruders.

Still, he couldn't shake the itch to scout further.

"I'm coming with you," Lexi said, grabbing her bow as she stepped forward.

Roman glanced at her, smiled, and nodded. "Sounds good."

As the two prepared to leave, Roman caught Seth winking at him out of the corner of his eye, followed by muffled chuckles from the others. He shook his head, waving them off before heading toward the palisade.

The newly constructed barrier marked the edge of their efforts—a sturdy wall erected after Roman had cleared enough trees. Once they passed through it and entered the forest, the chatter of the group faded, replaced by the subtle sounds of nature.

Roman broke the silence as they walked. "Hey, I just realized I don't know much about you. Where did you grow up?"

Lexi adjusted the strap of her quiver, her footsteps measured and quiet. The sunlight filtered through the canopy above, casting shifting patches of light across her sharp features. She didn't respond immediately, her fingers brushing the bowstring absently as she gazed ahead.

"Where I grew up?" she repeated, her voice low. A faint smile flickered across her lips, but it lacked warmth. "Not really a place worth talking about."

Roman tilted his head but kept his tone light. "Fair enough. I get that. Still, you seem like someone who's had to figure a lot out on your own. You handle yourself better than most."

Lexi laughed softly, the sound almost bitter. "That's a polite way of saying I've got a chip on my shoulder."

Roman chuckled. "Not exactly. But if the shoe fits..."

Her smile faded as her steps slowed. She stopped, her gaze distant as she stared at the trees ahead. "I grew up alone. My mom..." She hesitated, her voice tightening. "She left me. Guess her new husband didn't want to take me in, and she didn't feel like fighting for me."

Roman felt his chest tighten, but he stayed quiet, giving her the space to continue.

"For a while, I waited for her to come back," Lexi admitted, her voice softer now. "Every night, I'd sit by the road outside the village. I'd tell myself, 'Tonight's the night. She'll come back for me.' But she never did."

She shrugged, though the motion seemed hollow, more habit than emotion. "Eventually, I stopped waiting. Figured out how to fend for myself."

"That's awful," Roman said quietly. "I'm sorry."

Lexi waved him off, shaking her head. "It was what it was. I learned to survive. I fought for everything—food, shelter, even the clothes on my back. Nothing came easy."

They walked in silence for a while, the weight of her words lingering in the air. The rustle of leaves and the chirp of distant birds filled the void, soothing but not enough to drown out the sting of her story.

"Archery saved my life," Lexi said suddenly, her tone gaining strength. She lifted her bow slightly, as if grounding herself. "There was this hunter in the village. Quiet guy, always kept to himself. I used to follow him whenever he went into the woods. Watched him track, set traps, bring down animals with a single shot."

Roman smirked. "Bet he knew you were there."

Lexi's lips quirked in amusement. "Oh, he knew. One day, he stopped mid-hunt, turned around, and said, 'If you're gonna stalk me, you might as well learn how to aim.' Scared the hell out of me."

Roman laughed. "Sounds like a great guy."

"He was," Lexi said, her voice softening. "He handed me this beat-up old bow and started teaching me. I was terrible at first, but he was patient. He taught me how to hunt, track, survive. For the first time in my life, I felt like I was good at something. Like I had a purpose."

"What happened to him?" Roman asked.

Her expression darkened. "One day, he just... left. Never said why. Just disappeared. Guess he figured he'd taught me enough to make it on my own."

Roman frowned. "That's rough."

Lexi smirked, but it didn't reach her eyes. "It was. But it taught me something important: if you want something, you fight for it. You take care of yourself. Relying on others just sets you up for disappointment."

"Until you met the group," Roman pointed out.

She glanced at him, her expression softening. "Yeah... until then. I don't know why I stayed with them at first. Maybe I was tired of being alone. Maybe because they didn't try to take anything from me. They just... let me be me."

Roman smiled. "Sounds like they earned your trust."

Lexi nodded, a rare vulnerability flickering in her eyes. "They did. And I'll fight for them. For this town, too. Maybe because of how I grew up, but I can't stand seeing the weak get pushed around."

She paused, realizing how much she'd shared, and quickly looked away, her cheeks reddening.

Roman chuckled. "I get it. I didn't grow up like you, but... I lost a lot, too. My family, my girlfriend..." His voice faltered. The memories rushed back, sharp and vivid. He stopped walking, his fists clenching. "I was left bleeding on the ground, paralyzed. Couldn't even move a muscle."

Lexi placed a steady hand on his back, her touch grounding him. He looked into her eyes and found not pity, but understanding.

"I can't imagine what that was like," she said softly. "To lose everything and still find the strength to keep going."

Roman shook his head. "I don't know if it's strength or just... stubbornness. But now? I think I've found something worth fighting for again. People worth fighting for."

"Guess that makes two of us," Lexi said, her voice warm.

They stood in silence for a moment, the bond between them deepening in the quiet.

Lexi cleared her throat, gesturing to the trees. "Come on. We should keep moving. If there's trouble out here, better we find it before it finds us."

Roman smirked, adjusting his glaive. "Lead the way, sharpshooter."

Side by side, they walked on, their steps light but purposeful. The forest stretched ahead, dappled in golden light as the sun dipped lower, and Roman felt the weight of his past ease, if only for a moment. For the first time in a long time, he felt something close to peace.

Chapter 27

They trudged on, the forest alive with the gentle whispers of the wind weaving through the trees, the occasional burst of bird song, and the rustle of unseen creatures moving through the underbrush. Lexi's eyes darted around, absorbing the beauty of the untouched wilderness—the rich greens of the canopy above, the dappling of sunlight on moss-covered rocks, and the faint shimmer of a distant stream cutting through the land. She exhaled softly, the serenity of the scene a welcome reprieve from the chaos of the past few days.

Roman, however, was lost in thought, his steps steady but his mind far away. The peace of the moment stirred something within him, a question he hadn't dared to face fully until now.

If the opportunity arose… would I go home?

The thought sent his mind spinning, his heart caught between conflicting emotions. On one hand, he had friends back home who would miss him—friends who, in some way, might still care about him. But the shadow of guilt crept in, dark and suffocating. Would they blame me for her death too?

He hadn't spoken to a single one of them since the incident. How could he? After the shooting, he'd slipped into a coma for five years, and by the time he woke up, this world had pulled him into its grasp before he even had the chance to process anything. He hadn't had time to reach out, but then again... neither had they.

They would have visited him if they didn't blame him, right?

The thought was like a dagger, sharp and unrelenting. His mind replayed the loneliness of waking in the sterile hospital room, the beeping of monitors his only companion. *Five years,* he thought bitterly. *Five years, and not a single familiar face waiting for me when I opened my eyes. Not one of my so-called friends or family came to visit me when I woke!*

But then, another thought intruded, stopping him before he could spiral too far.

In the six hours you were awake?

It was a small voice, part reason, part reprimand, and it yanked him out of the depression threatening to consume him. Roman paused mid-step, inhaling deeply as he forced his focus back to the present.

"What's on your mind?" Lexi's voice cut through his reverie, light but tinged with curiosity.

Roman glanced over, startled, and caught her studying him with those sharp, perceptive eyes. Her bow hung loosely in her hand, her fingers brushing the wooden handle absentmindedly as she waited for his answer.

"Nothing important," he said with a faint smile. "Just... thinking."

She tilted her head, clearly unconvinced. "You've been awfully quiet, even for you."

Roman shrugged, looking around at the forest as if to deflect the attention. "Just... enjoying all this." He gestured to the sprawling landscape around them. "It's... peaceful. Makes you think about things."

Lexi smirked, raising an eyebrow. "And what's Roman, the mystery man, thinking about in all this peace?"

He hesitated, his gaze drifting to the trees ahead. "If... I had the chance to go back home... I'm not sure if I'd take it."

Lexi's smirk softened into something more thoughtful. "What's holding you back? Home not all it's cracked up to be?"

Roman sighed, running a hand through his hair. "It's not that. I had people who cared about me. Friends. A life. But... things happened. I got hurt. Someone I loved... she didn't make it. After that, everything just... fell apart."

Lexi was quiet for a moment, her steps slowing as she processed his words. "Sounds like you've had your share of hell."

"You could say that." Roman said, his voice low. He kicked at a rock on the path, watching it tumble away. "I guess it's hard to think about going back to a place where... I don't know if I'd even belong anymore."

Lexi nodded slowly, her gaze drifting to the horizon. "I get that. I mean, not the same way, but... I get it." She glanced at him, her expression softer than he was used to. "Sometimes, it's not about the place, though. It's about the people. You've got people here now, you know."

Roman blinked, her words catching him off guard. "Yeah... I guess I do."

They continued walking in silence for a while, the bond between them settling into something comfortable, unspoken but solid.

As they crested a small ridge, the forest began to thin, revealing a stretch of land scarred by jagged rocks and patches of burnt grass. The air grew heavier, tinged with the faint metallic scent of mana-tainted corruption. Roman's chi vision pinged faint signatures ahead, his senses sharpening as the pit where the monsters were being held loomed closer.

"This is it," Roman murmured, his voice quiet but tense.

Lexi nodded, her grip tightening on her bow. "Stay sharp."

They moved cautiously, their steps light as they approached the ridge where Roman posted up before to look into the crater. Roman glanced at Lexi, her expression unreadable but her movements precise, practiced. For all her vulnerability earlier, she was every inch the hunter now, her focus unshakable.

He crouched low, peering over the ridge to get a better look at the crater below. It was massive, the iron gates standing ominously at one end, while the monsters inside milled about aimlessly. Roman's enhanced vision picked out details easily—the scars on the beasts' bodies, the unnatural gleam in their eyes, the faint shimmer of mana binding them.

"Lexi," he whispered, gesturing for her to join him. "You seeing this?"

She crouched beside him, her bow at the ready as she scanned the scene. "Yeah. That's... not natural. Whatever they're doing here, it's bad news."

Roman nodded, his jaw tightening. "We need to figure out who's behind this... and how to stop it."

Lexi smirked faintly, her sharp eyes locking onto his. "Good thing we're not the giving-up type."

Roman chuckled despite the tension. "Yeah. Good thing."

Snap! Both of their heads shot to their right where the sound came from and Roman's heart sank.

"Well, I guess I have to move up my plans, huh." The assassin smirked as he locked eyes with Roman. Roman's blood ran cold. He turned, glaive at the ready, and his eyes landed on the figure stepping from the shadows of the trees. The assassin who had attacked him before stood there, a wicked grin splitting his face.

"Miss me?" the man said, his sword gleaming in the fading sunlight.

Roman narrowed his eyes, his muscles tensing. "Not even a little. What do you want?"

The assassin chuckled darkly, lazily twirling his sword. "Oh, I'm here to see you bleed, Roman. But I plan to enjoy every second of it."

Before Roman could respond, the assassin's free hand darted into a pouch at his side. He hurled something back in the direction of the crater, and Roman barely had time to react before it exploded with a deafening bang. A thick cloud of red smoke billowed into the air, spreading fast and clinging to everything it touched.

Roman winced, his ears ringing as he spun to check the source of the chaos. Below, the monsters erupted into a frenzy, their deafening roars shattering the air as they charged relentlessly toward the iron gates.

"What the hell did you do?" Roman barked, his gaze darting between the assassin and the wild scene unfolding below.

The assassin smirked, his stance shifting into readiness. "Oh, you'll find out soon enough. But first—let's see if you've learned anything since last time."

There was no time to answer. The assassin lunged, his sword cutting through the air toward Roman's throat. Roman barely managed to parry the blow with his glaive, the impact sending vibrations up his arms.

"Lexi!" Roman shouted as he sidestepped another brutal strike, his voice strained with the effort.

"I know!" Lexi's voice was sharp and urgent. She was already scrambling to her feet, her gaze locked on the pit below. The iron gates groaned and buckled under the onslaught of the monsters, the twisted metal straining against the relentless force.

With a final screech, the gates shattered. The monsters surged through, their massive forms thundering across the ground in a terrifying wave. They charged straight toward the smoke—and, beyond it, the village.

Roman gritted his teeth, deflecting another blow and countering with a sweeping arc of his glaive. "Go, Lexi! Warn them!"

She hesitated for only a second, her eyes flicking between Roman and the advancing horde. Then, without a word, she sprinted toward the village at full speed.

The assassin laughed; his eyes gleaming with malice as he watched her retreat. "Brave of you, sending her off. But she won't make it in time. And neither will you."

Roman's jaw tightened, his anger flaring. He pressed the attack, his strikes quick and unrelenting. "She'll make it. And as for you—you're not walking away from this."

The assassin's smirk widened. "Big talk. Let's see if you can back it up."

The fight raged on, each clash of their weapons a test of skill and will. Roman's focus was razor-sharp, every move calculated to keep the assassin occupied while subtly steering the battle downhill, toward the village.

He had to control the range, using the reach of his glaive to his advantage. Normally, he wouldn't favor the weapon in a duel against a swordsman, but now, he needed to dictate the flow of the fight.

The assassin noticed the shift in Roman's movements, a spark of realization flickering in his eyes. "Clever," he sneered, swinging in a wide arc that Roman narrowly parried. "But you're running out of time. And options."

Roman's breaths came hard and fast as he deflected another blow, the force rattling his arms. His mind raced, balancing the immediate danger with the distant screams now reaching his ears. The village was in chaos. He prayed Lexi had made it in time.

He feinted left, then spun, delivering a powerful side kick that sent the assassin stumbling backward. Roman seized the opportunity, surging forward and forcing the fight closer to the village.

"You're persistent," the assassin admitted, wiping blood from the corner of his mouth. "But persistence won't save you."

Roman didn't respond. His entire focus was on staying ahead, keeping the assassin too busy to exploit the chaos in the village.

As they neared the outskirts, Roman's chi vision flared, illuminating the shapes of villagers scrambling for cover and the monstrous horde tearing through the town. Flames raged along the rooftops, consuming crops and buildings alike. Screams echoed through the streets, mixing with the thunder of collapsing structures and the guttural roars of the beasts.

"I told you; you were too late!" the assassin spat, his voice dripping with triumph. He surged forward, his blade striking faster and harder than before. Roman's arms moved on instinct, his glaive deflecting the strikes before his mind could register the movements.

"How did you block that?!" The assassin snarled, his voice tinged with frustration.

Roman blinked, just as confused as his opponent. It was as if his body had acted on its own, driven by something deeper than thought.

But there was no time to process it. The assassin pressed the attack, his strikes relentless and precise. Roman parried and dodged, each move a desperate effort to stay alive.

Then, a sharp whistle sliced through the air. Roman heard the familiar *twang* of a bowstring and ducked instinctively as an arrow whizzed past his head. The assassin twisted, dropping to the ground just in time to avoid the projectile.

Roman smirked. "Looks like you're not the only one with a backup plan."

Lexi stood a few yards away, her bow drawn and another arrow already nocked. Her eyes burned with determination as she took aim.

"Guess we sped up your plans enough to ruin them," Roman taunted, his confidence returning.

The assassin's smirk twisted into a snarl. "You think this was my plan? Unleash some monsters on a random town?!" He laughed, a crazed, bitter sound.

Roman narrowed his eyes. "If not this town, then what? The capital?"

The assassin's laughter grew louder, almost unhinged. "The capital? You fool. We already control the capital! You don't even know why you're about to die!"

Roman's grip on his glaive tightened. "Then enlighten me," he said, his tone sharp. "If you're so confident, what's stopping you from spilling your master plan?"

The assassin's grin widened, his teeth bared in a predator's snarl. "You'll find out soon enough. Assuming you live long enough to see it."

With that, he lunged again, his blade flashing in the firelight as the battle raged on.

Chapter 28

The assassin kept pressing his advantage, his strikes unrelenting, a deadly dance of speed and precision. Roman, sensing the shift in the fight, switched from his glaive to his sword. The longer weapon had served its purpose, but now the assassin was too close, and Roman needed something more maneuverable for the tight exchanges.

He had tried firing off a few lightning strikes earlier, but his mana seemed completely inert, as if locked behind an unyielding barrier. Frustration bubbled beneath the surface, but he forced himself to stay calm. He couldn't rely on his chi either, not yet. Not until he was sure this psychopath didn't have some hidden countermeasure waiting to spring.

The assassin's attacks were relentless, forcing Roman to move, block, and counter at a pace that left his muscles screaming. *How is he this strong?* The thought clawed at Roman's focus, his frustration rising with every narrow dodge and barely-parried strike.

In this world, I should be invincible, Roman thought, bitterness creeping into his mind. *With all the cheats I've got—my titles, my growth rate—this shouldn't even be a fight.* But deep down, he knew the truth: power didn't make him invincible. The assassin wasn't just strong; he was experienced.

Maybe he's just been at it longer, Roman reasoned, gritting his teeth as the assassin's blade scraped his armor. The clang reverberated through his body, jolting him back to the present.

The assassin smirked, clearly enjoying himself. "What's the matter, hero? Losing your edge already?"

Roman ignored the taunt, pushing himself harder, faster. His blade moved in precise arcs, each strike aimed to disarm or cripple, but the assassin was too quick. He parried effortlessly, countering with strikes that Roman barely deflected.

If I had more time, I'd wipe the floor with this punk. The thought flitted through Roman's mind, but he crushed it. *Now's not the time for ifs. Focus on reality.*

Roman's breathing was labored, sweat dripping down his face as he forced himself to stay in the fight. His instincts screamed at him to draw on his chi, to unleash the power simmering just beneath the surface, but he held back. He couldn't afford to reveal everything—not yet.

The assassin's grin widened as he pushed Roman to the brink, his strikes coming in quick, brutal succession. "You're not bad," the assassin admitted, his voice dripping with mockery. "But you're not good enough."

Roman locked eyes with him, his resolve hardening. *I've come too far to lose now.* He adjusted his stance, his grip on the sword tightening. If the assassin thought he had the upper hand, he was in for a surprise. Roman wasn't just fighting to win—he was fighting to survive. For the village. For Lexi. For everyone depending on him.

And that meant he couldn't hold back much longer.

Roman roared, a guttural sound that tore through the chaos, as rage surged within him. His chi erupted, raw and untamed, spiraling outward with an intensity that made the air vibrate. He focused the energy, transforming it into lightning the moment it left his body. A massive arc of electricity crackled through the air, jagged and blinding, hurtling straight toward the assassin with a deafening crackle.

For the first time in the fight, Roman allowed himself a smirk. The assassin's infuriating grin—the one that had taunted him the entire battle—was about to be obliterated, wiped clean by the sheer force of Roman's power.

Except...

"About damn time," the assassin said, chuckling as the lightning barreled toward him.

Roman's smirk faltered, confusion flashing across his face. He had anticipated fear, shock, anger—

something. But the assassin laughed, his tone as casual as if Roman had just handed him a gift.

Before Roman could process what was happening, the assassin moved.

Fast.

Too fast.

The lightning crashed into the spot where the assassin had stood a split second earlier, sending up a shower of sparks and scorched earth. Roman's eyes widened, his heart sinking as he searched the battlefield. Where—?

A blur of motion streaked to his left, and then the assassin was there, unscathed, his blade gleaming as he casually rested it against his shoulder. His grin had only widened.

"That's more like it," the assassin said, his voice dripping with mockery. "I was starting to think you didn't have it in you."

Roman clenched his teeth, his hands tightening on his sword. *What is this guy?*

"But as happy as I am that you're not some weakling who can't even use chi," the assassin sneered, his grin turning vicious, "I'm afraid I'm out of time. So... goodbye. But don't worry—I'll leave you with a little parting gift. Something to remember me by."

Roman barely had time to process the words before the assassin moved.

The pain hit like a thunderclap; shattering Roman's senses. It wasn't like the searing heat of lightning or the sharp sting of a blade—it was worse. A raw, blinding agony that consumed him entirely. He couldn't even scream; his throat locked up, and no sound would come.

His knees buckled, and he collapsed, the impact sending shockwaves through his already battered body.

"Oh no, you don't," a voice cut through the haze of pain, sharp and commanding. Roman heard the distinct sound of steel slicing through flesh, followed by a wet, gurgling noise. He didn't even register the pain, he heard the sound of the attack but felt nothing.

All he could feel was the overwhelming agony radiating from his core, like his very life was being drained away.

This is it, he thought numbly. *I'm dead.*

His body hit the ground with a dull thud, the rough earth unyielding beneath him. He must have bounced slightly on impact, but he couldn't tell anymore. His senses were shutting down, one by one.

His eyes remained open, staring blankly ahead. The world blurred, but one detail remained painfully clear: the burning village beyond the swaying grass in front of his face. The flames devoured everything in their path, casting the sky in shades of orange and black. The grass swayed gently in the breeze, a cruel contrast to the chaos and destruction unfolding behind it.

It's so quiet here, Roman thought distantly, his mind slipping further away. *Why does it feel like nothing's happening?*

His vision began to fade, darkness creeping in at the edges. But just before it swallowed him entirely, something shifted.

A familiar warmth stirred in his chest—a spark, faint and fragile but unmistakable. His chi.

No, he thought, his mind clawing desperately for clarity. *Not yet. Not like this.*

Roman's fingers twitched, his body refusing to surrender. The spark grew stronger, fueled by a defiance that flared like a dying ember refusing to go out.

The sound of the assassin's voice broke through again, distant and barely audible. Roman only caught a few words. "…kill everyone you ever cared about."

Roman gritted his teeth, his fingers digging into the dirt beneath him. He pushed with everything he had trying to turn his Chi but each rotation caused more and more waves of excruciating pain to radiate through his body forcing him to stop.

The assassin stood over Roman, his blade glinting in the firelight from the burning village beyond. Roman could barely move, his body wracked with pain. Every attempt to channel his chi sent searing agony coursing through him, leaving him paralyzed and helpless on the ground.

The assassin crouched next to him, leaning in close. His lips moved, whispering something, but Roman couldn't make out the words. The ringing in his ears drowned everything out.

The assassin straightened, sheathing his sword with a practiced motion. "This was fun," he said, his voice carrying just enough to pierce the haze of Roman's mind. "But it's over now."

With that, he turned and disappeared into the shadows, leaving Roman alone with the smoldering wreckage of his body and the chaos he couldn't stop.

Roman groaned, the sound weak and guttural. He tried to push himself up, but his arms trembled and collapsed beneath him. *Move.* The command echoed in his head, but his body refused to obey. His chest ached with every shallow breath, and his vision blurred as exhaustion threatened to drag him under.

After what felt like an eternity, a sliver of strength began to return to him. He forced his eyes to focus, blinking away the haze. The grass in front of him was charred and blackened, still swaying faintly in the breeze.

And then he saw her.

Lexi lay crumpled nearby, her bow shattered and scattered beside her. Her body was still, unnaturally so, and the blood that stained her tunic seemed far too vivid against the ashen ground.

Roman's breath hitched, his chest tightening in a way that had nothing to do with his injuries. "No," he whispered, his voice cracking.

He dragged himself toward her, every inch a battle against his failing strength. The pain in his chest was unbearable, but it didn't matter. Nothing mattered except reaching her.

When he finally did, he collapsed beside her, his trembling hand brushing against her cheek. Her skin was cold.

"Lexi..." His voice was a choked whisper, barely audible over the crackling of the distant flames. Tears blurred his vision as he cupped her face, his thumb brushing over her pale lips. "No, no, no. Please."

He couldn't lose her—not like this. Not after everything.

A sob tore from his throat as desperation took hold. He placed his hands over her chest, his mind racing. *There has to be a way. There has to be something I can do.*

Without hesitation, he drew on his chi, summoning everything he had left. The pain was instant, white-hot and blinding, but he didn't care. His chi surged through his body, crackling and sparking like wildfire.

"Come on, Lexi," he begged, his voice shaking as he poured the energy into her lifeless body. "You don't get to leave. Not now. Not like this."

The pressure in his core built to unbearable levels, the pain so intense it felt like his very soul was fracturing. He gritted his teeth, tears streaming down his face as he pushed harder, forcing every ounce of energy he had into her.

Please, God. Please.

A sharp, shattering sensation ripped through him, and he cried out as his core gave way, breaking apart like glass under a hammer. His vision darkened, the world tilting as his strength left him entirely.

But then, just as the blackness began to swallow him, he heard it—a faint, fragile gasp for breath.

Roman's eyes fluttered open, his vision swimming as he looked down at her. Lexi's chest rose, shallow but steady, and her lips parted as she drew in another breath.

Relief flooded through him, overwhelming and all-consuming, but his body had reached its limit. His head slumped forward, resting against her shoulder as the darkness finally claimed him.

The last thing he heard was the sound of her breathing, weak but alive.

Chapter 29

Epilogue

Commander Athel stood atop the walls of Eidon, surveying the chaos below as the final remnants of the enemy forces were driven from the city. The once-thriving town was now a smoldering battleground. Smoke curled into the sky from buildings that had been burned and battered, but the Hydra Knights had done their duty. Eidon was theirs once again.

"Push them to the river! Don't let a single one slip away!" Commander Athel barked, his voice cutting through the din of battle. His armor was splattered with grime and blood, the golden crest on his chest dulled but still visible—a rallying point for his men.

Down below, Sergeant Smithson led the final charge, his towering frame cutting through the enemy ranks like a battering ram. His shield struck a fleeing soldier, sending the man sprawling, and with a brutal efficiency, Smithson's blade followed, silencing the enemy for good.

"Retreat is not an option!" Smithson roared, his voice filled with the kind of determination that ignited the spirits of his men. Around him, the Hydra Knights fought with the precision and brutality that had earned them their reputation.

The enemy's resolve shattered. Soldiers dropped their weapons, their flight turning into a panicked stampede. The riverbanks became a bottleneck as the enemy scrambled to escape, many throwing themselves into the frigid waters to avoid capture or death.

"Commander!" A lieutenant jogged up to Athel, saluting briskly. "The last of the resistance has been routed. The city is ours."

Athel nodded grimly, his gaze fixed on the battlefield. "Good. Send word to the medics to begin tending to the wounded, ours and theirs. Make it clear: we don't have the luxury to waste resources, but mercy today may save us tomorrow."

The lieutenant hesitated but nodded. "Yes, sir."

Athel turned and made his way down the stone stairs to the courtyard, his heavy boots echoing with each step. The streets were littered with debris, bodies, and the lingering stench of blood. The Hydra Knights moved with purpose, dragging bodies to a central location, extinguishing fires, and setting up triage stations wherever there was space.

Smithson approached, his shield slung across his back and his helmet tucked under one arm. "The city is ours, Commander," he reported. "But it's not pretty. Half the infrastructure is in ruins, and the people... well, those who didn't flee are hiding like frightened rabbits."

Athel grimaced. "We'll rebuild. This is the best location to establish a forward base. If we don't hold it, the rest of the kingdom will fall."

Smithson scratched at his beard, his expression heavy. "It's a start, but it won't be enough. The enemy has already dug deep into the kingdom. We're fighting on borrowed time."

Athel motioned for Smithson to follow him. They entered what had once been the mayor's estate, its walls still mostly intact. The room they chose was cluttered with broken furniture, maps, and hastily gathered supplies, but it would serve as a war room.

Athel gestured to a massive table in the center of the room, its surface covered in maps and hastily scribbled notes. He swept his hand over it, clearing away debris before planting both fists on its edge.

"We'll use Eidon as our base of operations," he began, his voice firm. "But we need more than just the Hydra Knights. We need alliances. Supplies. Reinforcements."

Smithson nodded, stepping forward to study the maps. "The southern regions have been hit hard, but Fairen hasn't committed their full forces. They're testing our defenses. If we can push them back here, we might have a chance to regroup and strike."

"Agreed," Athel said, his eyes narrowing. "What about the capital? Any word from the king?"

"None. All we know is that the city is under their control. But the enemy is splintered; they're spread thin trying to hold onto everything they've taken. That's our advantage."

Athel's jaw tightened. "Then we take it back. We'll retake the capital and rally the kingdom. If we fall here, there won't be another chance."

Smithson leaned over the map, pointing to key locations. "We'll need to secure these supply routes first. Without them, we won't last long. And if we can cut off their reinforcements from the north, they'll have nowhere to retreat when we strike."

Athel nodded. "Start making preparations. I want scouts sent out immediately to assess the situation. We need to know what we're up against."

As they strategized, the sounds of rebuilding filtered through the broken walls—men shouting orders, hammers pounding, the faint cries of wounded soldiers. The weight of their task was monumental, but the Hydra Knights had always thrived under impossible odds.

"One more thing," Smithson said, his voice quieter. "What about Roman? And the others who went to deal with the monster pit? If the capital's their stronghold, we can't afford to lose fighters like them."

Athel's gaze darkened. "We'll give them time, but not too much. Roman's power is undeniable, but we can't hinge everything on him. If he doesn't return soon, we move without him."

Smithson straightened, saluting. "Understood. I'll get the men ready."

As Smithson left, Athel stared down at the map, his fingers tracing the jagged lines of the kingdom's borders. The weight of the kingdom rested on his shoulders, but he would carry it.

He had no choice.

The hospital room was bathed in the sterile glow of fluorescent lights, their hum faint against the backdrop of muffled voices and distant footsteps. Roman's bed sat in the center, surrounded by machines that beeped steadily, monitoring a life suspended between moments.

Five figures stood near the door, their expressions a mix of sadness and quiet determination.

"I can't believe we're too late again," Jake muttered, his hands shoved deep into his jacket pockets. His broad shoulders hunched forward as if trying to shield himself from the weight of the moment.

"It's not your fault," Mia said softly, her voice gentle but firm. The petite woman, always the voice of reason among them, placed a hand on Jake's arm. "None of us knew what would happen today."

Chris, the tallest of the group, stood by the window, his gaze distant. "Five years," he murmured. "Five years he's been in that bed, and we still haven't gotten to tell him."

"Tell him what?" Sophie's voice broke, her eyes red from holding back tears. "That we're sorry? That we don't blame him? He already knew that. He has to know that."

Kevin, the quietest of the group, stood closest to Roman's bed. His hand hovered over the railing, fingers brushing against the cold metal as he struggled to speak. "He didn't deserve this," he said finally, his voice thick with emotion. "None of it. But if he ever wakes up... I want him to know we were here. That we're still here."

Silence fell over them as they turned their eyes to Roman. His face was peaceful, almost too peaceful, as if he were simply sleeping and might wake up at any moment.

"We made a promise, remember?" Mia said, breaking the quiet. "Every month. We come together, no matter what. For him. And we've done it. For five years."

Jake's jaw tightened. "Yeah, but it's not enough. It's never been enough."

Chris crossed his arms, his brow furrowed. "We all should've been there that day. Maybe if we had—"

"Stop." Mia's voice was sharp, silencing him. "Don't do that to yourself. Don't do that to any of us. We couldn't have stopped what happened."

The room grew heavy again, the weight of unspoken guilt filling the space.

A knock at the door broke the silence, and a nurse stepped in, her expression surprised to see so many visitors. "Oh, you're all here today. That's... fortunate."

"Fortunate?" Sophie echoed, confused.

The nurse hesitated before stepping fully into the room, closing the door behind her. "I've been meaning to tell you this for weeks. Roman woke up."

All five of them froze, the air in the room shifting as if it had been sucked out.

"What?" Kevin's voice cracked.

"When?" Jake demanded; his voice rough.

"About a month ago," the nurse said, her tone cautious. "He woke up briefly. It was only for a few hours, but he was conscious."

Chris's hands clenched into fists. "Why didn't you tell us?"

The nurse's face softened with guilt. "I would've, but... well, it wasn't exactly a typical wake-up. Two men from Genesis Creations were here. They spoke with Roman the entire time, asking him questions. He was coherent—alert, even—but he seemed... different. At the end of the conversation, he signed some paperwork for them, and then..." She hesitated, her voice dropping. "He slipped back into the coma."

"Genesis Creations?" Mia repeated, her brows knitting together. "The tech company?"

The nurse nodded. "Yes. They've been involved in Roman's care since shortly after the accident, but this was the first time I'd seen their representatives in person."

"And the paperwork?" Kevin asked, his voice sharp with suspicion.

"I'm not privy to the details, but..." She hesitated again, as if unsure whether to continue. "They've arranged to move Roman to one of their private facilities. He's leaving tomorrow morning."

The group fell into stunned silence, the weight of the news pressing down on them.

"Tomorrow?" Jake finally said, his voice low but furious. "They're taking him tomorrow, and we're just now hearing about this?"

The nurse stepped closer, her voice apologetic. "I know it's sudden, but... honestly, you're lucky you came today. If you want to see him before they take him, now's your chance."

Without waiting, Sophie stepped forward, tears streaming freely now as she took Roman's hand in hers. "We're not leaving," she said, her voice trembling but resolute.

Kevin nodded, his grip tightening on the bed's railing. "We'll stay until the last second if we have to."

Chris glanced at the others, his face set in grim determination. "He deserves to know we were here. Always."

The nurse offered them a small, understanding smile. "I'll give you some privacy." She slipped out of the room, leaving them alone with their thoughts—and with Roman.

As the door clicked shut, Jake let out a shaky breath. "Whatever this Genesis thing is, I don't trust it."

Mia crossed her arms, her gaze locked on Roman's peaceful face. "Neither do I. But for now, let's focus on what matters: being here for him. Just like we promised."

One by one, they nodded, the unspoken bond between them tightening. They would stay. For

Roman. For their friend. For the chance to tell him everything they'd been waiting to say.

Even if he couldn't hear them.
■■■

The Enemy King

Far beyond the borders of the ravaged Kingdom of Meridia, a sprawling encampment stretched across the foothills of a desolate mountain range. Torches flickered in the cold wind, casting long shadows over the tents and makeshift fortresses. At the heart of it all stood the enemy King's command tent—a structure of dark, reinforced fabric adorned with crimson sigils. Inside, the air was thick with tension.

The enemy King sat at a massive wooden table cluttered with maps and scrolls. His sharp features were twisted into a scowl, and his fingers drummed rhythmically against the table as he stared at the reports before him. Around him, his advisors and generals stood in silence, not daring to interrupt his thoughts.

"We've accomplished what we set out to do," the King said at last, his voice low and deliberate. "Meridia's King is ours. The throne is in shambles, the people scattered. Yet…" His eyes narrowed, glinting like a predator's. "We still haven't secured the heir."

A general stepped forward, his armor clinking softly. "Your Majesty, the prince managed to slip through our grasp during the chaos in the capital. Our scouts are pursuing him, but—"

"Find him!" the King snarled, slamming his fist on the table. The force sent papers flying, and his advisors flinched. "I will not allow loose ends to threaten our plans. The boy must be eliminated before he rallies any resistance."

The general bowed deeply. "Yes, Your Majesty. We'll double our efforts."

The King leaned back in his chair, his gaze burning holes into the map of Meridia. "Good. And what of the monsters?" he asked, his tone deceptively calm.

An uneasy silence filled the room before another advisor stepped forward, his face pale. "Your Majesty... the creatures we were collecting and training near World's End... they were all destroyed. The operation was lost."

The King's eyes widened, his lips curling into a snarl. "What?!" His voice rose to a roar, shaking the tent's very frame. "How could this happen?"

"We believe it was... outsiders, allied with the remaining resistance," the advisor stammered, visibly trembling. "They—"

"Excuses!" the King bellowed, rising to his feet. His towering presence seemed to fill the room, his anger palpable. "That operation was vital to our plans. Those creatures were the foundation of our army! Now you're telling me we've been set back by months?"

The advisor lowered his head. "Y-Yes, Your Majesty. But we can—"

"Enough!" the King thundered, his fury radiating like a storm. He pointed a finger at the gathered officials. "I don't care what it takes. Start gathering more monsters immediately. Triple the efforts. And this time, ensure they're properly trained. I want progress. Now!"

"Yes, Your Majesty," came the unified reply, and the room quickly emptied as the officials scrambled to obey.

The King stood alone for a moment, his breathing heavy as he stared at the map before him. "Soon," he muttered to himself. "Soon, this entire continent will bow to me."

Thank you for reading! Stay Tuned for Roman's story to continue in Roots of Rebellion!

Made in the USA
Columbia, SC
02 May 2025

57479162R00183